SIGNIFICANT
THINGS

For Ian and Nancy
and
David, William, and Simon

SIGNIFICANT
THINGS

a novel

HELEN McLEAN

SIMON & PIERRE FICTION
A MEMBER OF THE DUNDURN GROUP
TORONTO · OXFORD

Editor: Barry Jowett
Copy-Editor: Jennifer Bergeron
Design: Jennifer Scott
Printer: Transcontinental

National Library of Canada Cataloguing in Publication Data

McLean, Helen
   Significant things / Helen McLean.

ISBN 1-55002-441-8

I. Title.

PS8575.L393S54 2003   C813'.54   C2003-900347-7
PR9199.3.M42444S54 2003

1   2   3   4   5   07   06   05   04   03

Canada

THE CANADA COUNCIL | LE CONSEIL DES ARTS
FOR THE ARTS | DU CANADA
SINCE 1957 | DEPUIS 1957

ONTARIO ARTS COUNCIL
CONSEIL DES ARTS DE L'ONTARIO

We acknowledge the support of the **Canada Council for the Arts** and the **Ontario Arts Council** for our publishing program. We also acknowledge the financial support of the **Government of Canada** through the **Book Publishing Industry Development Program** and **The Association for the Export of Canadian Books**, and the **Government of Ontario** through the **Ontario Book Publishers Tax Credit** program, and the **Ontario Media Development Corporation's Ontario Book Inititative**.

Printed and bound in Canada.⊕
Printed on recycled paper.
www.dundurn.com

Dundurn Press	Dundurn Press	Dundurn Press
8 Market Street	73 Lime Walk	2250 Military Road
Suite 200	Headington, Oxford,	Tonawanda NY
Toronto, Ontario, Canada	England	U.S.A. 14150
M5E 1M6	OX3 7AD	

My sincere thanks to Cynthia Holz, wise friend and mentor, who has given so generously of her time to read many drafts of this book.

I am grateful for the unfailing support and encouragement of The Admiral Road Gang: Abby Pope, Louisa Varalta, Catherine Gildiner, Anne Koven, Barbara Bruce, and Colleen Mathieu.

My thanks as always to Ross.

1

Edward glanced at the eighteenth-cen-
tury Boulle clock on the mantelpiece
and then checked its none-too-reliable
time against his watch, just to be sure.
Five-thirty, half past eleven in Italy. The restaurant tables would
long since have been cleared away, the family would have finished the late dinner at the big table in the kitchen. Edward
could almost smell the aromas that filled the air of that kitchen,
just thinking about it. Paulo would be out in his studio among
the cypresses, putting in an hour or two at his easel before he
went up to the loft and stretched out on that big bed under the
skylight. Edward hadn't felt such a yearning to see and touch
another human being since they'd sent him away to boarding
school as a small boy and his loneliness for his mother had been
a constant anguish, a sickness. He went into the hall and picked
up the telephone, started to dial, put it down again. Not yet. He
would prolong the anticipation of pleasure a little longer, do a
last check around the place and then call and spring his surprise.
Paulo was going to be over the moon.

His Burberry raincoat lay neatly folded over the back of the
hall chair, ready to go. When had he put that there? Was there a pair
of gloves in the pocket? Probably wouldn't need gloves anyway; the
weather would be mild, almost spring in London. He looked at his
watch again. Half an hour before the airport limo would be here.
His suitcase was packed and standing in the middle of the hall with
his plane ticket and passport lying on top. He reached into his
trouser pocket to make sure the little silver penknife was attached
to his key ring; he wouldn't step out the door without *that*, the
plane might go down, God knows what would happen. He patted
the breast pocket of his jacket — probably for the third or fourth
time — to feel the reassuring bulge of his billfold stuffed with

credit cards and twenty-pound notes. He'd already crossed off every detail on the list he'd made the day before. He knew he was dithering, but to hell with it, it didn't matter as long as he didn't end up at the customs desk slapping himself all over in blind panic and suddenly remembering he'd left his wallet on the dresser in his bedroom. Some remnant of the man he used to be sat in a corner of his mind watching these antics, arms folded across his chest, eyebrows raised in amusement. What had happened to the meticulous unflappable fellow who couldn't have lost track of the time or forgotten his passport if he'd tried?

He began a tour of his second-storey living quarters in the tall, narrow house that was both his place of business and his home, making sure all the window latches were caught, checking the bolt on the door to the balcony off the kitchen. These rooms were becoming more and more of an obstacle course with all the furniture and objets d'art he'd managed to cram into them, to say nothing of the overflow of framed drawings and prints propped in stacks against door jambs and baseboards. He'd long since used up all the wall space; if he could have found a way to hang pictures on the ceiling he probably would have done it. He walked through the ever-narrowing channels between settees and armoires and breakfronts, tables and commodes, wondering wryly if the stuff was surreptitiously increasing and multiplying while he slept. Never mind, he was in the process of buying another house a few streets away, one built on simple Georgian lines some fifteen years before the turn of the century — old, by this city's reckoning. The new place had large rooms and high ceilings and tall windows, French doors that opened onto a paved terrace and a walled garden at the back, even a small east-facing solarium where he and Paulo would eat breakfast on winter mornings.

When he moved into the new house the stock-in-trade of the gallery could spread itself all over this place — large paintings and sculpture downstairs, smaller ones and works on paper on the second floor, and he'd fit what had been a little makeshift attic studio for Paulo with racks and shelves for storage. Living upstairs over his business had been fine while he was getting the gallery underway, but his life had changed. It could be a year or more before Paulo would be able to leave his family for good; the transition might even be gradual, a few months back in Sicily, a few in Toronto. However long it took, Edward would be waiting.

Before Paulo came into his life all these possessions of his — the works of art, the antique furniture, the silver and crystal, the various small collections — had been everything to him, his world. He would have run into a burning building to rescue any of them — and maybe he still would — but he no longer felt about them as if they were family, practically his flesh and blood. Oh, he still loved them, he found his treasures no less beautiful than before, but they didn't absorb him in the way they once had. His attachment to mere things had loosened, his passion had found another object that was infinitely, incomparably, more precious.

Just the same, the windows had better be locked properly, alarm systems notwithstanding. Somebody could be up a ladder and in and out with that irreplaceable French clock, for instance, long before the police got here. During his hurried walkabout Edward stumbled and cracked an ankle on a chair leg, hopped on one foot and grabbed what was to hand, which happened to be a heavy brass floor lamp. Man and lamp performed a short pas de deux before he set it back on its base and finished his meandering excursion. He sat down at the hall table, rubbed his ankle for a minute while he composed himself, and picked up the phone. Paulo answered on the second ring.

"*Pronto.*"

"*Sono io, carissimo.*"

"*Ah, Eduardo. Come stai? Tutto va bene?*"

"*Si, si. Molto bene.* Paulo, I have wonderful news. But how are things there? Is your father well?"

"He's fine, Edward, Mamma too, *grazie a Dio*. Everything okay in Toronto?"

"Better than okay. I hardly know where to begin. I sold the little portraits, all nine of them. The man who bought them thought he deserved a better price because it was a multiple sale, but he finally got it through his head there weren't going to be any bargains."

"What portraits?"

"You know, the little heads you painted when you were here."

"Of Mamma's relatives? The ones I left upstairs in the studio?"

"Why, yes —"

"You sold them? I was going to give them to my cous —"

"— all at once! Got a wonderful price, too. But here's the real surprise. You're having a show in London."

"What? When?"

"In ten days! Catch a flight to Heathrow as soon as you can and come straight to the hotel. Durrant's, on George Street. I've booked us a suite. God, Paulo, I think I'll go right out of my mind if I don't see you soon. I'm leaving tonight myself; I'll be at the gallery tomorrow afternoon to supervise the uncrating and hanging and whatnot. We can have a few wonderful days together before the —"

"Ten days! Edward, hold on! What are you talking about? You don't have enough work for a show. I haven't sent you anything new all year!"

Edward laughed. "Don't worry, I haven't lost my wits. I didn't tell you at the time, but I bought a number of paintings from your show myself, twelve of them, to be exact, and they've all gone over for this little exhibition."

"You bought my paintings? I don't understand —"

"It was business, dearest. I wanted your show to be a sellout. Good for your career, good for the gallery. It's a wrench parting with them, I couldn't have brought myself to do it if I didn't know there were going to be more. Gauthier, the man I'm dealing with in London, says we'll price them about a third higher than we did in Toronto. Of course you'll be getting the increase, Paulo, you know that."

There was a silence.

"Paulo?"

"I'm still here. I don't care about the money, Edward. I have new work, though, stuff I'd rather be showing in London. I wish you'd told me about this —"

"*Carissimo,* there'll be lots more shows. The work's already over there, the invitations have gone out, we've put announcements in the major papers. All you have to do is turn up. Oh, and the BBC wants to interview you at the opening. Gauthier arranged it, some series they're doing on London galleries."

"I appreciate what you do for me, Edward, but —"

"Did you write down the name of the hotel?"

"*Si si,* I've got it. What's this gallery called?"

"Gauthier Fine Arts. On Cork Street, near Piccadilly. Come as soon as you can, love."

"I've got some business to look after here first, Edward, I —"

"I miss you horribly —"

"— have to be in Rome for a day or two. I'll call and let you know —"

"I *want* you, Paulo —"

"*Ciao, Eduardo.*"

"*Buona notte, carissimo.*"

Just as Edward set the phone down the doorbell rang. Christ, the taxi, he'd forgotten all about it. He grabbed his coat and the tickets and passport, picked up his suitcase, and hurried down the stairs.

2

It had begun two years earlier, in the spring of '74. Edward had long been wanting to make a pilgrimage to the two small Greek temples at Paestum in southern Italy, and then to travel down through Sicily to visit the great archeological sites at Agrigento and Selinunte. The idea of those temples, and the remains of the cities around them, had always stirred his emotions, perhaps because he felt empathy with the men and women who had settled so far from home, in a kind of exile, and yet had managed to carry with them their aesthetic and religious philosophies and to express them so profoundly. That spring things were finally running smoothly enough in the gallery that he decided he could safely go away for a few weeks and leave his business in the hands of his assistants.

He began to cast his mind about for someone who might join him on the trip. At nearly forty-seven there was still no one special person or partner in his life. He'd been living in Toronto for eighteen years, the first ten of which he'd spent running the art department of Christopher's Auctioneers; for the past eight he'd been out on his own as an independent dealer. He was not without friends, on the contrary he had many, couples mostly, since people tended to come in pairs. There had been lovers, discreet liaisons, some that lasted several years, others only a few months, and the odd one that began and ended in the space of a couple of weeks. If he were to believe what his mother had told him about the circumstances of his birth, and if events had unfolded differently, he would undoubtedly have gone down in the history books as Edward the Ambivalent, because had never been able to decide on which side of the fence, sexually speaking, he was at home. His lovers had been almost equally divided as to male or female, with a slight tipping of the balance toward the male, relationships that invariably ended without regret on

Edward's part. In each instance, when his lover turned out not, after all, to have been *the one*, and the relationship had begun sailing irreversibly onto the shoals, he would divert his attention to acquiring a wonderful painting or a rare piece of antique furniture or a priceless carpet, and become so absorbed with whatever it was that he would hardly even notice when the affair was actually over and he was on his own again.

He had an obsessive idea, one to which he would not have admitted, that there was one person out there who was bound sooner or later to appear, his perfect mate, the love of his life. They would meet, they would *know*, and they would open their arms and hearts to each other. He was more than a little ashamed of this infantile wistful yearning, even while he still hoped the miracle would happen. It was pathetic, a man of his age daydreaming like a moony-eyed teenager about finding his one true love, searching the eyes of every new person he encountered. The years were rolling past. One of these days he'd be searching the eyes of the embalmer.

He wondered now if Jack Turner might feel like taking a little holiday with him. Jack had retired from the auction business; he ought to have plenty of time on his hands. Edward had worked with Jack for many years at Christopher's in London before he was offered the job in its Toronto branch. Back in London Jack had been first of all his immediate superior, then his mentor and friend, and during the last few years his lover. Edward wrote now, suggesting that if Jack would fly over and meet him in Rome they could travel together down through Italy by train, pick up a car in Naples, stop as long as they liked at Paestum, and then take the ferry across the straits to Sicily. It would be a relaxed trip; they wouldn't have to meet any deadlines other than their flights home. He knew Jack had never felt particularly comfortable behind the wheel of a car, especially driving on the wrong side of the road, so if Edward promised to do all the driving, how about it?

13

Jack sounded a little apologetic when he wrote back. He was by that time in his late sixties, some twenty years Edward's senior. He said the older he got the more phobic he'd become about flying, to such a degree that he hadn't set foot in an airplane in years. As a matter of fact he didn't fancy sea travel much either, especially in the spring, when gales were blowing and channel crossings were dodgy. The truth was he hardly left London anymore, let alone England. Edward would think he'd turned into an old fuddy-duddy, and he'd probably be right. He read a great deal now that he had the time to do it, he went to the new exhibitions and attended some of the major sales, and he had permanent seats for the opera and ballet. He would really hate to miss any of the spring season at Covent Garden. He thanked Edward for wanting to include him, it sounded like a wonderful trip, but he was afraid his travels were confined to adventures of the mind and spirit these days, sorry if that sounded a bit trite. All he could think of when he imagined leaving England was the discomfort the time change would wreak upon his bodily functions and the sleepless nights he'd spend tossing in strange beds. Europe had changed. The last time he'd been in Paris the waiters had all been Spanish and everyone was drinking Coca-Cola. England had changed too, he supposed, everyone was telling him so, but at least his little corner of it — his flat overlooking the river, Putney Bridge and the high street, the heath, the little restaurants where he had dinner now and then — still felt like home. If Edward were thinking of stopping off in London, now ...

After Jack turned him down Edward decided it was probably for the best that he wouldn't have to make compromises for anyone else's agenda anyway. A little solitude was the price you paid for being able to stop where you wanted and stay as long as you liked — or so he persuaded himself when he set out on his holiday alone. He landed in Rome in mid-morning, took a train directly to Naples, spent a single night in a hotel and started off toward Paestum in a hired car the next day before the sun had even appeared over the horizon. Warm spring air fanned his face through the open window of the car. He had the road virtually to himself.

Those temples, when he came upon them, presented a scene that looked almost surrealistic — two ancient edifices standing in the middle of a patch of goat pasture silhouetted against the morning sky, their still-erect columns casting long shadows on the dew-jewelled grass. There was no one in the little tourist office at that hour, but in any case there weren't any fences or barriers to keep him out. He got out of the car and picked his way through little heaps of rubble and fallen stone, aware of a growing feeling of delight, that same lifting of the heart that he remembered from his first trip to Italy, when as a young man he had set out by himself to walk the streets of Florence. He approached the temple of Poseidon now with an odd sense of being welcome, as though the men who had built the place still lingered in spirit and were pleased to have him drop in and look around. A small brown bird swooped and landed on a cornice where it had a nest, another creature making itself at home in these solemn temples built five hundred years before the birth of Christ. What wonderful things man has created from the raw materials the planet provides, Edward thought, artifacts that challenge the inventiveness and perfections of nature herself. He would have been hard pressed to think of something in nature as moving and beautiful as these ancient temples.

By the time he began to make his way slowly back to the car a feeling of hollowness had begun to come over him, a kind of heartsickness. He wished he could have shared what he'd just seen and felt with another soul, someone who would have found what he'd just been looking at as extraordinary and wonderful as he had himself. He shouldn't have come to a place like

this alone. His earlier sense of elation had almost entirely evaporated by the time he drove away. Maybe he was always going
to be on his own; maybe the kind of union with another human
being he'd been searching for as long as he could remember
existed only in childhood memories and dreams.

He crossed the Straits of Messina on the car ferry, spent a
night at a bougainvillea-draped pensione overlooking the sea at
Naxos, and the next day began travelling southward down the
coast. He stayed in small hotels and pensiones, taking his coffee
each morning on a terrace or balcony in air fragrant with the
scent of orange blossoms, but in spite of the beauty of the
Sicilian countryside and the archeological wonders he explored,
his mood didn't seem to lighten. The timelessness of those relics
of another civilization made him increasingly aware of his own
mortality, his own brief allotment of years. He was already more
than halfway through his life, and his future held what — more
exquisite paintings, still finer furniture, rarer objets d'art? All
those things would continue to exist long after he'd disappeared
from the face of the earth, which was well and good and as it
should be, but what did his own existence amount to? What
about the *now* of Edward Cooper?

He set his course back toward the centre of the island to see
the final site on his itinerary, the mosaic floors of the Villa del
Casale near Piazza Armerina. When he arrived he saw that a bus-
load of German tourists had just gone in ahead of him, so he
hung back and waited until they and their guide had done the
circuit. By the time he finished his own tour it was past noon and
the sun was straight overhead and scorching. He was tired and
hungry. He'd seen so many photographs of those mosaics over
the years that his eye had become jaded; the battling titans and
bikini-clad maidens with their barbells had seemed hackneyed to
him. He began to wonder why he'd wanted to come to Sicily so
much in the first place, what he was doing on the island at all.

He climbed into the stifling car, rolled down all the windows and made his way toward the nearby town, looking out for a restaurant recommended in his guidebook. *La Trattoria dei Gemelli* turned out to be an old house stuccoed in faded ochre, set back from the road among cypresses and oleanders, blending into the landscape as though it had grown there. *Gemelli.* Human twins, Edward wondered, or the zodiacal ones? A stone walkway and a short flight of steps beside the house led down to tables set up on a tree-shaded terrazzo that overlooked the dreaming sun-drenched countryside. A lovely spot. Maybe a good meal and a bottle of wine would restore his spirits.

A handsome woman of perhaps Edward's own age came out to greet him, narrow-waisted and full-bosomed, her smooth dark hair rolled into a chignon at the back of her head. Her unhurried walk seemed to invite one's attention while at the same time implying complete indifference to it. She asked Edward in limpid Italian to choose his own table, drew out his chair, strolled back inside to reappear moments later carrying a tray with a moisture-beaded bottle of white wine, another of *minerale,* and a hand-written menu. He followed her graceful figure with his eyes as she crossed the flagstones and disappeared again through the doorway before he turned his head to look around the terrazzo.

A frail-looking elderly man sitting at a table a few yards away appeared to have been watching him.

"*Buongiorno,*" Edward said, nodding.

"Good day to you," the man said in English. "Isn't she a lovely sight?"

Edward smiled and nodded in agreement. "Indeed she is. Beautiful."

"You're American?"

"Canadian," Edward replied, to keep it simple. "And you?"

"English, originally. I've been here a long time now. I fought up through Italy with the British army during the war, and after it was over I came back and stayed."

"I'd say you made a good decision."

A man came out of the restaurant just then and started towards Edward's table. The brilliance of the sun behind him put his features momentarily in shadow, but its rays lit up the red-gold hair that surrounded his head like a halo. Edward had read about the fair-haired Siciliani, inheritors of the genes of the Normans who had conquered the island during the eleventh century, and it crossed his mind that this might be one of them. As he came closer and Edward was able to see the man's face more clearly, he gasped out loud. The hand holding his water glass froze halfway to his lips.

He couldn't believe his eyes. He knew these beautiful features as well as he knew his own. He'd been seeing this face in his mind's eye for half his life, had dreamed of it nights beyond counting. He was looking at the face of Piero della Francesca's angel, the unearthly creature who had spoken directly to him all those years ago in the Ducal Palace of Urbino.

3

Edward's fantasy of perfect love had evolved over the years from formless memories of a sublime happiness that still floated, will-o'-the-wisp-like behind his eyes, whenever he allowed himself a moment of quiet meditation. He had been his mother's utterly beloved only child. What had been exceptional in the relationship between Edward and Dolly Cooper was the exclusivity of the attachment. Until he was past his sixth birthday, there had been no other person of any importance whatever in the lives of either one of them.

From the day he was born Edward and his mother had never been separated from one another for so much as an hour. Woman and child existed in a continuum so seamless that neither could have easily distinguished the place where one left off and the other began. Before he could even understand the words, Dolly had begun telling Edward that except for him she was alone, that there was not one other person in the whole world she loved, nor anyone but him to love her back. From a very young age he understood, too, that his mother was frail, a little helpless, that he would have to grow up as quickly as he could because she needed someone to look after her, and that person would be himself. He was like the little boy in the nursery rhyme, Weatherby G. Dupree, who took great care of his mother although he was only three.

By the time he was five Dolly was treating her son as though he were in every way an equal, a partner, sometimes even as though he might be the wiser of the two. She never insisted that she knew better than he, or that she was the one in charge, she made no rules as parents usually do — in fact she began looking to him for advice when he was little more than a toddler. In later years, looking back, he saw that she had always been a woman of very feeble inner resources, and he never thought of blaming her for the way things turned out. She had found it so difficult to stand alone that she looked for support anywhere she could find it. Even when he was a small child she asked his opinion and advice about practically everything.

"Do you like this dress, Edward?"

"It's beautiful, Mummie."

"Are you sure? Is it a bit too long?"

"I like it that way."

"Well, I won't change it then. What should we have for lunch, darling? Do you think if we invited Mrs. Macklehenny up for a cup of tea this afternoon she'd want to come?"

"I don't know. Maybe she doesn't like tea."

"I guess we won't, we don't want to hear her make excuses, do we?"

Edward was happy to play the part of the little man, proud of his mother's beautiful golden looks and gentle manners. He liked it when men got up and gave her their seats on the streetcar and smiled at the two of them. He would have done anything in the world to please her, and if she seemed to be in low spirits or unhappy, which she often was — in tears over her lack of money and her loneliness, and at having to live in that mean apartment on that miserable street in a city she hated — he took it upon himself to cheer her up. By the time he was six he and his mother were drinking tea and eating toast and marmalade in the mornings like an old married couple, glancing through the day-old newspaper the landlady left for them in the hall downstairs after she'd finished with it. As far as Edward was concerned there was nothing in the world he wanted that he didn't already have. He never had a reason to cry unless he'd fallen and hurt himself, and except for his mother's occasional fits of tears, his existence was cloudless, an idyll.

The two of them woke up together, spent the day in each other's company, and at bedtime — which was at whatever hour they both decided they were tired — he went to sleep curled in the crook of her warm arm, with his fair head snuggled into her shoulder, often with one small hand resting on the soft mound of her breast. If he happened to wake up during the night to find they'd rolled apart, he had only to look across and see her head on the other pillow to be reassured. No one ever intruded into their quiet domesticity; he had his mother entirely to himself, and she was devoted to him. What child could find such an arrangement anything but perfect?

In the mornings, when the sun came needling in through cracks and pinholes in the brittle dark green window blinds, Dolly would reach over and draw her son into her arms, stroke his head and hug him, and tell him how much she loved him. He hugged her back. "I love you too, Mummie," he would say. They gave each other this reassurance half a dozen times every day. After the ritual of morning greeting they talked about where they'd gone and the things they'd seen the day before, how they might spend today, maybe even give a thought to what they'd do tomorrow if the weather stayed nice. Edward was a sunny, good-natured child with a natural poise and charm about him and an air of being wise beyond his years that sometimes made strangers in the street pause and pat his little fair head before they walked on. He was not unaware of his appealing looks, and he enjoyed his ability to draw approving nods and smiles from strangers. He was mentally precocious, too. Dolly had begun teaching him to read when he was barely three, and by the time he was five he could read just about anything, and print and write very nicely too. He'd been drawing since he was able to hold a pencil.

Home for Dolly and Edward was part of the second floor of a house on Brunswick Avenue, which they called their apartment but was really just one room with a kitchen alcove at one side and a tiny bathroom in a kind of ell at the back. They ate their meals facing each other across an oilcloth-covered table in front of the window, and they slept on what Dolly called a "studio couch," a bed that folded in on itself and turned into a sofa by day. After she closed up the studio couch in the mornings she threw her brilliantly embroidered long-fringed Spanish shawl over the back of it to make the room look a little more cheerful. There was a worn blue Axminster carpet on the floor with the canvas backing showing through in patches, an easy chair covered in a faded pattern of red peonies and white lilies, a brass floor lamp with a mustard yellow shade, and a small bookcase. A green-painted dresser and a rickety wardrobe of yellowish wood with sagging doors held all their clothes. The room overlooked the street with two windows in a little bay, facing east.

Dolly received a cheque from England every month, with which by dint of careful management she paid for their rent and groceries and other necessities. They were poor — but then so was almost everyone in that old neighbourhood. By the time Edward was three the world had been plunged into the worst economic depression in history. Brunswick Avenue was on the way down, and most of the big one-family brick houses on that old midtown street were being cut up into apartments like the one Dolly and Edward lived in. The boy was unaware of their financial straits. They had everything they wanted as far as he could see, but their mean pinchpenny existence made Dolly so unhappy she thought she might go completely crazy if she had to go on living in that ugly room much longer, watching every single nickel so carefully. In winter the landlady didn't stoke up the furnace until midmorning, and the apartment was so cold at night that she and Edward had to wear sweaters and stockings to bed. She couldn't afford to buy nice clothes for them, and her good shoes had long since worn out and the cheap ones she was forced to wear didn't fit and looked horrible. Concerts and even movies were beyond her means; they could never have a proper meal in a restaurant; they had to buy little odds and ends they needed — a saucepan, or a toy for Edward — at second-hand shops and rummage sales. When she was out walking men often glanced at her with interest, but as she went everywhere with her child they naturally assumed she was a married woman — and indeed she wore a cheap wedding ring she'd bought at Kresge's, in case anyone should notice — so there was no possibility of her having a beau or finding a husband, of finding anyone at all who might rescue her from her miserable circumstances.

Dolly was a naturally gregarious person but she had no friends of her own age — no friends of any age, apart from her son, and in her present circumstances she didn't know how to acquire any. The women in the neighbourhood, mostly Catholics of Irish descent with large broods of children, eyed her with suspicion. She had begun calling herself Mrs. Cooper when she moved onto Brunswick Avenue, but there was never any husband to be seen, and the landlady, who lived downstairs and sorted the mail for the house, couldn't help noticing that Dolly's monthly envelope from England was addressed not to Mrs. Cooper, but to Miss. It didn't matter to her one way or the other as long as Dolly paid the rent, but it did to other women on the street when word leaked out. Edward seemed like a nice little tyke and it wasn't his fault if his mother was a slut, but they didn't fancy being friends with her or having their own children play with Edward. The likely truth, which they didn't put into words, was that they didn't want a loose-living woman as pretty as Dolly Cooper getting anywhere near their husbands. In any case Dolly was raised to view Catholics with suspicion and was even slightly fearful of them, what with their confessions and incense and the pope telling them what to do. There was a convent school almost directly across the way from their apartment, and the glimpses she got of those black-clad nuns made her shudder. What a way for a woman to spend her life. She hadn't attended church since she'd left home to study music in London at the age of seventeen, and even if there had been an Anglican church close to where she and Edward lived she would have had no interest in attending it. The neighbourhood took note of the fact that Dolly was never seen heading out on Sunday mornings wearing a hat, and that was another mark against her.

Edward was less than three weeks old when the two of them moved into that apartment on Brunswick Avenue. The landlady, Mrs. Macklehenny, met them at the front door when they arrived in the early afternoon of a dull wet day. Dolly handed the woman an envelope containing a month's rent and received in return the key to the front door and another to the apartment — second floor, the woman said, pointing up the stairs, first door on the left. With the keys in her hand and her tiny baby in her arms, Dolly climbed the stairs, followed by the taxi driver who came bumping up behind her with her small trunk, returned to his car for the two bags of groceries they'd stopped to buy on the way and the suitcase Dolly had borrowed from her Aunty Kay for Edward's things. After she'd paid off the driver and closed the door behind him, she laid her infant carefully in the centre of the sofa, shifted the cushions on either side of him to make sure he didn't roll off, and began to unpack the trunk and suitcase. She put her underwear and blouses and the baby's things into the one dresser the room contained, hung her beautiful evening gowns and her everyday dresses and skirts in the creaky old wardrobe, and lined up her shoes below. She stored the milk and eggs and butter she'd bought in the brown varnished wooden icebox where the landlady had already installed a block of ice, put the loaf of bread in the battered metal breadbox, and set the cans of soup and the packet of tea and a jar of marmalade on a shelf beside the stove.

She was just about to make herself a cup of tea when suddenly such a feeling of weakness came over her that she had to sit down. She didn't have the strength to do another single thing. Her baby was still sleeping soundly. She leaned back in the chair and looked around, taking in the stained oatmeal wallpaper, the fly-specked windows with the cracked green blinds and greyish net curtains, the sagging shelf of mismatched plates and cheap glass tumblers over the sink, the battered aluminum teakettle and old iron frying pan on the tiny gas stove, the radiator with blisters of brown paint flaking off its sides, the gritty-looking carpet. Suddenly she was overwhelmed with the most terrible feeling of despair. She was so tired, tired to the point of exhaustion. Everything that had happened, from the time the baby started to arrive back on board the ship until this very minute, had drained her of every ounce of energy and strength she possessed, leaving her so worn out and hopeless she didn't know how she was going to be able to go on. Twenty-six years old, and her life was over. She leaned her blond head against the back of the chair and let the tears pour unchecked. While the baby slept on, she wailed and sobbed as though she might never stop. How could those few most wonderful days of her life have brought her to this? How was she ever going to escape from this huge unfriendly country, this cold horrible city, this hideous flat? How would she ever get back where she belonged? What was going to become of her and her poor little innocent son?

As she lay in bed nursing her baby early the next morning, Dolly decided that if she were going to survive she must get out of that apartment as much as possible because if she sat around in it day after day she would certainly lose her mind. She wrapped Edward in his woollen shawls and carried him along Bloor Street until she came upon a second-hand store that had an old wickerwork pram for sale. The proprietor of the shop gave it a wiping out with a duster and Dolly put Edward into it right on the spot. After that she spent every morning out walking, came home at noon to feed and change her baby and make herself a little lunch, and then set out again for most of the after-noon, arriving home at dusk with just enough energy left to put together a meal for herself, unfold the studio couch, tuck Edward in beside her on the side next to the wall, and drop exhausted into a dreamless stupor. When the weather was fine she often didn't even come home at noon. When the baby was hungry or needed changing she would go into the women's lavatory of a public library, the museum, or a department store, even a cafe or luncheonette, to nurse him and change his nap-pie and eat the sandwich she'd brought with her for her own lunch. Nobody challenged her about using these washrooms. She looked so tired and sad, as if she had enough trouble as it was, poor pretty little thing.

When Edward was nearly two she exchanged the pram for a collapsible go-cart and pushed him around in that, even lifting it (invariably with the help of some gallant male passenger or the motorman himself) right onto the streetcar, and that broadened the scope of her travels. By the time Edward was three and could walk at a decent pace they began to go even further afield, rid-ing streetcars all over the city. In the summer they went down to the waterfront, or to High Park, or over to the Toronto Islands for the day, carrying their lunch in a paper bag.

About once a month they would board the Bloor streetcar and travel to the west end of the city to pay a visit to Dolly's Aunty Kay, who had taken her in when she'd first arrived with her newborn infant in Toronto, her one relative on that side of the Atlantic. It had been Aunty Kay who had read the newspa-per ads and found the Brunswick Avenue flat and arranged for Dolly to rent it. Kay had three boys of her own and a house and a husband to look after, so there was no question of Dolly and Edward moving into that little two-bedroom house on Garden Avenue. Over the following years when Dolly came to visit, Aunty Kay often seemed rather stern with her flibbertigibbet niece, ready with questions to fire at her the minute she walked in the door. Was she making sure Edward kept regular bedtime hours? Did his bowels move every day? Maybe he should be having a dose of milk of magnesia once a week. Was Dolly cooking him enough fresh vegetables? Since Dolly had no knowledge whatever of how to feed a young child she simply bought the things she liked herself and fed him those. Sometimes they both had cornflakes for supper or ate a lunch consisting entirely of some overripe bananas she'd got cheaply. Once when she had an absolute craving for chocolate cake she bought a whole one and they ate practically nothing else all day. Edward ate everything she offered him and seemed to thrive.

For Dolly the great attraction at Aunty Kay's house was the old brown upright piano with yellowed keys that occupied the main wall in the parlour. Uncle Alf was the musical one in that family, but he couldn't play anywhere near as well as Dolly. He never let one of her visits go by without persuading her to give them a concert, and after she'd played a few pieces from her repertoire he'd get out the sheet music for a little singsong. Alf had quite a nice light tenor voice, surprising for so large a man, but Aunty Kay could hardly carry a tune, so she didn't join in the music-making. The three boys were as unmusical as their mother and escaped out of the house as soon as Dolly sat down on the piano bench.

Plain stout Aunty Kay would sit on the sofa with Edward on her lap while Dolly played, Alf standing at one side turning the pages of the sheet music, his head bent down close to Dolly's so he could read the words. Kay's feelings about that scene were mixed, and they were mixed too about the child she held on her knees. He was so beautiful and sweet you couldn't help but love him, but the contrast between him and her own three clumsy roughneck sons disturbed her. Boys ought to be a bit knobbly and awkward, for how else would you know they were real boys? Dolly was probably turning Edward into a bit of a sissy. Just the same, Edward aroused tender feelings in Kay that she couldn't remember feeling for any of her own three — huge, bald, red-faced babies they'd all been, hard to carry and hard to give birth to with their big square heads. Her boys seemed to have been born shouting and bawling and banging their toys on the furniture and on each other, exhausting her with their wrestling and yelling and squabbling. She cared for her niece and sympathized with her plight, but her ambiguous feelings about her, and about her child, made Kay uneasy; she was just as glad that Dolly only visited every few weeks so she wouldn't have to think about it too much. Dolly sensed her aunt's reserve and prickliness, so she didn't come to the house on Garden Avenue too often, didn't overstay her welcome when she did.

Dolly became quite clever at finding ways to keep herself and Edward amused, places they could go that cost little or no money and filled the empty hours of their aimless existence. In really bad weather she and Edward might spend an entire day in one of the big department stores and as a special treat have a lunch of chopped egg sandwiches in the basement cafeteria. They drifted around from floor to floor, riding the elevators and escalators, looking at toys and children's clothes, furniture, ladies' dresses, washing machines, chinaware and linens, carpets, curtains, dry goods. And, of course, pianos. One day, when Edward was five, they were in the piano department of Eaton's uptown store on College Street. Dolly looked around, saw that there wasn't a salesman or customer close by, and with a boldness unusual for her she slid onto a piano bench and played the opening bars of her favourite Chopin étude. Suddenly someone spoke, right beside her.

"May I help you, madam?"

Dolly leaped from the bench so quickly she almost knocked Edward over. "Oh, no, I'm not buying a piano. I'm sorry. I just couldn't resist ..."

A middle-aged man dressed in a floor manager's black jacket and pinstriped trousers was standing behind the bench she'd just vacated. "Please go on," he said, smiling. "You play very well. I'd like to hear the rest of the piece."

"Oh dear, I don't get the chance to practise very often, I'm afraid my fingers are stiff ..." Dolly sat down again anyway and found her place in the étude.

"There," she said when she was finished, "you see — I really am rusty ..."

"You're a professional pianist, then?"

"Oh, I did play professionally when I was — before my son ..."

"I see. Where was that?"

"Well, actually, on the high seas," she said with a little laugh, "entertaining the passengers in the salon of the *Queen Mary*."

The man looked amused. He put his fist to his mouth and coughed into it. It was clear even to Edward that he didn't believe her. "Well, this is a far cry from what you're accustomed to, then," he said. "Do you know more pieces off by heart? Do you sight-read? Play by ear? Popular music, show tunes?"

"Oh yes, certainly, all of those, but why — ?"

"I've been thinking of hiring someone to play for a couple of hours in the afternoons, to give people an idea how the different pianos sound if they're thinking of buying. Then of course the music attracts customers to the department if they happen to be on the floor. Would you be interested in doing that?"

"Oh, I would, I'd be very interested — as long as I could bring my little boy along."

"I see. Well, I don't suppose that would be a problem, as long as he's well-behaved. Think you could behave while your mother plays, sonny?"

"Yes, sir. I like listening to her play."

29

"I can't pay you what you'll have been getting on the —
what was it — the *Queen Mary*? How about twenty-five cents
an hour?"

Dolly accepted. An extra fifty cents a day would be a big help.

4

A year later Edward and his mother were sitting down to his favourite midday dinner — a tin of pink salmon creamed with condensed milk (the recipe was right on the tin, even he knew how to make it) and canned peas — before they went off to her job at Eaton's College Street store. It was late October, cool, not cold enough for winter leggings, but when they headed out after lunch he was wearing his brown wool coat and thick knee socks and a pair of dark brown shoes the landlady had given him a few days earlier. The shoes were too big but the thick socks helped.

You'll have to let me pay you for them, Mrs. Macklehenny.

Well, if you insist, Mrs. Cooper. You can give me fifty cents if you like. There's still a lot of good in them. My Jimmy's feet are growing twice as fast as he is.

After lunch the two of them walked down to Bloor Street, crossed the road and turned west so they could pass the chemist's shop where there was a row of large bottles in the window, each containing a dead baby, starting with a little thing no bigger than a mouse and going right up to one as big as a doll, to show what they looked like before they were born. Dolly found that display a bit disgusting, but Edward never tired of looking at it. The two of them then proceeded to Bathurst Street where they boarded a streetcar. Edward put his own red ticket in the box and took his transfer from the motorman. He was an old hand at streetcars by then; he could have travelled around the city pretty well by himself if he'd had to. They changed to the southbound car at Yonge, got off at College, and went into the store.

Dolly had been playing the piano at Eaton's two hours every afternoon for more than a year now. She was playing when Harvey Rak stepped out of the elevator that day, congratulating himself, so he told them later, on having renewed a business contract in the executive offices upstairs. When he appeared in the piano showroom Dolly was seated, by coincidence, at a Rak upright, and Edward was perched on the end of the bench, hunched over, feet dangling, quietly drawing pictures of squirrels and birds in the Big 5 scribbler he had open on his knees. His mother's right arm moved in and out of his peripheral vision as she reached for the high notes on the keyboard.

Harvey Rak stopped in his tracks, his pendulous ears perking up when he heard the succession of effortless runs of a Fauré barcarole. When his eyes lit on the pretty blond pianist, their upper lids ascended into the tufts of eyebrow set like commas in his narrow squared-off forehead. He stood watching and listening, and when the lovely pianist had finished the selection, he made his sidling knob-kneed way across the floor, tacking this way and that between the pianos, and proceeded to compliment her on her musical ability, all the while eyeing the small waist and high bosom under the bodice of her dress of patterned artificial silk, noticing the way its skirt moved across her knees and slithered down between them when she moved her feet on the pedals, outlining her slim thighs.

"Very nice indeed," he said. "Fauré, I think? Do you play any of the English composers?"

She looked up and gave the man an arch little smile. "Oh, certainly!" She turned back to the keyboard, raised both hands, and plunged into a spirited rendering of "Land of Hope and Glory." When she'd brought the piece to its resounding conclusion Harvey Rak set down his attaché case and applauded.

"Beautiful, my dear, beautiful," he said, slapping his long bony hands against one another. "You may be interested to know that my own company is the manufacturer of the very piano you're playing."

"Really? Well that is a coincid —"

"And I must say I've never heard one of my instruments produce a lovelier sound."

Dolly put the tips of her fingers to her cheek.

"Oh, I'm no concert pianist, I'm afraid," she said, laughing modestly. "I'm sure a better musician than I could do your piano more justice."

Things went on in this vein for a few more minutes, and then this person straightened his shoulders and cleared his throat. He wondered, with a ducking of the head and lowering of the eyes meant to express diffidence, whether the lady — and the little fellow, of course — would care to join him upstairs for a cup of tea in the Round Room when she had finished her stint at the piano. He hoped she wouldn't think him forward, but what a coincidence it was, after all, that at the very moment he arrived she had been persuading one of his own pianos to bring forth such beautiful sound. He had just been on his way up to the Round Room himself and would be delighted if she would consent to join him. A little refreshment wouldn't be amiss, eh?

Dolly thought for a minute, and then she told the man she'd be through for the day in ten minutes and she would be happy to join him then. Why not? she asked herself. Tea in the Round Room would be a lovely treat for Edward — and for her, too, when it came to that — and the man seemed nice enough. Later, when they'd been seated in the elegant room with its high ceilings and graceful art deco ornamentation, and large tasseled menus had been set before them on the snowy tablecloth and consulted, Dolly told Mr. Rak she knew her little Edward would simply love the charlotte russe, and as a matter of fact she would like to have the same herself.

"Charlotte russe for a child of this age? Oh no. No no no," Mr. Rak said. "Most unwise. Simple fare for the young, I always say. You don't want to spoil the boy, Mrs. — ah —"

"Cooper," she supplied. "Dolly Cooper."

33

"Well, Mrs. Cooper — by the way, I do hope *Mister* Cooper won't object to my having invited you to tea on this rather special occasion."

Dolly blinked her eyes rapidly and then glanced toward her small son, her expression suddenly wistful. "Oh, no, you see Edward's father is — that is — my little boy and I, we're quite alone now —"

"Ah. I see. How sad," Mr. Rak said, his face brightening. He turned to the dark-haired waitress in black dress and frilled white apron and cap who hovered at his shoulder with her order pad at the ready.

"A banana sliced in a dish with a little milk and sugar on it, I think, and some plain bread and butter for the young man. That will do you nicely, won't it, little fellow," he said, dipping his long face in Edward's direction and giving him a whiff of stale breath. "The lady and I will both have the charlotte russe," he said, addressing the waitress again, "as long as you're sure the cream is perfectly fresh. Remove the maraschino cherries before you serve us our charlottes. They're coloured with the bodies of dead insects, did you know that, my dear? It's true. Insects from Mexico, of all the filthy places. In my opinion they are absolutely poisonous. I don't know how people can bring themselves to eat such things."

This last remark was addressed to Dolly, not the waitress. Edward knew his mother loved those cherries, and she looked as though she hadn't believed a word of what the man said about the bugs from Mexico, but she smiled sweetly and agreed with him all the same. She turned to Edward and winked. *Let's go along with him*, the wink said, *I'll make it up to you.*

A small matter, or so it seemed at the time, but that charlotte russe, as it turned out, was as pivotal to the story of Edward's life as Proust's madeleine was to his — not a talisman unleashing a flood of memories, but the first destabilizing tremor that set in motion an avalanche of unhappiness, the first of Harvey Rak's edicts against which his mother would never find the courage to argue. But for her acquiescence on the point of that cup of cream-filled sponge cake, her life and his would have evolved very differently. If she had been brave enough to face the man down, insisted that Edward be allowed to have what he wanted, obliged Rak to order a charlotte russe instead of fobbing him off with that filthy banana, Harvey Rak would have paid up the bill when they finished their tea, bowed to Dolly Cooper one final time, and gone on his way without a backward glance, having no further interest in a woman who would have the temerity to insist, ever, about anything.

"I don't want a banana, thank you," Edward said politely. Mr. Rak ignored him. A child's wishes were beneath consideration. When the banana arrived Edward stirred it around in the dish and slopped a little of the milk onto the white tablecloth, but as no one took any notice he finally pushed the dish away and sat with his chin in his hands, staring at Mr. Rak.

Everything about Mr. Rak was long and narrow. His features were more vertical than horizontal, his mouth a downturned thin-lipped curve, his pear-shaped eyes set in pouches that look weighted, as though they might contain small ballasts of sand. He had narrow angular shoulders and a caved-in chest under his grey suit and waistcoat. His shirt collar didn't begin to cover the length of his stringy neck, which reminded the boy of a tortoise he'd seen in the Riverdale zoo, stretching its neck out to an incredible length to reach its food. He watched with fascination as Mr. Rak ate his charlotte russe, his Adam's apple rising like a stone under the skin and plummeting down again as though dropping of its own weight. Mr. Rak talked on and on, telling Dolly all about himself.

"I'm a manufacturer of upright pianos, Mrs. Cooper, as I believe I mentioned earlier." He leaned back in his chair and addressed the slowly revolving black-bladed fan in the ceiling. "I do not boast but simply state the truth when I say the Rak piano is an excellent instrument, one suited for daily use in the home or classroom. There's reliable quality in every Rak piano, through and through."

"Oh, I'm sure that's true," Dolly said. "It must make you very proud to produce those beautiful pianos."

"Perhaps beautiful isn't quite the right word, my dear. I don't believe in putting the value into useless decoration. No no no. Plain cases. Solid, but plain. Every piano is made with a firm action, built to hold up well even with the heavy use it may receive in a school or from several generations of a large musical family."

"I'm sure that's very sensible," Dolly replied.

"But make no mistake, Mrs. Cooper. The keys of a Rak pianoforte are always of genuine ivory. Top quality there," said Rak, leaning down close toward her in a way that made Edward so angry he picked up his spoon and deliberately slopped more milk on the table. Mr. Rak did not deign to glance his way, and if his mother saw she pretended she hadn't.

"A middle-range instrument at a reasonable price," Rak went on. "I'm happy to say I produce something of real value to society. And what's equally gratifying," he said, smiling, or rather, scrunching his eyes so the pouches under them puckered up until they looked like little peach pits, "the financial rewards are in keeping with the quality of my merchandise."

"And they ought to be, after all," said Dolly, nodding vigorously.

"They are. They are. I own a substantial house in Richmond. Right on the river. Riverview, it's called, my house. Do you know Richmond, Mrs. Cooper? It's —"

"Well, I've never been —"

"— south of London. A short train ride. Reasonably close to the site of my manufactory in Kingston. I'll confide something to you though, my dear," he said, putting his face close to Dolly's again, "and it's this. I've been so busy building up my business through the years that I'm afraid I've neglected my personal life."

"Oh, one shouldn't do that, surely, Mr. Rak."

"You're a wise little lady. No, indeed, one shouldn't. But here I am in my late forties — although you might not guess it — feeling as though something were missing, as though my life were —"

"But what could that possibly be, Mr. Rak? Surely with your business, and your wonderful house on the river —"

"— not quite complete. To share a secret with you, dear lady, I've begun to think it might be time for me to take a wife."

Edward felt no wave of dread. The words "take a wife" meant nothing to him.

"You're not married then, Mr. Rak?" Dolly asked.

"Not for want of hoping one day to be so, Mrs. Cooper. No indeed. But here now, tell me about yourself," Mr. Rak said, straightening his narrow shoulders. "I've heard the evidence of your extraordinary musical talent with my own ears, and your — *feminine charms* —" he stretched out his horrible neck and inclined it obliquely toward her "— are evident for all to see. But you're English, too, Mrs. Cooper. Home Counties, I should say, judging from your accent. How do you come to be on this side of the Atlantic, my dear?"

His mother must have invented her story on the spot, because Edward had certainly never heard it before. She told Mr. Rak a strange tale about the untimely death of a beloved husband soon after they'd immigrated to Canada, and how she'd been left almost entirely without resources and a newborn child to raise alone. She seemed to have forgotten about her great days as a pianist in the grand salon of the *Queen Mary*, a time of her life she never tired of telling Edward about. She caught her son looking at her in amazement and winked again. He was baffled. He didn't know what was going on, but whatever it was he

37

knew it made him uneasy, that he didn't like it, and he knew he didn't like Mr. Rak, either.

"I was stranded, truth to tell, Mr. Rak. I can't tell you how much I've missed England. I've never felt at home here."

"But my dear, what a dreadful situation. However have you managed?"

"I have a tiny income from my father's estate," she said, "but it only covers the rent on a one-room apartment and the bare necessities for Edward and me."

Mr. Rak assumed a wide-eyed expression of mild horror, shook his head slowly from side to side as though he could hardly imagine such a plight.

"My job in the piano showroom is rather badly paid," she went on, "as you might imagine. I do my best," she said, smiling up into Mr. Rak's eyes, "but I do worry. Any time the department manager decides he wants a different pianist, I'll be out of a job. Only the other day he said I should try to play jazz."

Mr. Rak made a noise with his tongue. *Tsk tsk tsk.* "Dreadful," he said. "Jazz!"

"I might be forced to go into domestic service," Dolly said, looking very sad, "although even that work is hard to find when one has a child to look after." She fell silent, looking down into the scalloped white cardboard circlet that had contained her charlotte russe. Mr. Rak said nothing, but simply gazed at her, while his narrow chest swelled to the full extent of its capability, that is to say, almost an inch. Even then he didn't break the silence. He slowly lifted Dolly's hand from the white table cloth where it lay, so delicate and long-fingered and pale, and raised it until it was almost touching his lips, all the while looking soulfully into her eyes.

At last Dolly said that she must go, and Mr. Rak leaped to his feet to help her on with her black wool coat. Minutes earlier he'd been jotting her address in his leather notebook, and his little gold mechanical pencil was still lying on the table, partly hidden by the napkin he tossed down when he rose to help her. While Mr. Rak's back was turned, Edward reached across and gave the pencil a quick push so it rolled over the edge of the table and landed on the carpeted floor, and waited to see whether Mr. Rak would notice he'd forgotten it.

He didn't. He took Dolly's elbow and began steering her toward the elevator. "Come along, darling," she called back over her shoulder to Edward. He swiftly picked up the pencil and put it in his pocket, holding it tightly it in his fingers on the way down on the elevator. He was beginning to feel afraid, of just what, he wasn't sure, but all the same it made him feel strong to have that pencil in his pocket, as though Mr. Rak himself were trapped down there in the dark, under his control.

Edward already had a collection of beautiful things he kept in the wooden box that his mother had wheedled out of the man at the cigar store. There was a string of glass beads with a silver cross on the end that caught his eye where it lay sparkling in the grass in front of the convent school one day. Another of his treasures was a gold button with the raised outline of a king's crown on it, which he found on the floor when his mother was buying a card of bobby pins in Kresge's. He also had several marbles that he'd picked up in playgrounds, including a very large glass one full of wonderful swirling colours. He had pieces of silver paper that he'd pulled out of empty cigarette packages, smoothed out perfectly, and folded up small, but they weren't as important as the other things. Now he would put Mr. Rak's gold pencil in his box, and he'd be able to look at it any time he wanted, even draw or write with it if he felt like it, and smelly old Mr. Rak couldn't get it back, ever in the world, no matter how much he loved it, or needed it when he wanted to write in his notebook. It belonged to Edward.

"Just think, darling," his mother said a few weeks later, "we'll soon be out of this horrid little apartment forever. Won't it be wonderful when Harvey and I are married, and we'll all be living in his beautiful house? You'll be able to watch the swans and see all the boats going up and down the river."

"I like this house. I want to stay here."

"Oh Edward, this isn't a house at all. It's just a little piece of a house."

"I don't like Mr. Rak. I don't want to live in his house. I don't like swans, either."

"You've never even seen a swan, Edward. And you don't know Mr. Rak yet. He's going to be very good to us. He's going to be your daddy, you know."

The concept of a "daddy" meant almost nothing to him. He knew only a few children and had never met their daddies. What would you do with a daddy, anyway? Where would he sleep? He certainly wouldn't want the man in the same bedroom with him and Mummie.

"We don't need a daddy," he said. "I like us the way we are."

"You'll have a bedroom of your very own, Edward, and lots of toys and books to put in it."

"To sleep in all alone?"

"Of course. Won't that be wonderful?"

The boy gave a shriek and burst into tears. Next thing he knew his mother was crying, too, and they were hugging each other.

"Tell him we're not coming to Iglid," he snuffled.

"But Edward darling," his mother said, wiping away her own tears with the hem of her apron and then applying it to his, "we *are.*"

"Don't you love me anymore, Mummie?"

"Why Edward, of course I love you!"

"Then *tell* him we don't want to come, *tell him, tell him, tell him —*"

He punctuated these small explosions with sharp angry tugs on the sleeve of his mother's flower-patterned dress, one of the few nice ones she had. Later that evening when she was undressing she saw that the material had given way at the shoulder seam.

"Oh Edward," she said sadly, looking over to where he already lay tucked up in bed, "look what's happened to Mummie's good frock."

Dolly's one interest apart from her son had been the keeping of her scrapbooks and photograph albums, which she had always carried along with her on board the ship, before he was born. Edward had spent hours and hours leafing through these books with her, looking at pictures of Dolly when she was young, of her as a baby with her own mother, who died when she was nine. There was a young Dolly dressed for her first piano recital, another with her music teacher, Miss Smythe, Dolly at twelve holding a bouquet of flowers for having won first prize in a competition. There she was as a teenaged girl standing with her father in the cobblestoned courtyard of a Tudor inn in the English village of Amersham. "That's your grandfather, Edward. You'll never meet him. He's a harsh and cruel man." Sometimes she had to wipe tears from her eyes when she looked at these family photographs.

There were many photos of Edward's mother as a grown-up young woman, usually in the company of some good-looking young man, or a group of men and women, in parks or gardens where trees were in bloom, or in front of large buildings in a city that she said was London. Another album was full of photographs taken aboard the *Queen Mary*, mostly of famous or rich people, film actors and actresses, whose names meant nothing to Edward. Dolly had taken dozens of pictures of her son, too, with her little box camera, and put them into a special album, and she'd also kept a scrapbook especially reserved for nothing but pictures of the British Royal Family. Every Sunday while he was reading the funny papers, his mother went carefully through the sepia-tinted rotogravure section of the *Weekend Star*, looking for pictures of them to cut out and paste in her book, especially pictures of the handsome young Prince of Wales who was going to be king someday.

"There he is, Edward. Your hair is just the colour of his, did you know that? And his eyes are blue too. You have a stronger chin, though. That comes from my side of the family."

Every year since his first birthday, Dolly had taken Edward to have his picture taken in a photographer's studio over a store on Bathurst Street. She had two prints made, one for herself, to put into the album, and the other she sent along with a letter to London. Maybe the person she sent them to never even saw them. She never received a reply, but she went on sending them anyway.

Before they left the apartment on Brunswick Avenue for the last time, Dolly destroyed all the pictures taken on board the *Queen Mary*, all the pictures of herself with the young men and women in London, and the entire album of the British Royal Family. She wept while she did it, but it had to be done.

5

He sat stupefied, gazing up into a beautiful face whose every feature he already knew, scarcely aware of his surroundings or the murmuring sounds of the Sicilian noonday — the rustling of leaves in the branches overhead, sparrows chirping, the laughter of a group of women working in a vineyard below the terrace, cutlery tinkling at a nearby table, wine purling from the neck of a bottle. All this blended itself into a harmony that rose and ebbed in the perfumed air while Edward stared at the angelic being standing in front of him.

He felt himself suddenly overwhelmed with an uprush of unspeakable joy, an explosion of happiness so extraordinary that he began to tremble. Was this creature real or a hallucination brought on by the heat and sun? He took off his dark glasses and rubbed his eyes, struggling to regain a sense of reality. The angel in the white waiter's jacket was holding a pad of paper in one hand, a pencil poised above it in the other, and he seemed to be asking Edward something — for the second time, or possibly even the third: "Have you decided yet, signore?"

Edward looked down and scanned the menu, so flushed and dazzled he was hardly able to read what was written on it, and quickly ordered the first things that caught his eye.

"*Antipasti del casale*, then the house specialty — I saw it here somewhere — *il risotto con i funghi?*"

"*Bene, signore.* And after, a grilled breast of chicken, perhaps?"

"Yes, by all means, *il petto di pollo diavolo.*"

"*E, per contorni?*" The man seemed to move back and forth between the languages as though he were hardly conscious of doing it.

"Just a green salad," Edward said, still gazing into those astonishing eyes.

"*L'insalata verde.*" The waiter smiled, folding his pad. "*Benissimo.*"

It was a larger meal than he usually ate at noon, but he wanted it to go slowly, last long enough so that he could figure out what to do, find a way of getting into a conversation with this young man, as he absolutely must. As the waiter turned away after taking his order Edward surprised even himself by impetuously catching the man's elbow with his hand.

"I think you must be a descendent of the Norman invaders, with that blond hair," he said a little breathlessly — a weak reason for detaining him, but the only one he could think of on the spur of the moment. He was grateful now for his sporadic studies of the Italian language over the years and his recent reading on the history of the island.

The waiter turned back toward him with surprise, smiling.

"That's possible, I suppose," he said in his unaccented English, "but I think it's likely I got it from someone who came more recently. That's my father over there." He tipped his head toward the old man, who was smiling broadly.

Edward looked back at the son again, and now saw in his features a resemblance to the woman who had shown him to his table.

"Oh," he said, feeling foolish, "and the lovely lady who greeted me when I arrived must be your mother."

The young man and his father both laughed.

"No harm done," the father said. "I'm old enough to be his grandfather. I've been doubly blessed. Not only a beautiful young wife but handsome offspring as well to cheer me in my old age."

"You're a lucky man," Edward said. "I envy you both your blessings, since I have neither."

The food was good but he hardly tasted it. He did his best to stretch out the meal, eating slowly, engaging the young waiter's attention when he could, fabricating questions about the vineyards below the terrace, whether they belonged to his family, what other crops were grown hereabouts. He consulted him about the various *dolci* on the menu, finally ordering sliced blood oranges with toasted almonds and amaretto. It was just to slow things down; he'd already had more than enough to eat. When his oranges were finished and he'd asked for an espresso he still hadn't been able to initiate a conversation, as he desperately wanted to do.

He drank his coffee. The old man had nodded off to sleep, leaning back in what seemed to be his permanently reserved chair, hat tilting off to one side and his cane fallen to the stone paving. Edward noticed the tender way his son picked up the cane and laid it across the table, straightened his father's hat to protect the old head from the dappling sun. A party of six Germans had arrived, and a couple of Italian businessmen in dark suits, and he went to attend to them. His mother was seating another party, two fair-skinned elderly couples who could have been Dutch or British. If he couldn't manage to speak to him now, Edward told himself, he'd come back again in the evening, or the next day, as often as it took. He finished off what remained of his wine and went into the restaurant in search of the *bagno*.

The indoor dining room was large and cool, the tables laid with white cloths, large green plants in terra cotta pots set about in the corners. An espresso machine hissed at the bar. There were works of art on the white-painted walls, and when Edward's eyes had adjusted to the indoor light he began to look at them more carefully. For the second time that day he found himself gaping in astonishment. What in God's name was work like this doing on the walls of a tiny restaurant in the middle of Sicily?

He walked slowly from one painting to another. Each canvas was composed in areas of colour as glowing and pure as those Matisse might have used. There the resemblance ended.

45

These compositions were energetic and elaborately conceived, the shapes complex, the surfaces raised here and there in a rich impasto. The eye was not left sitting on the picture plane as it was with Matisse's later work, glued there by strong outlines, but was led into depth and brought out again a dozen times as it travelled across the canvas, all by means of contour and colour. Edward found his attention drawn away from the subject matter by the dazzling vibrant hues that reflected the glorious Sicilian sun. The artist, whoever he was, handled the paint with genius.

The subjects were commonplace — fruit, vases of flowers, a table in the sun with a few glasses or bowls, the natural shapes sometimes attenuated or warped to accommodate themselves to the overall design. Things seemed to be slipping in and out of focus so that no one area of the canvas or single object dominated the composition or captured the attention more than any other. There was a considerable degree of distortion from reality, but each picture had as its starting point some clearly recognizable natural motif. Several paintings were different versions of the same small collection of objects — pottery bowls, fruit, a jug, flowers — rearranged in different lights, sometimes viewed close up, and in others from a distance. It looked as though the artist could have gone on happily painting the same objects ad infinitum without ever becoming bored with them, because they were really of no importance in themselves, merely vehicles for his colour and composition. He had as clear a grasp of the possibilities of his little cluster of motifs as Cézanne had of his apples, or Edward's adored Morandi of his bottles and jars.

He was enthralled. He could imagine an entire exhibition in which the subject of every painting was that same little collection of inanimate objects. It would be a tour de force, a virtuoso performance. In addition to the still lifes there were several figure studies and one stunning large landscape, a scene framed by the architecture of a window giving onto a terrazzo and the distant countryside — in fact, he realized, shifting the focus of his eyes, the very window before him, the terrace on which he'd eaten his lunch, and all that lay beyond.

"They're my son's work. Do you like them?" The woman was standing a little behind him, on her way outdoors with a tray of little cups of coffee. She had spoken, as before, in Italian. Edward could hardly believe his ears. *He* was the artist! Again, he was stunned. Some things are too meaningful to be explained away by chance. He felt as though his coming here had been preordained from the day of his birth.

"They are absolutely beautiful," Edward said. "Marvellous. Your son is a wonderful artist."

"He sells his pictures, if you're interested. I believe his prices are quite reasonable. *Non troppo caro.*"

He looked through the open door and saw the young man bending over a table with the menu in his hand, explaining it to one of the stolid-looking Germans. It came to him at that moment that in this out-of-the-way corner of Sicily he had discovered what every art dealer dreams of — a painter of tremendous talent still unknown in the wider world, an artist who could become one's protegé in the fullest sense of the word, whose talent could be fostered, the work promoted, until it received the attention it deserved. What with his suddenly having been catapulted into a state of love, and then discovering that the object of his infatuation had produced these extraordinary paintings, his heart and brain were in such turmoil that he felt the need to sit down at one of the tables.

"I'd like to talk to him when he's free, if I could," he said, bringing the words out in a rush, "but I'll wait." He raised a hand to indicate his patience. He was still breathing rapidly. "There's no hurry, none at all. What's the young man's name? *Come si chiama, il giovanotto?*"

"*Si chiama Paulo,*" she replied, smiling.

6

When he first walked through the massive iron-studded front door of Harvey Rak's house in Richmond, Edward couldn't believe this was really a place where people lived and ate their meals and went to bed. It was immense and dark, crammed full of heavy furniture and strange terrifying objects. In the gloom of the front hall there was a huge vase covered in a design of purple flowers, a jar so big it could have held a dwarf, or a genie. Next to it was a big black dragon whose scaled back rose in writhing coils to support a brass tray, and on the tray a vase of dusty-looking peacock feathers arranged like a bouquet of flowers. He caught a glimpse through a partly open door to the right of a ferocious grinning figure, carved from some kind of green stone, sitting cross-legged on a pedestal — an ogre, maybe. The staircase facing him was as wide as a room, with blackish carved wooden newel posts and a runner of purple carpet going up the middle of the steps. The walls and ceiling of the hallway were made of rough-looking yellowish plaster, like the inside of a cave. Were they really going to live here? The place was horrible, ugly, frightening, not a beautiful house at all, but some sort of dungeon. Edward was exhausted from the ocean voyage and the long train ride to Richmond. The thought that he and his mother were going to have to stay in this house was too much for him. He collapsed on the slippery oak parquet at his mother's feet and howled in despair.

"Tell the child to stand up!" Rak barked as Dolly bent over her son patting and cajoling. "He'll learn to behave if he's going to live in this house!"

That night Dolly pleaded with her new husband, and Edward was allowed to sleep, as a purely temporary arrangement, it was understood, in the bedroom next to the one they occupied rather than in the nursery on the floor above.

"Just until he gets used to being in a room by himself, Harvey," Dolly begged. "He's never been alone at night before."

"Thoroughly spoiled, I'm afraid. You should have been stricter with him, my dear."

"I'm sure I never meant to spoil him, Harvey. I was doing the best I could."

"Well he'll stay down here only until I find a woman to look after him. After that it's up to the nursery with him."

"I'm sure that will be fine with Edward — won't it, darling, when your new daddy finds a lovely nanny to look after you?"

Edward wanted none of it, not a lovely nanny, not a bedroom of his own, not this horrible house, and not, not, not this new daddy. He hated Mr. Rak. It was clear to him that his mother was afraid of the man, that they were both his prisoners, and so he was afraid too. The so-called nursery was a large room with sloping eaves up in the attic, along the hall from the tiny bedrooms where the servants slept. When he and his mother had explored the house together she'd told Edward it was a playroom for rainy days, but it seemed Mr. Rak expected him to live up there and hardly see his mother at all. Anyway, after what happened that first night, even the dreadfulness of sleeping so far away from her almost seemed better than being down there where Rak was.

Some noise wakened him during the night. He was frightened at finding himself alone in a strange room, so he slipped out of bed and crossed the floor, padded along the hall to his mother's room where a strip of light shone under the door. He heard a coughing noise, turned the knob very quietly, and peeked in. His mother was sitting on the low bench of the dressing table with her pink nightgown pushed down off her shoulders so it was around her middle, leaving her top all bare. Mr. Rak was standing in front of her, naked, blotchy, hairy, horrible, clutching her head with both hands, bending back her neck with his fists full of her blond hair, pushing his stomach against her face again and again while she scrabbled at him helplessly with her hands. Edward screamed and ran back to his bed and hid under the blankets, terrified. He knew Rak would be coming after him next, as soon as he'd finished killing his mother.

A few minutes later Dolly came into his room. "Edward, it's all right, darling," she said, crying a bit. "That was just something grown-up people do sometimes. It means they love each other, that's all. Mr. Rak wouldn't do anything to hurt Mummie."

Edward knew she was lying. He turned over in the bed and hid his face so he wouldn't have to look at her.

The very next day Nanny appeared, a sour-faced old woman dressed all in grey, with a veil over her head like those nuns back in Toronto, the ones his mother had always given wide berth to when she met them coming and going on Brunswick Avenue. This person now became Edward's constant companion. She was way past retirement age, his mother said, which was why she was available on such short notice. Harvey Rak informed the woman in Edward's hearing that her charge was to be kept in firm check, she wouldn't be expected to go running after him from morning to night. When he came home from school in the afternoons she took him for slow, slow walks by the river, clutching his hand firmly in her own to keep him from tumbling mindlessly into the Thames, or so she said, more probably just to check his speed to match her own varicosed and bunioned pace. As soon as she was installed in the house he was banned forthwith from eating at the table with Mr. Rak and his mother, excepting on Sundays when Nanny had the day off. The rest of the time she trudged up the two long flights carrying Edward's meals on trays and sat beside him while he ate under the glare of her beady eyes, listening to her hectoring nasal voice.

"Hold your fork properly, the way Nanny taught you. Don't drink your milk with your meat. Chew that bite thoroughly before you swallow it. Eat those sprouts, I didn't give you too many. No! There won't be any pudding until those creamed onions are all eaten. I don't care whether you want your pudding or not, those onions will be on your plate at breakfast if they're not finished now."

Edward learned before long how to bring on a fit of gagging merely by thinking about such disgusting things as creamed onions for breakfast, and when his retching reached the point of threatening to return the whole meal Nanny relented, no doubt to save herself trouble, and slapped down the dish of cooked apple drenched in unappetizing yellow Bird's custard.

"You're a wretched picky boy. Poor people in the London docks would think those onions were a feast!"

He had been enrolled in a preparatory day school in Richmond soon after Nanny arrived, and his loneliness at being separated from his mother all night and most of the day became a chronic ache, a pain he couldn't get used to. He felt weak and hollow inside as if something had been torn right out of his body. He cried off and on during the nights, and spent his days waiting for the little time he and his mother now spent together. He knew she must be missing him just as much as he missed her, but sometimes she seemed not even to notice how sad and desperate he was.

Mr. Rak announced one day that he was going to take Dolly up to London to shop for new clothes —"a wardrobe properly suited to my lovely wife's station in life" — and afterward they would have dinner at the Savoy Hotel "to celebrate." Dolly kissed her son goodbye while Nanny was getting him ready for school and left in the car with Harvey Rak. By teatime that afternoon Edward was frantic with worry. Sleeping so far from his mother was one thing, but having her absolutely gone from the house was another, and it was terrible. He had no idea where Mr. Rak had taken her or whether she was even safe. That man might be planning to hurt her again. Maybe he was going to kill her and never bring her back, or he might leave her in some dark place where Edward would never find her. He lay awake in an agony of worry until at last, when it was nearly midnight, he heard the car roll up on the gravel drive in front of the house. He slid out of bed and hurried to the top of the stairs. Through the railings he watched his mother and Mr. Rak ascending from the ground floor, his mother carrying a large box before her in her two hands. Rak carried two more parcels in one arm while his other hand seemed to be holding onto his mother's bottom. While he watched the slow procession up the stairs, Mr. Rak moved his hand in some way he couldn't see, and his mother squealed and jumped a little, but when she turned her head back toward Mr. Rak, Edward saw that she wasn't really upset or hurt: she was laughing. Until they disappeared into their room he stayed hunched there, motionless, gripping the spindles of the stair rail so tightly the palms of his hands still had red marks on them the next day.

During the next few weeks, after Nanny had begun to snore in her room adjacent to his, Edward would creep as far down the stairs as he dared to watch what was going on below. There were often guests to dinner, big men in black suits and their pale grey-haired wives wearing floaty dresses, none of the women as young and pretty as his mother. After those long, late dinners, when the chokey smell of cigars came wafting up the staircase, he watched while everyone crossed the hall into the drawing room where his mother always finished the evening by playing the piano for the guests. The sound of her playing overwhelmed the boy with grief and longing for those days when his mother had played in Eaton's College Street store and they'd been so happy together. These days Dolly had so many things to do that she and Edward hardly even saw each other at teatime as they had during their early days at Riverview. Now other ladies invited her out to tea practically every day, or she was at the shops, or getting her hair done, or having fittings on new dresses and coats. She seemed not even to notice how unhappy he was, how he yearned for things to be the way they'd been before they met Mr. Rak, how much he missed her. It was almost as though she didn't want to understand how he felt, because she hardly seemed to listen when he tried to tell her.

As months passed Edward began to notice something else about his mother: her figure was becoming stouter and wider. On Sundays, the only day he was allowed to eat dinner downstairs, he watched her as she waded into helping after helping of the heavy food that was served at that table — the thick brown soup, the slabs of beef or roast pork, potatoes drowned in gravy, blistered wedges of yellow Yorkshire pudding running with fat. By the end of the first year his mother's fine-boned face had filled out until it was all cheeky roundness, and her slender body was well on the way to becoming a shapeless bolster. Even Rak had begun to chide her.

"I don't think it would be good for you to have another eclair, my darling," he said one evening, raising a hand to dismiss the maid hovering beside Mummie's chair with the tray of pastries. "I've heard eating too many sweets can lead to sugar diabetes."

"Oh Harvey, just one more." She reached up to stop the maid from taking away the tray, gripping its edge with one hand while she helped herself with the other. "I *do* love them so." She swiftly took not one but two eclairs, and began shoving great forkfuls of the creamy pastry into her mouth as though she were starving.

Of course there was no question of Edward's having eclairs. Even on those evenings when he was allowed to eat with them at that long table, under two massive crystal chandeliers that he decided in later years must have come from the lobby of some bankrupt hotel, his plain nursery food somehow followed his trail through the house and turned up triumphantly before him in the dining room. He was forbidden gravy, Yorkshire pudding, all dishes baked with cheese, fried foods, butter, cream, sausage, smoked bacon or ham, pastry, trifles, chocolate, tarts, flans, gateaux, and sweets of all kinds. While Mummie bloated herself with whipped cream, Edward ate blancmange with stewed blackberries and munched on detested arrowroot biscuits or cardboardy Social Teas.

When he turned seven Rak dismissed Nanny and arranged for Edward to attend a boarding school near Cheam. The thought of actually living entirely away from his mother seemed to him so absolutely unbearable he could hardly believe it was really going to happen. The worst of it was that Dolly didn't even seem to be putting up a fight to keep him at home.

"It was the lesser of two evils, darling," she explained. "Cheam's quite close by, don't you see? At first he was talking about a school in Scotland, hundreds of miles away. If you go to this school at Cheam I'm sure I'll be able to visit during term sometimes, and if I can't, why at least you'll be home for holidays. Oh darling, it's a little hard at first, but you'll really love it, I know."

In reply he threw himself across her lap, wailing.

"Edward dear," she murmured, putting her arms around him and patting his head, "it'll be all right. You'll see. You'll have lots of lovely new friends at school, and think of all the wonderful games you'll be able to play."

Why had she said that? She knew he hated games, kicking footballs and running races, all of it. Unless they absolutely made him do it he never joined in at school. He clung to his mother, inhaling the perfume she'd just dabbed on her wrists and throat from a small glass bottle. He couldn't imagine how he was going to be able to live without her.

When the day came that he was to leave for Cheam, Edward went to his mother's room while she was downstairs and took that tiny scent bottle from her dressing table. Even if it upset her when she couldn't find it, he had to have it. There was hardly anything left in it, only a drop or two, and she'd have to buy a new bottle soon anyway, so it didn't really feel like stealing. He pushed the glass stopper into the tiny neck as tightly as he could, wrapped the bottle in a handkerchief, and put it in the sponge bag he was taking with him to school.

The dormitories at the school were damp and frigid, and the blankets so thin his legs ached all night. Often he couldn't sleep for the cold and the dreadful loneliness that all seemed to pile up in him after the lights went out. When the other boys had settled down he would open his sponge bag and take out the little handkerchief-wrapped bundle with the perfume bottle in it, press it to his cheek and inhale its delicate scent, and after a while he'd begin to feel a little better and be able to sleep.

The boys were obliged to run about the playground wearing short pants and thin shoes however cold and damp the weather; in those days painfully chilblained fingers and toes were dismissed as the price children paid for a healthy outdoor life. The food was so similar to what Nanny had always fed Edward that he took no notice of it at all, although the other boys never stopped complaining about it. Most of the masters were somber grey-haired men, strict, but never so grim as Rak. Sometimes the blond-haired housemother reminded him a little of Dolly. He neither hated that school nor enjoyed anything about it. It was a colourless, shapeless time for him, a sort of limbo, and later, when he looked back on it, he found he could remember almost nothing about it, could hardly distinguish any one of the five years he spent there from another.

During summer holidays in Richmond, Edward idled away the rainy days alone up in the nursery, reading or drawing or working at some puzzle. He could fill in hours just leaning on the windowsill, looking down at the comings and goings on the tow path and the river. His mother didn't seem interested in taking walks or playing games with him anymore, and often stayed in her room all day, only getting dressed in time to come down to eat dinner with Harvey when he came home from the piano factory. If Edward asked her what was wrong, why she stayed in her room so much, she'd tell him she thought she must be a little bilious, and maybe he should just run along and play now because she needed to rest. If his stepfather noticed him at all it was to drive him out of doors "to get the stink blown off," as he charmingly put it. Bleak unrelenting loneliness, no less painful because it was chronic, was Edward's constant condition.

He took to walking around Richmond by himself, making his way up to the green where he'd sit on a bench reading or drawing, or he'd go drifting through the quiet residential streets to the centre of town where he'd visit the public library or browse around in the shops. Nobody seemed to pay any attention to him. He often threaded his way through the Richmond Lanes, in and out of the tiny antique shops that lined those narrow walkways. The things they sold were interesting to him, and the proprietors must have got used to seeing him wander about, because they didn't seem to mind when he'd spend fifteen minutes or so peering into their display cases full of antique watches and rings, try out one of the silver-headed Victorian canes, run his fingers over an ivory letter opener or a massive silver-topped cut-glass inkwell.

One day his attention was drawn to a tiny silver pocket knife that lay beside others under a glass-topped counter. When he leaned over to look at it more closely he couldn't believe his eyes. The knife had his initials on it, E.C., plain as day, engraved on an oval medallion on the side. A thrill went through him. That knife belonged to him, he knew it did. It had been there waiting for him. He absolutely had to possess it. He was jumping up and down as he pointed it out to the shopkeeper.

"That silver penknife there, the little one — no, the other — yes, that one — look at it, sir, it has my initials on it!" The man smiled and drew it out from under the glass display counter and held it in the palm of his hand.

"What's your name, laddie?"

"Edward Cooper, sir."

He peered at it. "Then you're quite right, Edward. Fancy that. Maybe it belonged to some relative of yours. Here, want to have a closer look?"

Edward held the little knife in his palm and gazed at it. Sunlight from the window flashed on the silver, and the metal felt almost hot against his skin. It was the most beautiful thing he had ever seen in his life. He opened its single blade very carefully and closed it again, almost breathless when he spoke.

"How much is it, sir?"

"Not too much. A pound, I guess, son."

Edward's face must have fallen. He didn't have a whole pound at the moment.

"But I could do, oh, let's say ten shillings, since it has your initials on it already."

He had seven shillings at home saved out of the pocket money his mother gave him. Even Rak tossed him a few sixpences or a shilling now and then, as one might pitch coins to an urchin on the street.

"If I went home and got seven shillings now would you save it for me until I can bring the rest?" He knew he had only to ask his mother out of Rak's earshot, and she would give him enough to make up the difference.

"Of course I will, young fellow. Bring in your seven now, and when you've got three more it'll be yours. How's that?"

Edward ran all the way home, pelted up the stairs to his bedroom, emptied his treasure box, and ran as fast as he could back to the shop.

"Here's the seven shillings," he said, gasping for breath as he proffered the fistful of coins. "I'll bring the other three shillings tomorrow morning. But sir ..."

"Yes?"

"You won't sell it to anyone else before I come back tomorrow, will you?"

The man laughed. "As far as I'm concerned, sonny, it's as good as sold. I won't even put it back in the showcase."

Edward hardly slept that night for thinking about the penknife, woke up the next morning beside himself with impatience to hold it in his hand again, to feel its warmth in his palm. His need for it was stronger than any pang of hunger he'd ever felt, almost as strong as the love he felt for his mother. His yearning for it made him forget everything else. He knew, somehow, that when he had that knife in his possession he would be happy again, at last. As soon as Rak left for work he rushed to his mother's room and asked her for three shillings, and with the money clutched in his hand he hurried back to the Lanes to claim his knife.

Owning that little silver knife thrilled him so much that for the next few weeks all he had to do was hold it in his hand and look at it to forget how much he hated Harvey Rak and his house, how unhappy it made him that his mother was lying upstairs half-asleep in bed day after day, even how bored and lonely he felt so much of the time. He could take that knife out of his pocket and press it to his cheek, or to his lips, take it to a window to let the sun shine on the beautiful silver, run his fingertip over the initials incised in its side, and feel the same burst of joy he felt the first time he set eyes on it.

It was some months before the knife began to lose some of its magic, and the loneliness and misery came ebbing slowly back, but now he knew what to do about it. He was already saving up for another knife, a bigger one this time, a more beautiful and expensive one. He looked at penknives with great concentration now whenever he went to the antique shops in the Lanes, thinking hard about which one he'd buy next. Of course that first precious one was in his pocket every day, and it always would be, but as soon as he found another one he liked, why, he would buy it and start feeling happy all over again.

7

Britain's declaration of war on Germany brought about few immediate changes in the Rak household. Harvey still went off to his piano factory in Kingston every morning, Dolly continued to lie in bed most of the day, and when he wasn't at school Edward still spent long hours by himself. He had been finding a little companionship with the young gardener who came do the lawns and flower beds twice a week, but when that lad quit to join the army he was replaced by an older man who wouldn't tolerate having Edward trail around after him, so the boy was even more on his own than before. He listened to the cook's terrible tales about the trenches in France during the Great War, how soldiers had their arms and legs blown off and were drowned in the mud. "It's going to be much worse this time, mark my words," she told him darkly. He enjoyed the gruesome stories, but they were like something from an adventure book and had nothing to do with him or anybody he knew.

After breakfast one Saturday morning Harvey Rak called Dolly and Edward to his study and announced to the two of them that he had just completed arrangements to send Edward to a school in Canada where he would be safe, far away from the threat of bombs. To Edward, Canada was now simply a large red area on the map, no longer the place where he and his mother had once lived happily together.

"I don't want to go to Canada," said Edward, who was by that time twelve years old. "I want to stay here with my mother. I don't care about the bombs."

Dolly protested that Canada was too far away, but Rak was adamant. Didn't she want the best for the boy?

"Of course I do, Harvey," she said, "but I've heard that lots of London children are being sent to schools in Wales, or Scotland. Couldn't Edward go to one of those?"

"I assure you, my dear, he'll be safer in Canada than any-where on this island," Harvey said. "Who knows what Mr. Hitler's going to do next? May invade England before we're done. Bomb us off the map. Wouldn't be a bit surprised."

"But Harvey ..."

"I don't want to hear any more about it, my dear," Rak said. "I've made up my mind. The school's going to cost me a pack-et and he's lucky to be going there. Lots of games in the cur-riculum. Make a man of him."

Soon after Rak had revealed his plan about sending him to Canada, Edward came home for a mid-term break with several folded copies of recent newspapers, which the boys had been required to read and discuss in class so they'd know what the war was all about. He had gone through some of those articles with growing excitement, and as soon as he found a chance to be alone with his mother he brought the newspapers to her room and spread them out on her bed. He still believed that the two of them were virtually Harvey Rak's prisoners and that she wanted to escape his clutches as urgently as he did himself.

"Mummie, look!" he said. "We don't have to stay in this house anymore. I won't have to go to Canada at all. Look what it says!"

He jabbed a forefinger at the headline on one of the papers. *Britain calls on her women to share the burden with our brave fighting men!* "They need ladies to take all kinds of jobs, to go to work on farms and in the hospitals and factories and schools and everything, even help build airplanes!"

"Oh, I know, darling," she said wistfully. "It's wonderful what some of these women are doing. I admire them so much ..."

"But don't you see? *You* can get a job in a hospital or a school or something, and we can tell Mr. Rak we're not stay-ing here anymore. We can go away and live by ourselves and be happy again. I can work, too. I'm old enough. I can do errands or be a helper somewhere after school. We can get away now, and Mr. Rak can't stop us! We'll be just us again! Isn't that wonderful!"

His mother looked at him with a pained expression. Tears sprang to her eyes.

"Oh if *only* I could, Edward dear, but I'm just not *strong* enough. I could never go to work every day like that. Oh, I just wish it were possible. I know how sad it is for you having to go away, I can't bear to think about it — Edward, you look so angry darling, Edward, what —"

He could hardly remember what happened next. His mother was sitting on the side of her bed and he was standing near her with the newspaper in his hand. When he tried to picture the scene afterward it seemed as though he were seeing the two of them through a tiny keyhole, and they were both small, unreal, like little dolls. Edward loved his mother more than anyone in the world, and she loved him back just as much, so how could he have suddenly run at her and driven both stiff arms against her shoulders and pushed her down flat on her back on the bed, and then, while she was trying to lever herself up onto one elbow, how could he have raised his foot and driven the toe of his heavy school shoe against her leg, twice, so hard she threw herself back with her arms over her head, shrieking in pain.

He didn't believe he'd really done that, he couldn't have. His mother always had what she called "bad legs" and often leaned over to rub them slowly with both hands. Maybe he *wanted* to kick her for letting Rak send him away, but he could never have actually done such a thing. Anyway, his being sent away was probably worse for his mother than it was for him. When she said it broke her heart he knew it was true.

He was doing his best to fix things, though. He believed he could make the war stop if he kept his promise — although to whom he made that promise he wasn't quite sure. He had found out how to do something wonderfully enjoyable but so absolutely wicked that he hadn't dared speak about it to anyone. He suspected it was what was talked about in a little health pamphlet the headmaster handed out to the bigger boys at school, something called *vice*. The pamphlet said any boy who engaged in it would get weaker and weaker until he couldn't play games and his brain would stop working and finally he'd go blind, but even before the onset of these symptoms it would be evident to anyone who looked at him that he was a secret practiser of *vice* because of his bad complexion and the bags under his eyes and the slack way his mouth drooped. He made a promise, anyway, that he would never ever do it again, and in return he required that some concerned entity — God, or someone like Him, maybe that bishop who visited the school one day — would stop the war right away. If that couldn't be managed it was to stop at least before he was put on board that ship for Canada, or at the very worst, immediately after he landed, so he could turn right around and come back. For all Edward's efforts God failed to come through.

Dolly packed his clothes very carefully into the one suitcase he was allowed to take with him. Everything else would be purchased through the school in Canada after he arrived.

"You were born on an ocean liner, darling," she said, "so it should feel just like home. Remember me telling you about that?"

"I remember," he replied a little sullenly, watching the packing with growing hollowness in the pit of his stomach.

"We had lovely talks, didn't we?"

"We used to eat breakfast in bed Sunday mornings," he said, smiling a little, in spite of himself.

"Clever boy! Fancy you remembering that! Toast dripping with butter and brown sugar and cinnamon, and lovely cups of tea. It was so delicious. I can smell it right this minute. And here you are such a big boy now, twelve years old, I can hardly believe it. Never mind, this war is going to be over soon and you'll be coming right back home to Mummie."

She finished packing the suitcase and began filling out a label with the name and address of the school in Canada toward which he would soon be dispatched. "Why," she said, putting the cap back on her fountain pen, "I went back and forth across that ocean so often I sometimes lost track of which direction we were going in." She smiled dreamily, thinking about those early days. "I had such beautiful gowns, Edward, you can't imagine. They used to give me a special allowance for the dresses I wore when I played in the grand salon. They wanted me to look glamorous for the audience."

"You used to put those fancy dresses on sometimes and walk around in them for me."

"That's right, I did." She gave a rueful laugh. "They certainly wouldn't fit me now." She gazed out the window with a wistful expression on her face. "I sold them all to a second-hand shop before we left. I was afraid of what Harvey might think of me owning dresses like that. I never told him about the *Queen Mary* or any of it, you know."

On those Sunday mornings in the apartment on Brunswick Avenue, Dolly used to lie against the pillows with Edward tucked in beside her fingering the fringes of the Spanish shawl, regaling him with tales of those great days in the grand salon of the *Queen Mary*, the wonderful dinners and romantic evenings during the stopovers in Southampton and New York. He imagined the scene, his mother looking so beautiful, dressed in layered chiffon or gleaming peau de soie, smiling down from her dais upon the first-class passengers, playing popular songs in the afternoon: "Lola," "Tea for Two," "The Wedding of the Painted Doll." In the evenings she would be bare-shouldered, with diamanté clips winking in her blond hair while she played Chopin études, transcriptions of Puccini arias, divertissements by Poulenc.

"I should have thought ahead a little better, shouldn't I? I knew you were bound to arrive sometime, but I don't think I paid too much attention to the dates, you know? Wasn't I a silly? I must have just got used to growing bigger and bigger and never thought about a real baby actually arriving one day. The funny thing is, nobody noticed. I suppose they just thought I was getting stout."

As Edward grew inside her Dolly busied herself during her off-duty hours letting out her clothes and remaking them to conceal her increasing size under overblouses and tunics, cleverly lowering the necklines of her gowns to expose more of her ever-lusher bosom in order to keep the eyes of her audience on her décolletage rather than farther down. Toward the end she draped herself in the brilliantly embroidered shawl that had clothed the gleaming lid of the grand piano. On that particular afternoon she concluded a rendering of Debussy's "Clair de Lune," rose with difficulty from the tufted velvet piano stool, and made her way to her cabin, bent over at the waist, with her arms wrapped around her abdomen as though she were trying to keep it from falling off.

"Dynamics were horribly off during that last performance, I'm afraid, Edward," she told him, laughing. "I must have put in all kinds of *fortissimi* Debussy never intended. Everybody was very kind. They even put together a lovely layette for you. The nurse who helped me when you were being born said she couldn't imagine a person not paying attention to her dates like that, and whatever could I have been thinking of? I've never been too good at looking ahead, have I darling? Your mother's a bit of a Dumb Dora." She leaned over and kissed the top of his head.

When the ship docked in New York the captain instructed the purser to give Dolly a month's extra pay, wished her well, and informed her that her services would no longer be required by Cunard Lines. Dolly rested for a few days in a hotel in New York and then boarded a train in Pennsylvania Station. She travelled all day and arrived unannounced on the doorstep of her only relative on that side of the Atlantic, her father's younger sister Kay, who lived in the west end of Toronto with her husband, a streetcar motorman. When Aunty Kay cabled the news to Dolly's father at the inn he managed in the village of Amersham, Bucks, that stern man informed his daughter by return cable that he would send her an allowance on a regular basis as long as she didn't disgrace him by coming back to England with her bastard. Edward's mother became a remittance woman.

Edward and Dolly and Harvey Rak had paid a farewell visit to Aunty Kay before they left for England to live in his house in Richmond. Kay ushered them into the front room where the three of them sat in a row on the green plaid sofa, Dolly on Edward's right, twittery and nervous, twisting the pair of black kid gloves she held in her hands, Harvey Rak on his left, too close, smelling unpleasantly of tobacco and his own particular sourness. Aunty Kay sat across from them in a dark brown plush armchair with a crocheted antimacassar along the back, her eyebrows knitting together over the top of her nose and a disapproving expression on her face.

"Would you care for a cup of tea, Mr. Rak?" Aunty Kay asked in a rather sharp tone.

"No. No tea. I don't take anything between meals, Mrs. Garden."

"Edward," Aunty Kay said, "why don't you go back to the kitchen and play with the boys? They have a puppy. Run along."

He did what she said. The three big boys were playing some noisy game at the kitchen table, and when Edward appeared at the doorway the puppy, so called, although it stood nearly as tall as he did, came out from under the table and barked at him, which made the boys laugh. He sidled back down the hall with his shoulders against the wall and stood listening behind the jamb of the living room door.

"— know there won't be any more cheques from Amersham after you marry," Aunty Kay was saying. "That was one of his — one of the stipulations."

"I am quite capable of supporting my wife, Mrs. Garden," Mr. Rak said. "She will have no need of cheques from Amersham. She will have charge accounts at any of the shops she chooses to patronize."

"Did I tell you about the beautiful house we're going to live in, Aunty Kay?" Dolly asked. "Harvey says it's right on the Thames. It's called Riverview. Won't that be lovely?"

"Oh, it'll be very grand, I'm sure," Aunty Kay said. "Damp, though, I should have thought. Rather be higher, myself, if I had to live in England again."

Mr. Rak stood up and looked at his pocket watch. He tugged down his waistcoat and took hold of Dolly's arm to draw her to her feet. She kissed Aunty Kay and told Edward to give her a kiss, too. They called goodbye down the dark hall to the boys, who appeared not to have heard. As they filed out the front door Edward looked up at his mother and saw she had tears in her eyes, so he surreptitiously squeezed her hand, and she squeezed back without looking at him, while she arranged her face in a smile for Harvey Rak.

8

Was it the horror of so irrevocable a separation that fixed everything in Edward's memory so precisely? Even the smells came back to him — the cold, soapy, boiled-tea air of the railway station, the stifling dusty plush smell of the carriage during the train journey, the fishy-salty fog on the docks at Liverpool, the stink of oil day after day in an airless cabin, which, along with the incessant thudding of engines, made him sick most of the way across the Atlantic.

He'd been herded into a train with a crowd of other boys, all of them in caps and navy blue coats and short trousers, the straps of satchels and bags criss-crossed over their chests, identifying tags in glassine envelopes pinned to their coat fronts. After they'd boarded the train and found seats, Edward peered through the dirt-spattered window and scanned the crowd standing on the platform, searching for his mother's blond head and round figure, his last glimpse for many long years of the only person in the world he loved. At last he spotted her, frantically blowing kisses toward a window several seats ahead of him.

"I'm here," he shouted, waving frantically from his side of the rapidly fogging glass, but he knew she hadn't been able to see him. The train pulled slowly out of the station and began rocking and creaking its way out of London. One or two of the youngest children had started to cry, while others were already getting up to rough-and-tumble games as though they hadn't a care in the world. A pair of adult supervisors, a man and a woman, patrolled the car, trying to comfort the weeping young ones, admonishing the rowdies. He wished he could shut it all out, those red-faced boys, the doggy smell of damp raincoats and ancient stained upholstery, the cindery allotments that flashed past the window, marking the miles that were separating him from his mother. He opened his satchel and felt for the leather drawstring bag that held his collections, each item carefully wrapped in cotton wool. He had added three more treasured perfume bottles to the original one he'd taken from his mother — a tiny Lalique bottle that he'd also picked up from her dressing table (unnoticed, he thought, she had so many, and it had been empty anyway) and two little silver-topped Victorian glass vials he'd bought in the Richmond Lanes. His penknives were in there, too — five of them now, the original silver one and four more: one in genuine tortoiseshell, two larger ones in silver, and another with gold inlay in a floral design on the silver in the shape of a lily. He'd seen another he yearned to have, the whole case in ten-karat gold, but it cost much more than he could put together.

In his bag he also had a small red oblong box that held the brand new writing set his mother had given him just before he left. He took it out now and lifted the lid, drew the marbled red fountain pen and matching pencil out of the elastic loops that kept them in place. While the train hurtled on toward Liverpool, he leaned back against the seat and closed his eyes, holding the pen and pencil tightly, one in each hand, breathing very quickly to keep from crying.

The very road divided itself humbly and split in two, to the left and to the right, as it approached the school. The building looked very much as Edward had imagined the workhouse in *Oliver Twist* — a massive forbidding facade of soot-darkened red brick and worn red sandstone pierced with small secretive windows. A tall solemn clock tower kept a lookout in all four directions for unwelcome intruders. Arriving in the middle of a heavy thunderstorm did nothing to soften the impression. Things weren't any better inside — shiny brown-painted woodwork, mustard-coloured walls, long corridors with newly varnished wooden floors in whose mirrorlike gloss a distant figure became a pair of Siamese twins joined at the soles of the feet. He was assigned to one of the junior dormitories along with five other boys from faraway places — four, including himself, from the British Isles, a Spanish-speaking boy from South America, and a Dutch boy whose family had been stranded in Canada by the war. Their beds were separated by small three-drawer dressers, of which the top drawer was fitted with a hasp and combination padlock so they could keep their letters and other precious possessions safe — an out-of-character courtesy provided by a place that otherwise allowed virtually no privacy or scope for individuality. The bathrooms smelled of carbolic, and the whole place smelled of boys. It was an improvement over his school in Cheam in one respect — the building was actually warm, not just in the daytime, either, and the air was so dry indoors that his hair crackled and clung to his comb when he tried to part it, a phenomenon he'd never encountered before. The heat came billowing out of fat radiators that clanked and hissed all night and got so hot they could scorch you if you laid a hand on them.

Each boy was handed a booklet upon arrival that listed the school rules for every situation, followed by a list of punishments for their infraction. Lesser offenses like tardiness, failure to do prep, or having food in the dorms would result in loss of "tuck" privileges, while for the worst crimes such as cheating, stealing, lying, plagiarism, damaging school property, bearing false witness against a student or teacher, or deliberately causing another boy physical harm, they could receive canings or expulsion or both.

Mandatory participation in sports constituted for Edward a form of unearned punishment that was inflicted daily. From his first day in class he was called "Limey" because of his accent, which quickly became "Slimey" when it was discovered how little aptitude he had for athletics. He was the team member who

70

was never chosen, always assigned, amid the groans of the side obliged to take him on. North American football, or rugby, as they called it, was to Edward an incomprehensible wrestling match in the mud. By the time he got back on his feet after a tackle he no longer knew which goal his team was supposed to be aiming for. When winter arrived he was pressed into playing brutal Canadian ice hockey even though he could hardly stay upright on his skates, but he usually managed to hurt himself early on in the game so he could spend the rest of the afternoon slowly freezing to death on the unprotected wooden bleachers beside the hockey cushion.

One evening, soon after he arrived, a strapping prefect from the senior school was sent into the juniors' showers with instructions to make sure the smaller boys were washing their hair.

"C'mon over here, Slimey. Gotta wash your hair for you, baby."

"I already washed it myself."

"Oh yeah? Well I'm going to wash it again."

He came at Edward with the cake of soap, gripped his shoulder with one hand, and began rubbing soap into his scalp. In a few minutes Edward's eyes were stinging, and when he tried to clear them by tipping his face up into the shower the big boy snatched the opportunity to shove him face-first into a corner of the stall behind the jet of water and splay his body against the tiles. There was enough steam and shouting and horseplay going on all around that no one paid the slightest attention to Edward's shriek of pain; it was over in a minute, and he was shoved back under the streaming spray.

That was the first of several assaults about which it seemed there was nothing to be done. The word went around that one of the boarders who had reported a similar incident to his housemaster had received a caning for telling lies. None of the boys in Edward's little foreign enclave spoke about what happened to them from time to time in the showers and locker rooms, but there was a sort of unspoken solidarity among them that took the form of offering a handkerchief when another boy cried at night, of sharing tuck with whichever of them seemed the most sad or damaged, lending one another small items like erasers or toothpaste when needed, even a pair of socks or a shirt when one of them had forgotten to put out his laundry. Sometimes they opened their locked drawers and showed one another their treasures. The others had photographs and letters and religious objects, prayerbooks and rosaries like that one Edward had once found on the lawn of the convent school. None of them had a valuable collection of beautiful things like Edward's knives and scent bottles. He kept his pen-and-pencil set in his locked drawer too. He wouldn't have dreamed of using it in class in case it should be stolen when his back was turned, or simply taken from him by a bigger boy.

"This school is and has always been the breeding ground of statesmen," announced the portly, blue-suited, black-gowned headmaster at the first assembly. "Those of you who have just arrived from the Mother Country will find yourselves in the company of the sons of some of Canada's leading citizens. Do not imagine you have fallen among members of an inferior colonial race." He laughed, and the assembly laughed with him.

Many years later, when Edward came back to Toronto to live, he learned that many of those loutish seniors had indeed become noted barristers and physicians and captains of industry, even turned themselves into high-ranking politicians who got their pictures in the papers with their attractive wives and sons and daughters. When he read one day that a well-known jurist had given that very school credit for being the making of him, Edward managed a wry smile. Perhaps it was the making of him, too, in its awful way — maybe a childhood of loneliness and pain is just as energizing and instructive as one of cloudless bliss.

9

Some of the teachers were amiable and well-liked, while others were simply to be endured. Monsieur Olivier, the French teacher, was sympathetic and kindly toward Edward from the very first day, and even gave Edward what appeared to be his special attention. As the term progressed Monsieur began touching Edward's head or patting his shoulder approvingly as he walked up and down between the rows checking translations and declensions.

"*Très bien, Edouard, très bien.*"

"Are you playing in the rugby match, *mon petit?*" he enquired one day, putting a light hand on Edward's shoulder as the class was filing out. The burly lad ahead of him gave a snort of derisive laughter.

"No, sir," Edward said.

Monsieur held onto his shoulder, keeping him back until the rest of the boys had gone. "Then perhaps you would do me a small service," he said, touching his cheek with his palm in such a fatherly and affectionate way that the blood rushed to Edward's face.

"Yes, sir."

He handed the boy a slip of paper. "Go to the library and borrow me these books. *Dépêche-toi.* Bring them to my office *tout de suite, s'il tu plais,*" he said with a smile.

On his way to the library Edward stopped in at the washroom, and as he stood at the washbasin he looked in the mirror and saw a pale mark on the shoulder of his navy blue blazer, the print of Monsieur's chalky hand. He stared for a moment, and then bent his cheek to his own shoulder, rubbed his face against that chalky mark, caught a whiff of something sweet and pleasant. His heart thudded in his ears.

The librarian was a pale older man who moved about behind the desk leaning heavily on a cane. He pushed the little list back across to Edward without looking at it, rolling his eyes up to the ceiling.

"Mr. Olivier has those books out already."

"But he told me …"

"Run along. Never mind about the books. Go on outside and watch the game. He'll forget all about it."

"But …"

The old man turned away, shaking his head.

Edward ignored his advice, but when he went to M. Olivier's office empty-handed, the man stood looking down at Edward with a sad expression on his face. "You disappoint me, little Edouard," he said. "Such a simple thing I have demanded, to bring me a couple of books. Come in and sit down with me, and we will talk. Boys must do what they are told. Is this not true?"

"Yes, sir."

He took hold of the Edward's arm, drew him into the room, and closed the door and locked it. Edward looked around, saw an old oak desk on which were a stained blotter, a reading lamp, a pile of students' workbooks, a white bowl containing two red apples, and an apple core that was turning brown. Maybe the apples accounted for the sweet smell on his blazer where Monsieur had touched it. He wondered if he was going to get a caning. He'd heard other boys talking about canings, but had never earned one for himself. If that was what was coming he wouldn't let himself yell, because he'd been told that yelling always made the punisher angrier and increased the number of strokes a boy would get.

M. Olivier took his time before turning his attention back to Edward. He slipped off the jacket of his dark suit and hung it carefully on a hanger suspended from the hook on the back of the door, crossed the small room and sat down in his swivel chair. Once seated, he reached forward and drew Edward toward him by his arms until the boy was standing between his knees.

"Now, little Edouard," he said, "perhaps we can learn to understand each other."

Before he unlocked the door and sent Edward on his way, Monsieur put his arms around him and hugged him one last time, holding him close, whispering in his ear that he was an angel, that he adored him. Edward no longer had any thought of resisting, he felt no desire to pull away or try to escape. His sobs had long since ceased, his tears had been gently wiped away with Monsieur's white handkerchief. Now he nestled his face under Monsieur's firm chin, inhaling the clean, fresh-bread man-smell of him, almost wishing he could stay wrapped in those strong arms for the rest of his life, drowsy and melting. He was in a state of utter confusion. Deep inside he felt shame, knowing with certainty that what Monsieur had done with him had been wrong — but how could it be wrong, when part of it, at least, had been so wonderful — not just *that,* but the beautiful feeling it gave him to have Monsieur hold him close like this, and kiss him, and tell him he adored him.

"I have loved you from the very first tiny moment you came into my classroom," Monsieur said. "You are precious to me, *mon petit ange.* You must always trust me. You must always come to me when you are troubled. Promise?"

"Yes, sir," Edward mumbled, dreamy in the snugness of that manly shoulder, the warmth of those strong arms.

"*Je t'adore, mon petit Edouard. Je t'adore.*"

The affection the man had lavished on him made his heart feel as though it would burst. After the office door closed behind him Edward went up to his dormitory and threw himself down on his bed, weeping, not caring who saw him, sick with grief and confusion, loneliness and yearning. In the days that followed he could think of nothing but the melting happiness he'd felt

75

when Monsieur held him in his arms and told him he adored him. One evening, a few days later, he could bear it no longer. He excused himself from prep and made his way to Monsieur's office. He could see a light through the crack in the door, hear Monsieur's voice speaking in French, pausing, speaking again. He must have been talking on the telephone. Edward raised a hand to knock, but suddenly his stomach felt as though it were rising and flopping upside down inside his body, and he barely made it to the bathroom in time to retch up his supper into the nearest toilet. He didn't go back that day, but the next morning M. Olivier again held him back behind the rest of the class.

"You're doing very well with your French, Edouard. I have some little storybooks I think you could manage. Would you like to come along to my office after your last class and borrow them?"

"Yes, please, sir."

"*En Francais, mon petit.*"

"*Oui Monsieur, je voudrais …*"

"*… emprunter …*"

"*… emprunter les livres, s'il vous plait.*"

His life now began to revolve around his encounters with this man who loved him so much and whom he loved in return. His heart raced when he so much as thought of M. Olivier. Now, in that same office, with the door securely locked, M. Olivier sometimes undressed him completely, gazed at him, caressed the smooth skin on his chest and arms, his back and buttocks and the lengths of his limbs, telling him over and over what an exquisite creature he was, how absolutely lovely, a veritable young god. Perhaps it was this new pride in himself that emboldened Edward to do something about the intermittent attacks in the showers. He got hold of a partly used cake of soap and embedded the broken-off point of a compass in it so the merest sharp tip protruded, and the next time he was in the shower and one of the hulking older boys laid hands on him, that boy found himself leaping backward, bellowing in pain and outrage, with blood streaming from a long gash in his thigh. The housemaster stuck his head into the steam-filled shower room.

"What's going on in here? What's the matter with you, Jameson — where's that blood coming from? Turn the water off." Several half-clad boys now appeared in the doorway, goggling at the spectacle.

"Slimey did it," Jameson hollered, pointing back toward Edward, who stood empty-handed, dripping and innocently naked. Jameson was bawling outright, dabbing at his bloody leg with a washcloth.

"Don't be a fool, Jameson. How could Cooper have done that? Get something on and go up to the nurse. Wrap a towel around that leg. Pick up that soap, Cooper, before someone breaks his neck. Get your pyjamas on, the rest of you. The show's over. *Did you hear me?*"

The word must have got around that Edward was a dangerous little bugger, not the angel he appeared to be, and by the time that term came to an end the big boys appeared to have lost interest in him.

| **10** | Summer holidays, for those who had no homes or families to go to, consisted of two months of mosquitoes and rain, sunburn and poison ivy, mildewed clothing and blistered feet at a boys' camp in Algonquin Park. Edward was a poor |

swimmer, couldn't dive without filling his sinuses excruciatingly with water, hated spiders and the sickening smell of skunks at night, was terrified of the bears that everyone assured him were snorting around in the trees only yards from the cabins. He loathed the ugly so-called "crafts" of birchbark and leather the boys were forced to create. Boats scared him, death by drowning always seemed only inches away. He got angry when the boys played practical jokes, like swamping the canoe he was assigned to paddle with another hopeless misfit, but when he gave vent to his emotions and yelled at his tormentors he was labelled a "poor sport," which was the worst thing a camper could possibly be.

All that first summer he had been able to think of nothing but getting back to school and being with Monsieur again, but when the new term began he realized, with the dawning of a sickening clarity, that Monsieur didn't love him anymore. Nothing Edward did or said pleased him. There were one or two invitations to visit the little office, and then no more. On those occasions Monsieur had seemed disappointed with the boy, looked at him with an expression of distaste that reminded him of Rak's cold glare. Eventually there were not even smiles when their paths crossed, and during lessons Monsieur's manner was abrupt, even harsh. The more Edward tried to please, the more he was ignored. To make matters worse, Edward saw that Monsieur had begun drawing a curly-haired Welsh lad aside for the little private chats he had once enjoyed, had begun letting his hand rest on the smaller shoulder of this new so-called war guest, who was a year or two younger than he was himself.

He was filled with rage at the other boy, so wretched with jealously he could have killed him. He couldn't believe Monsieur could love this false red-faced giggling little creature the way he had loved him, but everything he saw told him it was so. He was desperate, sick with anxiety, when he finally summoned the courage to go uninvited and knock on the door of M. Olivier's little office.

"Ah, Cooper. What is it?" M. Olivier glanced at his watch. "I have no time, I'm afraid. *Je suis très occupé a ce moment —*"

"Sir, please ..."

He began to weep, couldn't speak, dropped to his knees right there in the doorway and wrapped his arms around Monsieur's legs, pressed his head to the man's thighs. "Sir, please, please ..."

"Get up! Get up, you stupid boy, before someone sees you!" He took Edward's shoulders in his strong hands, hauled him to his feet, pushed him out into the hall, backed into his office, slammed the door and turned the key in the lock. "Go away," he growled through the closed door.

Edward was so grief-stricken and heartsick that he became ill, couldn't keep his meals down, began to run a fever and had to spend a week in the infirmary. He lay curled up in bed sobbing silently into the pillow, wishing he could go to sleep and never wake up. The nurse came to his bedside to wipe his face and offer drinks and little meals of soup or oranges and tea and toast, and eventually he pulled himself together and returned to classes, pale and thin, but outwardly, at least, recovered.

He was taking some books out of the library one day when the old librarian caught his eye and delayed him by holding onto the books instead of pushing them across the counter.

"I hear you've been sick."

"Yeah."

"Don't take it personally, son."

"What?"

"Nothing to do with you. He likes 'em young, that's all."

At fourteen Edward's limbs had grown to stringy length and his knees stuck out like doorknobs. By the time he moved up to senior school a year later he'd begun to fill out, even though he continued to avoid those bully-boy field games. A slight case of acne cleared up, his chest expanded, and eventually he became, from what he saw in the mirror, quite a decent-looking human being of average height, square-shouldered and agile, reasonably good at fencing and badminton, which were the only sports that interested him. All the boys were required to do military drill in the school cadet corps, every one of them prime officer materi-al, they were assured, should the war go on long enough to require their dubious talents in the armed services. Every so often a real sergeant-major from some reserve unit came to put them through their paces, motley collection of musical-comedy soldiers that they were, in their dark blue serge outfits with a red stripe down the pant leg and the one-size-fits-all forage caps stuck this way and that on their variously barbered heads. The boys who played at being officers ordered the others around with such stern and earnest expressions on their faces you'd have thought they were all headed for the battlefield the next day.

Edward had little interest in joining the shoulder-punching, dirty-joke-telling camaraderie that appeared to bind so many of his schoolmates to one another. He spent his spare time reading his way through the poetry and literature shelves in the school library, almost entirely the works of English novelists and poets, as there didn't seem to be any Canadian writers to speak of — although his English teacher did his best to persuade them that Canada should take credit for John Buchan, who had been the country's Governor General. He maintained good enough grades neither to stand out as a scholar nor appear to be in need of extra tutoring, which meant that through all those years he went more or less unnoticed by students and staff alike, which was exactly the way he wanted it. As for his sexual urges, *vice* sufficed. He had long since ceased to attribute to that activity any occult powers or threat to his moral or physical integrity. If there'd been any truth in the myth every boy in the school would have been a gasping hollow-eyed wreck.

As an upper school student Edward was allowed to go about the city on his own on the weekends, but even to one who had been leading as cloistered a life as he, Toronto didn't offer much excitement. The art gallery's collections and the artifacts at the museum were good for a few excursions; there were movies, of course, and a single burlesque house the boys all talked about which he visited a few times by himself, pleased with his own depravity. He occasionally trailed aimlessly through the department stores on Saturday afternoons, one day even dropped in on the piano department of Eaton's College Street store, which he remembered clearly from the afternoons spent there while his mother played for the customers. He was allowing himself to be carried away in pleasant nostalgia until he realized, with a jolt, that this was the very place where Rak had entered their lives, which spoiled his daydream entirely.

It wasn't until he discovered a cluster of pawnshops downtown on the fringe of the business district — one in particular that specialized in antique fountain pens — that Edward began to look forward with any sort of eagerness to his Saturday outings. His first sight of those rows of beautiful pens displayed alluringly on a length of black velvet made his heart beat faster and his fingers itch to hold them. He bought his first one the day he discovered the place, a Waterman with a smooth dark red barrel, the 1940 so-called hundred-year pen that had been designed with the military-style clip right at the top so it wouldn't stick up out of an officer's breast pocket. That modest purchase only whetted his appetite. Pens quickly became a passion.

Whether from a feeling of guilt, or what was more likely, a wish to appear benevolent and open-handed to the people in charge of his stepson, Rak had been sending quite generous quarterly drafts of money which were deposited in a sort of private account for Edward to draw on whenever he needed it, to buy extra sports equipment, clothes to wear on weekends when he was out of school uniform, hobby materials, tuck, books, gifts to send home to his mother. When he reached senior school the rules changed and he no longer had to account for what he spent at all, just filled in a chit and withdrew cash, no questions asked. He'd had little interest in money or what it would buy in the early years, and the stuff had snowballed into quite a tidy sum. Now he had become passionately interested in those fountain pens, and by the time the war ended and he returned to England he had bought a Waterman 552 Sheraton, for which he paid eighty dollars; a sterling silver Waterman 456 with a beautiful floral overlay in a pansy design; and the prize of his collection, a solid gold 556 that cost more than two hundred dollars and all but wiped out his little account at the school.

There was an upper-floor room in the school reserved as a place where students could go and listen to classical records, and to that place Edward often slipped away, carrying with him a couple of flimsy airmail-letter forms, a bottle of blue-black Quink, and the case in which he kept his beautiful pens. He'd choose one of them to use that day, fill it with ink, and settle down to write to his mother. First, though, he would pick out some music. The records were in brown paper sleeves inside cardboard-backed albums, and he worked his way slowly along the shelves — Bach, Beethoven, Bizet, Borodin, Brahms. He would pull a record out of its sleeve, blow on it to remove the dust, set it carefully on the turntable, pick up the arm, clean the ball of dust from the needle with the tip of his finger, and place it delicately on the rim of the record. In a few seconds the room would be full of music that somehow gave Edward a feeling of being at peace with himself and the world.

He would read his mother's most recent letter again and compose one in reply, filling the little blue form with his smallest writing. After he'd licked the flaps and pressed them into place, he would fold his arms on the table and lay his head down on them, close his eyes and open his pores to the symphony or concerto or, what he loved best, a recital of piano solos. The music conjured up images in his mind — perhaps not images, exactly, but tender feelings that reminded him of something beautiful he'd seen somewhere, although he couldn't have said quite what. Sometimes he found himself almost in tears when he was listening to a lovely piece of music, without knowing what he was crying about, perhaps remembered happiness. His mother often seemed near him then — especially when he stumbled on a piece she used to play long ago. That little room filled with beautiful sound was a refuge where for an hour or two his chronic loneliness and yearning faded and he felt a sense of safety, as though nothing bad could happen as long as the music was playing.

During his final year Edward became a little worried about his mother. A few of her letters sounded strange, as though she were occasionally confused. Once she said how happy she was going to be when her dear Edward got home from Scotland. She didn't say a word about being in poor health, so her condition was a complete shock to him when the war in Europe finally came to an end. He sailed to England along with a horde of other evacuees on the return voyage of a British ship that had carried Canadian troops home to Halifax. It was late in the summer of 1945, almost six years since he'd caught that last glimpse of his mother through the window of the train.

Dolly had become an almost total invalid. The diabetes Rak had wished on her and the gangrene that followed had cost her part of her left foot, and there was something wrong with her heart so she panted for breath and her lips turned blue when she exerted herself. Rak brought her to meet Edward at the Liverpool docks, that man looking quite unchanged from the day he'd come sidewinding through the piano department in Eaton's, while Dolly was almost unrecognizable, a pale shapeless creature in a wheelchair that was pushed along by a good-looking redheaded nurse. They looked like a family in which the nurse and Mr. Rak were the unfortunate parents of a gross retarded child.

11 Edward watched as the young man came through the door into the comparative gloom of the dining room, his dark figure silhouetted against the brilliance of the day as he approached, square-shouldered, youthful, self-confident, so handsome it made Edward's heart race just to look at him. He tried for a moment to imagine how he himself must appear to this man — another pale middle-aged tourist from some dreary cold country, dressed in drab foreign-looking clothes. Did he suspect that Edward's mouth had gone dry, that his heart was racing and sweat had broken out in his palms? He wiped his right hand surreptitiously on his trouser leg before he stood up and held it out. Paulo extended his own, square and muscular and beautifully shaped.

Edward spoke in Italian, thinking that would put the younger man at his ease, which was foolish of him, as it turned out.

"I'm Edward Cooper," he said. "I was admiring these wonderful paintings. Your mother tells me you're the artist."

The young man smiled and returned the handshake with a firm grip. He seemed to be considerably more self-possessed than Edward was himself.

"Paulo Jones. I'm glad you like them. Mamma said you might be interested in buying one," he replied — in perfect English.

"Yes, I'd like to buy one, maybe more than one. Do you have a minute so we can talk?"

"About prices, you mean?"

"Yes, prices among other things, but — maybe you could tell me a little about yourself — how long you've been painting, where you studied? You have an extraordinary talent —"

"I don't know about that," he said, dropping into the chair facing Edward. "It's a bit boastful to start calling yourself an artist in this country."

"You mean Leonardo's a hard act to follow?"

He laughed. "Something like that. Anyway, as far as the studying goes, I didn't spend much time in art schools."

"But you've had some training, surely —"

"Some. I learned more in the museums and churches than I did from any teachers. When we —I — started, I wasted a lot of paint. I went to an art school in Palermo for a while because Mamma wanted me to, but I didn't like it."

"No? Why was that?"

"The teachers were a bunch of stuffy old *uccelli*, all they wanted was for us to learn a set of rules and follow them. They were all still somewhere back in the last century."

Edward laughed. In some parts of Italy the word *uccello* can mean a bird or the male member, depending on your intention.

"So you're almost entirely self-taught. That's astonishing."

"I go to the museums and exhibitions. I read books on painting, study the theory behind modern movements. Anyway, nature's the best teacher."

"What's the situation, then? You work here in your parents' restaurant and paint in your spare time, is that it?"

He laughed again. "No, it's the other way around. I work to support myself so I can paint. If I ever make enough to keep me going just from selling paintings I'll quit working in the restaurant. Mamma and Papa tell me to just go ahead and paint and forget about working, but a man can't just live off his parents at my age."

"Which is?"

"Twenty-four. Why?"

"You started to say 'we' a minute ago. Who's 'we'?"

"Mamma and me. She was always drawing pictures for me when I was a boy, and she got me drawing, too. Then one day she came home with the car full of canvas and paints and books on how to stretch the canvas and prime it. Brushes, turpentine, linseed oil, gesso, everything. She said, 'Come on, Paulo, let's teach ourselves to paint.'"

"How long ago was this?"

"Oh, I was twelve or thirteen, something like that. That's when I started to get serious about art. Mamma and I began by copying pictures we liked, reproductions in books — it wasn't a bad way to learn. After a while you start to see what's under the surface of paintings, the composition, what holds it all together, the different things colour can do for you."

Edward indicated a painting that included a seated figure as part of the composition. "You seem to be pretty sure of your anatomy too, under all that brushwork."

"We used to sit around the piazzas and draw from the sculptures like all the rest of the art students. Then Papa asked us why were we copying statues when we had him to pose for us. He's always been thin, all the muscles showing under the skin — the best kind of model." Paulo paused and smiled at what he was remembering. "He'd take off his clothes and get up on our little stand any time we asked him — 'at the drop of a hat,' as he likes to say. He thought Mamma and I were a pair of geniuses. Are you a painter yourself?"

"No. I've often wished I were. I'm one of those people who loves art but has no talent for making it. Tell me though, you do intend to go on with it? It's not just a — what's the word — *passatempo?*"

He gave Edward a quizzical look as though he might be a little thick in the head.

"Painting's the most important thing in my life, apart from my family. It's an addiction." He paused. "Why are you asking me all these questions? Is it just because you want to buy a painting?"

"I'm sorry. I've been very rude. I'm just so taken with your work —"

Paulo suddenly leaned across the table with that amused expression on his face, a curious half-smile. "Is it really my art you're interested in, signore? It isn't just *me,* by any chance, is it?" He laughed. "The way you stared at me out there when you were ordering lunch I couldn't imagine what was going on. Well, that's not true, I could. Or I thought I could!"

Edward laughed, convincingly, he hoped. "I did stare, didn't I. I'm sorry. It was because you looked so much like a figure in a painting I saw years ago, one of the angels in Piero's *Virgin with Two Angels*. Have you seen it? You could have posed for it — your hair, your features, especially your eyes."

"I'll have to go and have a look at it. Nobody's ever told me that before."

"But aside from that, yes, it's your pictures that interest me. Dealing in art is my business. Here, let me give you my card. I'm from Toronto, if you know where that is."

He fished in his wallet for a card with trembling hands, desperately wanting to capture the man's interest and horribly afraid he might decide Edward was some sort of roving con man, or just an old lecher on the prowl. He could imagine this Paulo tossing his card in the wastebasket the minute he left. There was no reason why he should trust him or be interested in what he had to offer. He finally got the card out and handed it to him.

"Have you ever thought of placing your work with a dealer, showing it in a gallery?"

"*Di sicuro.* Sure I have. I don't sell much here. They take a few paintings in a shop in Taormina, but they only want little landscapes the tourists can take home in their suitcases. I've sent slides to galleries in Milano and Roma but most of them don't even bother to reply. One of them sent my slides back and said sorry, but they were only interested in contemporary work." He threw his head back and laughed. "I should have sent a canvas with the paint still wet, ask them if that was contemporary enough for them. I suppose they wanted abstract art."

"Well, they were fools, but it's the same everywhere. Whatever's in fashion this week."

"I get a few portrait commissions, somebody's daughter in her wedding dress, kids in their first communion outfits. That's okay. The worst is working from photographs after somebody's died, trying to make them look wise and holy and beautiful all at once. I end up giving a lot of my paintings to relatives and friends."

"Would you be interested in having me try out some of your work in my gallery, to see how it goes? There would be no financial risk whatever to you."

He held my card in his hand and sat looking at it for a few moments.

"It sounds good," he said. "I've never imagined showing my paintings outside Italy. I've heard plenty about Toronto, though — a lot of my relatives have gone over there. Half of Sicily must be in Toronto by now." He paused, as though there were some question he hadn't asked.

"Do I sense some hesitation?"

"I'm just wondering how it would work. Canada's a long way off."

"All right, how much would you ask if I wanted to buy one of these paintings?" He named a sum in lire that was equivalent to about two hundred Canadian dollars.

"I'd probably price them at something like ten times that," Edward said, "of which you'd get sixty percent and I'd take the remaining forty as a commission. Would that interest you?"

He smiled broadly. "I'd be really stupid if it didn't."

"I'd pay you outright the amount you've just quoted, and take, let's say, six paintings. I'd get you to remove the canvases from the stretchers and roll them up for me to take home. When I've sold them I'll deduct what I've paid you from your share."

"Sounds like I can't lose."

"I wouldn't want you to lose. I'll pick out the ones I'd like to have, if you agree to all this, and come back for them tomorrow. I'll write up a little contract in the meantime, and you could even take it to your *avvocato* to look over."

"Look, if you want to buy six pictures, that's good enough for me. They're all for sale. The rest of the deal is up to you. I don't need to talk to any *avvocato* about it."

"I won't disappoint you. I know I'll be able to sell your work."

"I'm happy you came by, signore —"

"Edward, please. If we're going to go into business together —"

"Okay, Edward." He paused, looked down at the card, finally spoke again. "It was just about the art, then. That's all you wanted to talk to me about?"

"How do you mean?"

He raised those beautiful dark-lashed eyes to meet Edward's. "I had the feeling earlier — I thought maybe there was — something personal. *Mi dispiaci.* Sorry. My mistake. Anyway," he said, squaring his shoulders, "will tomorrow morning do for you to pick up the canvases? You choose the ones you want and I can take them off the stretchers tonight."

Edward's heart raced. He was sure he blushed scarlet, the curse of a fair skin. Had Paulo meant what he seemed to be saying? *Something personal.* Could Edward have misunderstood?

"Paulo," he began, leaning across the table toward him, "it was no mistake, you weren't wrong. My interest in your work is perfectly genuine, but yes, there is something personal — I don't know whether you …" He trailed off lamely.

Paulo looked at Edward steadily for a few seconds. "Are you staying around here? Are you fixed up with a hotel or a pensione?"

"No. I don't know where I'll be staying. Before I saw these paintings of yours I was going to drive on, maybe go to Taormina for a day or two. But now —"

"Now …?"

"When I caught sight of you out there on the terrazzo I wondered if I was hallucinating. I thought you were the most beautiful human being I'd ever seen in my life. Piero's angel, incarnate."

He sat looking into Edward's eyes for a long moment before he spoke.

"I was watching you from in here when Mamma was showing you to your table," he said slowly. "I thought you must be some English lord or something. You have that air about you, you know — the way you move and gesture with your hands — sort of elegant and aristocratic."

"Please, you're embarrassing me."

"I mean it. You do. I was very attracted to you. I wanted you to notice me. I was hoping you would. But when you did, and then you just stared and stared I didn't know what was going on. Know what I thought? Don't laugh. It sounds really *a pazzo* — what's the word — crazy? — I wondered if you'd come here looking for me."

Edward's heart leapt. Seconds ticked by before he could speak.

"Maybe it's true," he said slowly. "Maybe I *was* looking for you. I think perhaps it was — ordained — that I was to come here and meet you."

"Mamma would call it God's will. That's how she explains everything, good or bad."

"Well, if it was I'm grateful. Paulo, is there some way I can spend a little time with you? So we can get to know each other?"

There was too much urgency in his voice, he sounded too eager. If he kept on like this he'd scare the boy off. He told himself to cool down. Maybe this man just wanted a casual fling with a tourist he happened to like the look of, the here-today-gone-tomorrow aspect was probably part of the attraction for him. He might not have the slightest interest in getting to know Edward. He waited, holding his breath, while Paulo sat looking at him, apparently turning over what Edward had said in his mind.

"You don't care about going on to Taormina?"

"Not a bit. I haven't arranged anything. In a couple of days I have to start driving back to Napoli to return that car, and then I catch a plane to Rome and fly back to Toronto."

"We keep a room here for guests. You could go off this afternoon and look at the countryside or whatever you want to do, and have dinner with us later. We all sit down to eat around ten or ten-thirty after we close for the night. It's the only time in the day we have to talk to each other."

Edward couldn't keep the excitement out of his voice. "It would please me very much to do that."

"Then I'll go and tell Mamma you'll be staying. Let's get your bags, and I'll show you where the room is. After dinner tonight we could go over to my studio if you like, and you could have a look at the rest of my work. And as you say, we could get to know each other."

Edward could no longer resist touching him. He reached across the table and covered Paulo's hand with his own. At that moment he happened to glance toward the door where Paulo's mother was about to enter, and quickly withdrew his arm.

"Don't worry," Paulo said. "They know about me. I told them a few years ago I was *omosessuale*."

"Were they upset?"

"No. Maybe they already knew. They just said love is love, everybody has to find his own way."

"Your mother and father seem like wonderful people."

"They spoil me."

"Are you the only child?"

"I am now."

"Now?"

"My twin brother died when I was three. I hardly remember him at all, but Mamma still talks about him like it was yesterday. She says she was the only one who could tell us apart."

"*I gemelli*," Edward said. "The twins."

Paulo nodded. "They renamed the trattoria for us when we were born. After Pietro died they couldn't bear to change it again, as though he'd never existed."

"What happened? An accident of some kind?"

"No. The doctor said most likely there was some kind of brain damage when we were being born, not enough oxygen or something. Or maybe something happened before, when Mamma was carrying us. My brother took — *convulsione* — what's that in English?"

"Same word. Convulsions."

"He took convulsions and died in Mamma's arms. Mamma didn't believe what the doctors told her. She says one of the strangers who came here must have been the devil, *l'invidia,* in disguise. When he saw how happy she was with her two babies he envied her so much he couldn't let her have both of us, so he cast the *mal occhio* on my brother."

"The evil eye. Do you believe in that?"

"No, not really, but I guess Mamma couldn't bear it unless she had some way of explaining why such terrible things can happen."

12

"My library in ten minutes, Edward."

Harvey Rak rose from the breakfast table, pulled out his pocket watch, studied it for a few seconds before starting to leave the room, and then paused to toss his peremptory summons back over his shoulder. Edward obeyed, more or less, allowing himself fifteen rather than the stipulated ten minutes to finish his toast and marmalade. When he finally appeared Harvey Rak was seated behind his massive mahogany desk, as Edward knew he would be. Rak almost never spoke to him while they were both on their feet these days. One of the first things that struck Edward when he came back to England was how much smaller his stepfather appeared to have become, that far from being the giant he'd always thought him, Rak was actually quite a small man and less than heroically built, with his narrow shoulders and pigeon chest, and a little pot belly that he carried before him as though with pride. At eighteen Edward was considerably broader than his stepfather and half a foot taller, quite towered over him, and it amused him now to see how the wretched little man was careful to avoid being on his feet when they were in the same room, even when they were alone.

Rak didn't suggest that Edward should sit down, so he stood in the middle of the airless dark-panelled room that Rak dignified with the term library, although it contained few books — Rak was hardly a reader — with his hands in his pockets, which he knew irritated his stepfather, and waited to hear whatever it was he had to say.

"You're eighteen years old, if memory serves. Nearly nineteen, in fact. Schooldays are over. Exactly what do you have in mind for yourself now, young Mr. Cooper?"

"I was thinking about going to university, sir. I'm interested in history and literature. My teachers at school seemed to think I ought to go on with my education."

"Did they indeed? And you're thinking about going to university, if you please. Well here's what I think. I think it's time you got off the dole around here and began standing on your own two feet. To that end I've arranged an apprenticeship for you." He leaned back in his chair with his elbows tight to his sides, wrists bent at right angles to his forearms so he could interweave his long knobby fingers over his narrow chest. He glowered up at Edward. "You ought to be grateful, though I don't suppose you will be." He pursed his thin lips.

"Oh, I'm grateful for everything," Edward said.

Rak clapped his two hands down flat on the desk and thrust his face forward. "I can tell you this, young man, I worked my way through every step of making a piano before I ever earned a farthing. We knew what work was in those days. Learned to build the case and finish it. Installed the sounding board and action. Oversaw the casting of the harp. Learned how to string it. Any idea how many pounds tension on the bass strings?"

"No."

"No. Didn't expect you would. Nose in a novel all the time. Lit-tra-ture! Too much trouble to read up a few facts about the business that's keeping you in luxury. Well, Mr. Bookworm, let me tell you something. I learned every single step of the business I'm in by working a twelve-hour day, six days a week, for four years."

He wagged a bony forefinger in Edward's direction, as was his irritating wont. "World's changed for the worse. Lads these days aren't willing to work for pocket money while they learn a valuable trade. Expect wages for their clumsy efforts, take no pride in what they do. I never saw a wage packet 'til I'd served my apprenticeship. Time better spent, I'll tell you, than the same number of years playing silly buggers in straw hats on the Cam. Toffee-nosed twits, they come out of those universities just about fit to sell Kewpie dolls on the Brighton Pier." He paused to give Edward a good long unblinking stare.

"I've taken your measure," he said finally. "You haven't got the bottle for an apprenticeship in my works. Never make a go of it. Fortunately for you, it happens I'm acquainted with one of the high-ups at Christopher's Auctioneers. Spent a lot of money there over the years. Persuaded them to give you a try. Starting Monday you'll be working for them. Seven a.m. sharp, mind. Employees' entrance at the rear of the building. Get cook to put you up a lunch. There'll be no money wasted on fancy meals in caffs, not while I'm supplying room and board, I'll tell you that right now. I'm advancing you two pounds." He pointed to Edward's side of the desk where two one-pound notes lay side by side. "They'll be giving you a small wage at the end of the month and you can pay me back then." He rose from his chair and went across the room to hold the door open, signifying that their interview was at an end.

"You were always a great lad with the lip," he said as a parting shot, "so maybe they can make an auctioneer of you. I told the Christopher brothers you were to start right at the bottom, so don't expect to be poncing around the showrooms in a velvet jacket. Coverall and boots will be more like it. You'll be shifting furniture, nailing up crates, sweeping floors. Get your hands dirty. Do you good."

The sleeping arrangements of the household had been altered during Edward's absence. Since she had become ill his mother had moved, or been moved, out of the large master bedroom facing the river that she had shared with Rak and was now in a room on the other side of the central hall. Her nurse occupied a slightly smaller one next to it. When Edward came home Rak seemed to expect he would go back up to the old nursery, but Edward stated with all the firmness he could muster that he wanted to be nearer his mother at night in case she should need him.

Rak started to object, but the nurse, Miss Flagg, who had been listening to this discussion, spoke up. "I wonder if Edward mightn't like to have my room, where he'd be right next door to his mother. Then I could take the unoccupied bedroom on the front — next the master bedroom — that is, of course, if you wouldn't mind, Mr. Rak." She smiled seductively and batted her eyelashes. "I do love watching the boats go by on the river."

Light bulbs popped on in Harvey Rak's eyes at that suggestion, and he quickly agreed to the arrangement. It was a while before Edward twigged to the fact that Miss Flagg wouldn't mind at all being the new Mrs. Rak if his mother were to succumb to her illnesses, although the idea that Miss Flagg could bring herself to be intimate with Harvey Rak was beyond his imagination, even if she was past her prime.

After he began working at Christopher's Auctioneers Edward was up and out the door before anyone else in the household was awake, and when he returned in the late afternoons the house was again silent and still. The kitchen staff and maids would be in their bedrooms at the top of the house or giggling over some game in their parlour off the kitchen; Harvey Rak wouldn't be expected home from his factory until seven or eight o'clock in the evening, and his mother would be having her afternoon nap. Occasionally he would encourage Miss Flagg to leave Dolly in his care and go for a walk along the tow path if she cared to, browse on the high street or in the Lanes, an offer she was glad to accept, and he thus cleared the way for himself to spend an hour or two prowling through the house, opening drawers and cupboards, going carefully through the papers and letters in his stepfather's desk. On the principle that knowledge was power, he wanted to know more about the man under whose roof he was obliged to live.

The desk was disappointing. Edward wasn't sure what he

hoped to discover, but he found no personal correspondence from friends or relatives, nothing to tell him how large a fortune there might be locked away in vaults, no solicitors letters suing for alimony on behalf of ex-wives or evidence of Rak's having spent time in prison — merely dull stuff like house insurance and taxes, accounts of wages paid out to the servants, and bills from the various shops he and Dolly patronized.

The house was crammed with ornate furniture, elaborate objets d'art, and large gilt-framed paintings, but after Edward had worked at Christopher's for a while he came to realize that Harvey Rak was not the collector and connoisseur he no doubt thought himself so much as an undiscriminating accumulator, a purchaser with an unerring eye for the spurious, the ugly, the grotesque. If you had something to sell that was ungainly in shape, preferably decorated with adders displaying their fangs or carved with rampant alligators, Harvey was your man. His table silver was larded with scrolls and squiggles and curlicues; wallpapers were flocked and flecked and printed in such richly three-dimensional designs that you couldn't easily tell where the flat of the wall was, and it made Edward dizzy to look at them. Plush draperies and pelmets fringed in gold could have come from the stage of some Victorian theatre; murky oriental carpets muffled the floors in every room, and all that dark panelling gave off the smell of the beeswax that he obliged the household staff to anoint it with regularly. Heavy corded velvet or thick brocades in mustard and oxblood tones covered the chairs and sofas in the downstairs rooms. Although the house was officially called Riverview, house-proud Harvey kept those wool-lined draperies drawn across every window at all times to guard his possessions against the depredations of whatever small glimmer of pallid English sunshine might seep through the high cedar hedges surrounding the house, so the place was perpetually in a gloomy half-light.

Edward invaded Rak's bedroom, went through his vast

mahogany armoire full of stuffy-smelling suits and shoes and hats. He examined drawers containing shirts and handkerchiefs, lifting garments with careful fingers and putting everything back exactly in place so there would be no trace of his snooping. Sometimes he stole a monogrammed linen handkerchief purely for the enjoyment of the theft and not because he wanted a handkerchief, or slipped a silk tie into his pocket from the dozens hanging on the rack and wore it at work for a few days before dropping it into a trash bin. He smirked over the old-man's gear in his bathroom — the badger shaving brush, the strop hanging on the doorknob, the set of pearl-handled straight razors in their case. What, he wondered, were these powders for, little folders of white grains, half of them wrapped in blue paper and half in white, what did they cure, or prevent? What did Rak do with this duo of blue glass eyecups? Maybe his eyes came out at night to soak! He didn't know what he was looking for, but he felt any knowledge he could glean about Harvey Rak couldn't fail to strengthen his position and eventually be to his advantage.

As Edward went through the sideboards and massive Victorian tallboys in the downstairs rooms he made something of a mental inventory of their contents, trying to assess their desirability and value. He pulled things out of shelves, removed silver objects from flannel cases — entrée dishes, gravy boats, salvers, teapots, filigreed bread trays, jugs, sugar basins, almost all of them elaborately scrolled and incised, bulging with reliefs of grapes and flowers, ugly as sin. The dinner services were no better, vulgar chalky-blue Jasperware and overly ornate Bavarian and Bohemian stuff — nothing with line or grace, no glazes or patterns beautiful in their own right.

Since he'd started working at Christopher's Edward had taken careful notice of the objects that went up for sale. He was interested in learning all he could about the china and silver and period furniture, and he enjoyed handling those beautiful objects.

Somehow, even before Mr. Love, the head auctioneer, and the others had begun to teach him which characteristics made something a particularly good example of its kind, he knew instinctively which were the best and most valuable. Their superiority to other pieces in the showroom was simply evident to him, their elegance seemed to leap out, there was a peculiar lustre that emanated from the objects themselves and caught his eyes with their lines and surfaces and volumes; they took possession of the space that surrounded them in a way that lesser examples never did. If this was a talent or a gift, an "eye," as Mr. Love called it, Edward had no idea how he came to possess it. He supposed it was similar to the perfect pitch some people have for music, or the facility with words that poets are said to be born with.

He decided to put his judgment to a test. He went to the Portobello Road one Saturday morning with two pounds in his pocket, and after a couple of hours of searching and haggling came away with a graceful etched-glass claret jug with a silver top. He gave the badly tarnished silver a careful cleaning and found the piece was from a respected English silversmith of the early nineteenth century. When he put it up for sale in one of the auctions at Christopher's his pound came back to him six-fold, even after the house commission had been deducted.

Edward's employers took an interest in bringing him along, were willing to take time to answer questions and explain the marks and symbols that identified makers and dates of silver and china. That little coup with the claret jug had amused Mr. Love, who then often invited Edward to accompany him as he walked around the floor before a sale, asking him to pick out the things he thought were the most beautiful or the best of what was there, and to his surprise and Edward's own, their opinions almost invariably coincided, although neither could explain what seemed to be Edward's innate good taste and sense of discrimination.

After he learned to check pedigrees reasonably accurately,

Edward began to give Rak's stuff a more thorough comb-through, and found that now and then something of real virtue had managed to slip into his stepfather's so-called collections by mistake. He would transfer the object to his mother's room and leave it conspicuously on her dresser or mantel for a while. He suspected that Rak was making no more than a daily visit to her room, if that, and in any case he could hardly object to her having a few nice things to look at. After a few weeks he would put the little cream jug or whatever it was into his satchel and take it off to Christopher's where he would tell Mr. Love, if he were asked, that it was another of his finds from the barrows in Portobello Road. In this way he supplemented the very small wages which were his only source of money.

"I do wish I could help you out more," his mother said when he was starting his new job, "but I don't really have any cash to speak of."

"You mean he doesn't give you an allowance? How do you pay for things? Clothes, and hairdressers, and all that?"

"He's opened charge accounts everywhere for me, dear, the local shops, my milliner in London, Harrods, Fortnum's. I buy what I want or order it by telephone and he gets the bills at the end of the month. Oh, I can have just about anything, I mean, he's always wanted me to dress well and he never questions what I spend on myself or on things for the house, but I never have cash except for a few pounds. That's the way it's always been. To tell you the truth, Edward, I carry a purse but there's never much in it but a handkerchief and my powder compact." She gave a little laugh. "I'm like the Royal Family, dear — I hear they don't carry money, either."

Edward vowed that things would change for his mother and for himself, that somehow he would get her away from that man and his hideous house. During the next few years he moved steadily upwards in the auction business, from general dogsbody in the storage rooms to arranging furniture and bric-a-brac on the display floor, packing delicate small objects for shipping, even participating in the sales themselves, carrying the lots up to and off the dais as they went under the hammer. Eventually he was given the task of taking down the names and addresses of successful bidders and entering them in the books, and one afternoon was allowed to auction a couple of small lots himself, under the patient teaching of Mr. Love. He did his best to learn, and his efforts were noticed.

He'd been at Christopher's for a little over four years when an elderly man who had been assistant to the director of the fine art department died in his sleep one weekend. After the news got around there was a lot of speculation among the rest of the staff as to who might take his place. A few days later he was checking off a list of items for an upcoming sale when Mr. Love caught his eye and jumped his eyebrows up and down mean- ingfully two or three times, just as the pretty secretary from upstairs appeared in the doorway to tell him he was wanted in the partners' office. He followed her up the stairs and she ush- ered him into a panelled room with tall arched windows, before which, silhouetted against the light, sat the brothers Christopher side by side, at a desk as big as a dining table. They looked very much alike, those two, substantial grey-haired men in dark pin- striped suits with old-fashioned gold watch chains draped across their waistcoats. The senior brother, Mr. Wilfred, remained com- pletely silent during the interview, elbows propped on the arms of his chair, hands clasped in front of his chin, index fingers pressed steeple-fashion to his lips, while Mr. John, the younger of the two, did all the talking.

"We're going to take a chance on you, Cooper," he said, in his clipped patrician tones. "We've been given to understand that you have a good sense of discrimination and an eye for quality. That's important in this business. From all reports you're a bright lad with a pleasing manner, interested in learning about the fine things in which Christopher's deals." He paused, as though waiting for some acknowledgement of what he'd said.

"I'm glad my work has been satisfactory, sir."

He went on as though Edward hadn't spoken. "So we're giving you, on a trial basis, a considerably more responsible position in our business. We're hoping you will prove our confidence justified." Another pause.

"I'll certainly do my best, sir."

"You'll be taking a recently vacated place in the art department as assistant to the director, Mr. Turner. At a very nice rise in pay, by the way. Any questions?"

"I can't think of any, Mr. Christopher."

"No? Then that will be all, thank you, Cooper. You may go across to Mr. Jack Turner immediately."

"Thank you, sir," he said.

In his own home, as he was obliged to call that house in Richmond, Edward generally tried not to look at the so-called art, the job lots of big gilt-framed works Rak had acquired from God knows where and hung on every wall, dark crackled canvases — as though a mucky surface of varnished-on dirt were a sign of great age and value — showing heathered glens strewn with sheep, or possibly large white rocks, it was difficult to tell. There was a portrait of a sword-bearing Scottish highlander with cauliflower knees, one foot planted threateningly on a convenient stump; a painting of a stout woman with rosy cheeks and nose to match, with a dark forest looming behind the garden bench she shared with a pair of curly-haired boys in kilts and ruffled blouses. Did Rak hope to pass himself off as a descendent of Scottish lairds? Edward wondered. Mac Rak?

On his first day at the new job in the art department, Edward took a long, long look at a work of art that Mr. Turner ("No, no relation," he said, smiling) told him was to be the jewel of the upcoming sale. As he stood looking at it, Edward found himself overwhelmed by a storm of emotions he'd never felt before. He had no idea why the painting affected him this way, moved him so deeply it almost made him weep. The work in question was a seascape in oils by the great English artist J.M.W. Turner, a canvas thirty-four inches high by forty inches long — it was part of Edward's job to prepare the labels giving names and dates and exact dimensions — showing a small dark craft on a stretch of water that Edward took to be the ocean, at sunset. The boat was near the horizon, if one could distinguish a horizon at all, which was almost impossible because everything, the water, the air, the sky were caught up together in a swirling mass of colour, a whirlpool of orange and yellow and pink and scarlet and purple, even brilliant strokes of vivid lime green. Up close the surface of the painting looked messy and unreadable, while from further away it obviously represented the sea all right, but one that was nothing whatever the like the slab of rough, dark slate with a curtain of watery grey hanging above it that Edward had seen on his Atlantic crossings day after tedious day. Here the water was exploding upward into the orange and purple sky in great plumes, the two elements blending and intermingling until they were virtually inseparable from one another. Reason said that the little boat ought to have been teetering on its bow, about to sink, or that it would have been snatched up out of the water into that colour-filled sky where it would be flapping its sails like a bird. And yet there it lay, perfectly stable, as peaceful as though it were becalmed.

Why that work of art made his heart beat faster, why he lost track of time when he was looking at it, why he kept slipping away from his other tasks just to stare at it, stepping backward across the room to see it from a distance, going up to peer at it with his nose practically touching the canvas — to none of these questions could he supply an answer. All he could find were more questions.

Was that the point of art, he wondered — that it draws us to itself, not because it represents the world faithfully and looks just like what we see every day, but because it doesn't? The idea was a strange one. Would the ocean look to him like Turner's ocean, now that he'd seen how Turner saw it, or did you have to be an artist yourself? Was beauty, as they say, all in the eye of the beholder, the artist? In that case, a work of art like this was some sort of sign language, a kind of translation of the world for people who couldn't see beauty for themselves. But then why did this painting look so beautiful to him, when Rak's highland meadows didn't? He'd have to think about it.

He felt a completely new kind of excitement. The rectangle of canvas that kept filling his senses that day seemed like some sort of token, an intimation, a symbol of something, perhaps even a ticket of admission, if he chose to accept it, to a realm of richness that had nothing to do with pounds sterling. He knew instinctively that wherever or whatever it was, mean spirits like Rak could never share it, they wouldn't even be capable of recognizing it, but that he himself could have access to this unnameable something if only he could figure out what it was. So he stared at the Turner, trying to decipher its meaning, gazing mutely at the pointing finger, trying to grasp what it was toward which he was being directed. He slowly began to understand, as the months went by, that in one way or another, art would be his life's pursuit.

13

Jack Turner had listened to what John Christopher was telling him, he was obliged to, the man was his employer, but he couldn't imagine how he expected some green young fellow to come up here and fill the shoes of old Marley, who'd been in the art department for thirty years — long before even Jack himself had come into the business. Jack was still having a hard time believing Marley was really dead, he simply couldn't accept that the old man wouldn't be coming back. If he could possibly have managed the department alone, he would have told them not to bother finding him a new assistant at all.

"They tell me downstairs the boy has an eye, Jack," John Christopher said. "A real eye. We're just asking you to try him out. Bob Love has been bringing him along, giving him a good bit of responsibility. If he doesn't work out or if you find you don't like him, why, we'll start looking around."

It seemed they'd taken this lad on downstairs a few years earlier as a favour to a client, put him to work fetching and carrying, helping to load and unload the vans and set things up for sales. John Christopher was now telling him that the boy had turned out unexpectedly well, had worked in various areas, moved up in the ranks, had even been allowed to auction the occasional lot. Jack's own contacts with young Cooper had been few — he'd come up to the art department now and then to deliver consignment papers or memos, which Jack would sign and hand back, or just wave the boy on his way if it were something he was to keep. He recalled being amused at the way Cooper's inquisitive blue eyes would dart around the art rooms when he was there, as though he were looking for an escape route or a place to hide. He wondered now if it had been the works of art on the walls that had interested the boy.

A few times Cooper had emerged from the ancient creaking freight lift, an antiquated machine that sent shudders through the whole building when it began its Herculean ascent from the base-ment, halting at the second floor minutes later with a crash that sounded like a lorry slamming into a wall. He and one of the other fellows would be carrying between them a large framed painting swaddled in white cotton, or would guide a wheeled platform with a wooden crate on it, roll the unsteady load into the work-room, and shift the crate carefully onto the floor. After that Marley would take over. You didn't turn a couple of boys loose with a crowbar on a crate containing a ten-thousand-pound painting.

John Christopher admitted that Cooper had no particular experience or specialized training in art or auctioneering — or anything else, for that matter — but he'd proven steady and reli-able at whatever he undertook and learned fast, so maybe he could teach the boy enough to make him useful. He hadn't recovered from the shock of Marley's sudden death; he still caught himself looking for the old fellow to come puffing up the stairs, excusing his absence with a "Sorry, Jack," peering up from under bushy brows, his mouth stretched in that apologetic grin that meant he'd been putting back malt whiskies with some old friend until closing time the night before. All those years Marley had been at Christopher's he'd never sought promotion, had even turned it down when it was offered. He'd found a comfortable niche and stayed in it, a place where he didn't have to take charge or make the serious decisions, particularly in the financial realm, and that suited him down to the ground. He knew exactly what his job was and performed it well, would shoulder extra responsibility if Jack were away for any reason — look after the phone, manage the consignments, hang the work for exhibition when a sale was coming up, all of it — but only to oblige, only as a stop-gap measure. It was the money side of this business he wouldn't touch. He would give his opinion of a piece of work when asked but would never have undertaken to make evaluations or set reserve bids.

He and Jack had been working together for some eight years when war broke out in '39. Old British bulldog Marley wanted to join up, but he was far overage. Jack had immediately joined the air force. After basic training they proceeded to make a cartographer of him, and he spent the war years flying a drafting table in a station near Oxford, which pleased his mother no end but was a disappointment to Jack. He'd fancied himself in leather helmet and goggles with a white silk scarf around his throat, saluting the ground crew from the open cockpit as the engine caught and sputtered into life — a romantic image left over from that other war that had come to an end when he was an impressionable ten year old. It seemed he wasn't destined for a life of adventure. John Christopher himself took over the art sales when Jack was away, and when he was welcomed back into his old job after the war, there was Marley, still the valued assistant, no more, no less.

One morning the previous week Marley's wife had gone down to make the tea as usual, carried a cup up to Marley and set it on the bedside table, opened the curtains, and turned back to the bed. Marley was lying on his back with his two arms bent at the elbows, hands behind his head like a sunbather on the beach at Brighton, asleep — peacefully and permanently. Jack still couldn't think about him without tears springing to his eyes. He'd loved the old fellow, and he was only giving half an ear to John Christopher when he began to talk about this young chap he was now trying to persuade Jack to take on.

As to this claim for the boy's so-called eye, it was just so much codswallop as far as Jack Turner was concerned. Might as well go in for palm reading. The knowledge he himself had been able to bring to his job was the result of years of looking, reading, studying, and comparing, diligent work, nothing magical about it. A general interest in art and a modest talent for drawing had spurred him into enrolling in extra-curricular painting classes during his grammar school days, but he'd quickly seen that if he wasn't the worst artist in the class he was a long way from being the best, and certainly didn't have what it took to make a profession of painting. He didn't turn away from art, however, just the practice of it. He was in his second year of studying art history at Leeds when his father died. He'd quit university, come to London, and taken a job in the art department of Christopher's Auctioneers, and there, apart from those years in the air force, he'd been ever since.

His own judgement and ability to discriminate had developed slowly. When he was very young he'd admired the sort of second-rate academic painting in which everything is rendered to look as three-dimensional as possible, with lots of surface effects — dew on the blossoms, down on the peach. As his understanding matured he learned to look past the subject and dismiss the cloying overdone realism in which the main object of the painting seemed to be to deny its two-dimensionality to the cost of everything else. After a time he began to lose interest in the anecdotal and sentimental that had once appealed to him — the exotic landscapes with camels and palm trees, neo-classical scenes of war and pillage, rosy girls with lap dogs — even just dogs. He'd been a wholehearted admirer of Landseer's dignified hounds and impudent terriers until he began to see, with a developing sense of the ironic, that whether or not Landseer had worn a straight face while he was painting them, those dog portraits slyly mocked what was quite possibly the silliest side of the English character, and compounded the silliness by presenting themselves as high art. It was a while before he recognized the prurience lurking in Alma Tadema's sleazily erotic depictions of life in Imperial Rome and ceased to be stirred by the quasi-religious sentimentality of Holman Hunt and Dante Gabriel Rossetti. When he was first becoming familiar with the art of the Renaissance he had much preferred a contorted mannerist virgin by Parmigianino to the flattened, even amateurish-looking (to his eye) painting of the same subject by Giotto. He'd had much to learn. He was still learning. If this young man had some magical inborn sense of discrimination, Jack Turner remained to be convinced.

"I'll just fetch him, then, shall I Jack?" John Christopher said, his voice rising questioningly, but leaving no room for disagreement. "Have a word with him, and send him along to you? Good chap!" He bustled down the steps and across the hall to his office without giving Jack time to reply. Jack sat down at his desk, from which he had a good view of the hall, and waited. Protocol was closely observed. Juliette, John's pretty young secretary, emerged from his office and went tip-tapping down the main staircase in her high-heeled shoes, re-ascended just as briskly a moment later with young Mr. Cooper in tow, and the two of them disappeared into the Christopher brothers' lair. In another few minutes the young man emerged alone, crossed the hall and ascended the short flight of stairs to the art room, smiling broadly as he approached. Jack couldn't help but smile back, the lad looked so pleased. He was a handsome specimen of the human race, had it all over poor old Marley in that department.

14

Soon after his return from Canada Edward waited at the foot of the stairs one afternoon to waylay his mother's doctor before he departed after one of his visits. He demanded to know what was wrong with Dolly, what was being done for her, and whether she was going to get better. It horrified him to think she might have to spend the rest of her life in a wheelchair or confined to bed, but if that was true, then he wanted the doctor to tell him so. He couldn't find out anything from his stepfather or the nurse, and he didn't want to upset his mother by asking her about the state of her health.

"I understand your concern, my boy," the doctor said, laying a kindly hand on his shoulder. "Primarily it's the diabetes, of course, which has in turn produced some heart problems and bad circulation. That's what caused the gangrene in the foot, and why the toes had to be amputated. Making sure she gets her insulin injections and takes her other medications is of the utmost importance. And sticking to her diet. She isn't inclined to be very cooperative that way. I believe she sometimes gets the maids to bring her things she shouldn't have, even though they've been told not to."

"What about that nurse, doesn't she —"

"Oh, Miss Flagg does her best. She's a good nurse, you need have no fear there."

"Are you saying my mother's going to be an invalid for the rest of her life, then? She'll never be well again?"

"I never like to look on the dark side, ah — Edward, is it? — but ..."

It was clear he thought she was never going to recover, but if his mother knew how ill she was she never gave any indication of it. When he went up to her room a little later he found her lying on her chaise longue by the window, a light knitted shawl over her knees, a magazine in her lap. A tea tray was on a small table beside her.

"Hello, darling," she said. "Have you had your tea?"

Before he pulled a chair close and sat down beside her, Edward picked up a little atomizer bottle of Houbigant's Quelques Fleurs from her dressing table and bent over her to spray her neck and hair with it, the same scent he'd surreptitiously taken when they'd sent him off to his first boarding school in Cheam at the age of seven. He'd needed it then, needed to have something of *her* when he was going to be so far away all by himself, and that flowery fragrance still had powerful nostalgic associations for him. Perhaps it was due to her illness, but since he'd come back from Canada he'd found the odour of his mother's person very unpleasant, rather sharp and ammoniac, and he had gone out and bought another bottle of that same beautiful Houbigant essence he'd always associated with the beloved Mummie of his earlier days. He made a little ceremony now of misting her with a little cloud of it whenever he came to her room. She seemed pleased with the attention, but in truth, without it he found it quite repugnant to be close to her.

Since he'd had that conversation with the doctor he'd been afraid the time might come, and possibly before very long, when it would be too late to find out something he very much needed to know.

"Will you tell me something, Mummie?" Edward asked.

"Of course, darling, if I can."

"I don't want to upset you, but — well — I'd really like you to tell me who my father was, or who he is."

"Why, Edward, you know Harvey took out adoption papers when we were married, darling. That was the one thing I really insisted he must do — in case anything happened to me. You

112

were only six at the time. We let you keep my surname because that was the name you were accustomed to." She smiled a little ruefully. "Rak isn't a very pretty name, but I didn't have any choice for myself."

He hadn't known Rak had actually adopted him. He wondered momentarily why Rak hadn't objected to Edward's keeping his mother's name, but then he obviously liked Edward so little that he was probably just as happy not to give him his own. The thought that he was legally that man's son made his stomach turn.

"I didn't mean him. I want you to tell me who my real father was."

Dolly raised herself on one elbow and turned to stare at him.

"But Edward, you *do* know. I told you when you were a little boy. I named you after him. The Prince of Wales was your father, dear, the prince who became Edward the Eighth and then abdicated. You were unacknowledged, to be sure, but his son nevertheless."

"You don't have to keep on telling me that story, you know," Edward said, not unkindly. "I'm a big boy now. I don't have to have royalty for a parent. I'm sure you wouldn't have loved anyone who wasn't a good person." He almost choked on the words, thinking of Rak, but then he couldn't believe that his mother had ever loved that one.

"Doubting Thomas," she said, with a little laugh. "I'm telling you the truth, dear. It was during one of the ship's longer layovers in Southampton. There were parties every night in the hotels, wonderful parties. Dinner dances. You should have seen the gowns, the jewellery, the women so beautiful and glamorous. Well, the Prince and his friends were over from Cowes where the yacht races were taking place. He danced with two or three of the ladies, women he knew, I suppose. Everyone had their eyes on him, poor man. He could hardly turn around without someone reporting it in the newspapers and magazines. There was always lots of gossip about his women friends, of course, everyone wondering which of those beautiful aristocratic women he might decide to marry. He was very attractive, I'll say that. The ladies would have been after him even if he hadn't been a royal."

His mother paused, a little breathless from her recital. She picked up her cup and took a sip of tea.

"Well, anyway," she said, setting it down again, "there we all were, me and a little group of officers from the ship and some other ladies they'd invited to join them. We'd just finished our dinner and the orchestra was playing, when all of a sudden this man appeared at our table, some kind of equerry in a naval uniform, who bowed to me, to *me*, Edward, and announced in one of those terribly posh voices that His Royal Highness had asked him to convey his compliments and requested the honour of having the next dance with me. Can you imagine it? Everyone at our table was simply stunned."

"And you said you would," Edward said, going along with the story.

"What would any young woman have done? The equerry gave me his arm and led me over to the Prince's table, and the Prince stood up and bowed slightly, more of a nod, really, and said, 'Charmed, Miss Cooper.' I don't know how he knew my name. I made a little curtsy because I didn't know what else to do. Then he took my hand and led me out onto the floor. It was a quickstep. He was a lovely dancer. I don't think there could have been a woman in the room who didn't envy me."

"And then?"

"And then we danced the next number, a foxtrot, I think, and just as it was ending he said he was giving a late supper to a small party of friends on his yacht, and would I care to join them? And I said yes, I'd be delighted. And he said in that case his equerry would escort me to a launch when the dance was over, and he would see me aboard the yacht at about midnight."

"Go on."

"Well, that's exactly what happened. I could hardly breathe, I was so excited. There were maybe half a dozen other people besides the Prince and me, young men and women, although I don't know if they were married to each other or not, and we sat around the table and talked, all of us a bit silly on champagne. They served us smoked salmon and caviar and scrambled eggs, and more champagne, and pastries, and some beautiful imported fruit, those great big blue grapes, and the next thing I knew the Prince was leading me along the corridor to his private suite. When we got there he opened the door and then he stepped aside and waited, just smiling and not saying anything, as though he were asking me to decide if I wanted to go in."

"And?"

"I went in."

"So it was just — that one time?"

"Oh no, darling." She laughed. "I don't know what you'll think of me, but it's too late to worry about that now. As a matter of fact, we didn't come out of that suite for two days. He just called for food, coffee, champagne, whatever we wanted, and they brought it. It was a large suite — a sitting room with pretty chintz sofas and chairs, and a small dining table and chairs, and two bedrooms, each with a separate bathroom. He showed me into one of the bedrooms and shut the door. In a few minutes a maid came and helped me undress, and I had a lovely bath in a huge tub that had gold faucets in the shape of swans' heads. Then the maid brought me a bathrobe and brushed my hair for me, and opened a wardrobe where there were several lovely satin nightdresses and tea gowns hanging, and asked me to choose what I wanted to put on."

"Then what happened?"

"I picked a blue satin nightdress to set off my hair, and a white lace peignoir."

"No, I meant, what about him, the Prince."

"I remember it all so clearly. The maid left and I was sitting there in an armchair, a bit nervous, you know, putting a shine on my nails with the silver-backed buffer that was part of the set on the dressing table, when there was a little tap on the door. I said 'Come in,' and in he came. He had on a paisley-patterned silk dressing gown, with a blue foulard tucked into the neck that matched his eyes, and navy blue silk pyjamas. We stayed in those rooms that night, and all the next day and another night, too. There was a section of the deck completely private, screened off by canvas on either side, nothing in front of us but the sea and sky, so we could sit out there in the sun in the morning, or in the cool of the evening. He had a gramophone, and after supper we put music on and turned the lights out and danced, just the two of us, in the moonlight. I'll tell you, Edward, it was like a wonderful honeymoon."

"What happened when the honeymoon was over?"

"Well, when it was time for him to go he put that gold bracelet on my wrist, you know, the one made like a vine of roses that you used to love to play with. Then he kissed me and left me in my room. And then that maid came with some beautiful daytime clothes — I'd just come in my evening gown, after all — boxes from the best shops in London, every-thing folded in tissue — a beautiful violety blue silk dress and a little cashmere coat in the same colour, and some pale furs, and lovely handmade satin underthings from France and pure silk stockings, even a pair of blue kid shoes and a handbag. And a white leather case for carrying the evening things I'd arrived in. And after a while that equerry came back and escorted me ashore on the launch."

"And that was that. He never knew about me?"

"When I found out later I was expecting I did write a letter, to Buckingham Palace, you know. I didn't know how else to reach him. I never received a reply."

"That's all fantasy, isn't it, dear. That's how you would have liked it to be, your baby the son of a prince."

"Edward, you are making me extremely cross! I'm telling you the truth. As a matter of fact, I can prove it! Bring me my red writing case. It's right over there on the dresser."

She held the case on her knees and lifted out a tray, took a piece of brocade cloth from the bottom and unfolded it. Then she turned to Edward with an arch expression, holding up between the fingertips of both hands a small white linen hand towel, yellowed with age, that was finely embroidered in blue at one end with the royal coat of arms and the word *Advantage*.

"I took this from the bathroom before I left and put it in my handbag, and I've kept it ever since. That was the name of the yacht, do you see, *Advantage*. They used to make jokes about it, the Prince taking advantage of all the smitten young women. Well, I was one of them, whether you believe me or not." Her bright-eyed look suddenly changed to one of sadness, and she fell back on her pillow with a sob.

Edward leaned over and kissed her. "Of course I believe you, Mother," he said. "Thank you for telling me."

15

"Oh, that little drawing's D.G. Rossetti all right," Jack said, on one of Edward's early days in the art rooms. "No mistaking that wiry line. See if you can find a date on the old man with the pipe over there, Edward. Get it under the light. I don't see a signature, but there's so much varnish on it the date and signature may have gone under. Look at the back, too. The consignor says Joseph Wright but I have my doubts. I think we'll say 'attributed to' on that one."

It was Jack's responsibility to categorize and date works that were to go up for sale, track down their provenance whenever possible, and finally to appraise them and set a reserve bid, which was not always as high as — although occasionally considerably higher than — the value set on them by the consignor. His new assistant was eager to learn, continually bombarding him with questions, which certainly didn't displease him. Jack had a strong didactic streak. When he asked Edward about his own art education Edward told him that at school in Canada he'd been shown slides of famous paintings from time to time, but he hadn't absorbed much from the experience. The art teacher would busy himself with the projector and read from his notes while the boys took naps or got up to various kinds of monkey play, and when an outburst of hooting laughter could no longer be contained the teacher would switch on the overhead lights and tell the boys they were going to be uncultured louts all their lives, and the session would be over.

Edward remembered that his teacher had revered the work of a brotherhood of Canadian painters called the Group of Seven, who were famous for their scenes of the bleak Northern Canadian landscape, but he thumbed through a dictionary of art and artists from the department's shelves of reference books without finding so much as a mention of them. Jack had never heard of them either, collectively or individually.

"Regional schools are an odd phenomenon," he said. "I doubt if your group is known outside Canada." He told Edward he mistrusted all so-called groups anyway. Could he imagine serious artists sitting around swapping paint brushes and comparing notes? Any painter worth his salt was first and foremost an individualist. It was evident to Jack that apart from what Edward had been exposed to at school he knew nothing of artistic theory or aesthetics and had hardly even seen any great works of art. He seemed eager to learn, and Jack would often find him browsing through books he'd pulled from their little library during his lunch break. One day he came to Jack with a small volume he'd found in the shelves called *What is Art*. He'd thought it sounded like a good place to begin, but he couldn't make head or tail of what the author was saying.

"Mr. Turner —"

"Just call me Jack, Edward, unless there are clients around. You make me feel like an old man."

He smiled. "All right, Jack, what does this person mean by 'form'? He's always talking about 'significant form.' I don't even know what 'form' is, let alone what makes it significant. Then he talks about 'content.' Does content mean what the picture's about? The story of it? Because he says the content or the story or whatever it is has nothing to do with art anyway and should-n't even be taken into account."

"Clive Bell loved that particular conundrum. What he means by form or forms is simply the coloured shapes the artist has painted onto the two-dimensional canvas, quite apart from what they represent. He insists that it's the shapes and the arrangement of them, or in other words, the forms, that affect us aesthetically, and he'd like to persuade us that what the shapes represent doesn't have anything to do with our emotional response to the painting. That may be partly true, but in my opinion human beings can't help but be interested in what a painting's 'about,' even if we're looking at one of these completely abstract paintings that are coming out of New York these days. Our eyes go on searching for recognizable objects from the real world. I personally believe it's something almost instinctive, maybe from the days we prowled through forests looking for the particular shape in the greenery that was something good to eat — or maybe the shape of something that wanted to eat us. Ever lie in bed when you were a little boy, finding faces in the wallpaper? What Bell is getting at is that if the arrangement of shapes and the colours aren't aesthetically pleasing by themselves it's a bad painting, no matter how interesting the so-called content may be, and I'd have to agree with him there."

Jack's little lecture seemed to satisfy Edward. Another day he saw his assistant poring over a large volume on French Impressionism, gazing intently at a reproduction of a painting by Camille Pissarro. Jack looked over his shoulder and tapped the page with his finger. "That one's right here at the National Gallery," he said. "Go have a look at it, why don't you?" He started to move away, and then he turned back. He had watched Edward the first day he came up to the art department, standing transfixed in front of that wonderful little Turner with an extraordinary expression, as though his senses were exploding, his face suffused with pleasure and amazement like the face of a baby who's just been given its first taste of honey. Every time Jack turned around that day Edward was back in front of the Turner wearing that look of astonishment, as though his eyes were beholding glory.

There had been a time when Jack himself had reacted to works of art in just that way, in fact those overpowering emotional experiences had been what got him hooked on art in the first place. Being thrown at an early age into a feeling of rapture over a work of art was a bit like first sex — so thrilling it makes you mad to have those feelings again and again. He had thought the way to pursue that aesthetic ecstasy was to read about art, to study and analyze it, understand the motives of the artists, find out what they themselves wrote on the subject, dig into theory, develop critical opinion. Whether his capacity for that direct emotional response was not terribly strong in the first place, or if by intellectualizing the whole process he put an insurmountable barrier between his vision and his heart, he don't know, but the more he studied and learned, the weaker his immediate reaction was. He became knowledgeable, even authoritative; he could say with certainty whether a painting was a good or great one and tell you why, and he could identify the school or movement the artist belonged to and what the work's value on the market might be, but he became less and less able feel it directly, until finally, after some time had passed, he realized he had lost that ability almost completely. Looking at a painting now had become a cerebral process, simply ticking off a list of its attributes. The kind of experience Edward was having when he gazed so raptly at that Turner was by then to Jack only a memory. He had no idea whether his capacity for that immediate response had always been weak, or if he had destroyed it forever by delving too deeply into the academic side of art, and he hadn't really decided whether his studies had resulted in a net gain or loss for him. He had fitted himself for his work at Christopher's, and maybe that's what he'd been meant to do with his life, but watching Edward that day stirred up something in him, a combination of nostalgia and regret, and — well — affection — of the kind he might have felt for a son who reminded him of what he'd been like once himself.

"If you're trying to learn more about art, Edward," he said, "look at the pictures first, *feel* them. Pictures were made to be looked at, not read about. That's like reading the score of a symphony instead of going to hear the music. Get out some books afterward if you must, but don't contaminate your eye with a lot of theory and critical writing before you've studied the work."

"What if I look at something and what I feel about it is all wrong?"

"How could it be? How could your reaction to a painting be wrong for you? Anyway, could you change the way you felt about it just because somebody said it was the wrong way to feel? As far as I'm concerned, the proper study of art is art."

Edward gobbled his sandwich on the run the next day while he sprinted down to Trafalgar Square to spend his lunch hour among the Impressionist paintings at the National Gallery. He stayed longer than he should have, grabbed a passing cab back to Christopher's and took the stairs up to the art room two at a time, as usual. He was full of questions, such as why had he had loved the Pissarro, but hated a painting of an almost identical subject by Renoir.

"All right," Jack said, "what was it about the Renoir that put you off?"

"Well, for one thing, it looked as though he'd painted it with jam. And the girl looked — I don't know — empty-eyed, as though there was nobody there. She was just a doll, Renoir's idea of perfection, I suppose. I got the feeling he was leering at those puffy little breasts as though he'd like to eat them for lunch. To tell you the truth, I thought it was sort of obscene."

"Spot on, Edward," Jack said, smiling. "I've always found Renoir a little obscene myself, especially the later work. All those overweight nude women looking about as intelligent as a pile of pink sofa cushions. Old boy was in his dotage. What about the Pissarro?"

"Oh, in that one the girl was a real human being, but — the painting was more than just a picture of a girl. You wished you could see what was going on outside the frame. She seemed to be part of something bigger. And the figure was sort of fused into the natural setting around her, not just stuck onto it, or rather, not as though the landscape was just there as a background to the figure, she was part of it. She looked serious and thoughtful. The colours were more earthy."

"Not painted with jam."

"No. And every brush stroke seemed important. I had the feeling he'd painted it very slowly and thought a lot while he was doing it. It was beautiful."

"You have a natural sense of discrimination, Edward, there's no question about that. I wonder if the best thing for you to do might not be to start with the Impressionists and work your way backwards. Take a good look at everything there is to see right here in London. That's a lot, more than you might think. Then in time, if you're still interested, you could consider going abroad on your holidays, when you know what you're looking for — Paris, Florence, Rome, Athens. Travel's cheap on the continent these days."

"I certainly want to see all that great art from the past, but I don't know anything about contemporary art either, you know? I feel so ignorant."

"Ah, the contemporary scene! That's a horse of another colour. These days they're abandoning representation altogether and just expressing their own emotional states. 'Action painting,' it's called, nothing to do with the visible world whatever, just a record of how the artist was feeling at the time. I suppose it's very self-indulgent, but sort of exciting too. Or it is to me. Maybe because I have to look at so much of the tired old academic stuff that finds its way in here, and this new painting is the very antithesis of it."

"Do people buy that kind of art?"

"Buy it? I assume American collectors do. The museums are embracing it over there, and the big-name critics promote it for all they're worth. I think I'm somewhere in the middle. I can appreciate Matisse and Picasso and the German expressionists, but maybe that's about as far forward as I'm prepared to go." He laughed. "One thing's sure, we aren't likely to see any Jackson Pollocks or Franz Klines turning up in Christopher's in the near future. It's an entirely different market. I think the New York dealers go right to the lofts where these painters work and cart the stuff off to their galleries."

Jack walked over to the window and looked down on the street. A drizzling rain was spattering the glass, a typical London November day. "Christopher's has started up a branch in New York City. It seems New York's becoming the hub of the art world, whether we like or not. It's certainly not Paris anymore, not since the war. Christopher's is planning to open auction rooms in Canada, too — possibly Toronto or Montreal. Did you know that? John Christopher was up here talking about it a few days ago, wondering if I'd be interested in working in America for a few years."

"Would you?"

"Oh good God no. Not even slightly. I'd never live anywhere but in England."

Jack's own home when he was growing up had been a plain little pebble-dash house in a row of identical houses on a narrow street in Walsall, the black country, England's midsection — steel mills, smokestacks, soot. When he first came to live in London he'd thought the city was the most beautiful place on earth, and with some small reservations he still did. He never stopped marvelling at the elegance of the Regency terraces and the splendid

public buildings and churches; he was enthralled by the art collections, the theatre and opera, the ballet, the music, the gardens,
the parks, the river — all of it. Since the war he'd seldom had
the desire to go anywhere, apart from the occasional trip to the
continent or a few days down in Dorset with an old friend. His
job at Christopher's, his life in London, and his flat overlooking
the river in Putney suited him perfectly.

16

"It's all fixed, Jack! They're giving me the first two weeks of September. What should I do? Should I go to Rome straight off?"

Edward had come running up the stairs waving a memo he'd just received from the office. He'd visited Paris twice during the two years he'd been working in the art department as Jack's assistant, spending almost the entire week of his vacation each time looking at the great works of art in the Louvre and La Musée d'Art Moderne, with brief interludes of wandering around Montmartre. Recently Jack had been guiding him through books on the art of the Italian Renaissance, and he was longing to see some of those works at first hand. With two whole weeks at his disposal, a trip to Italy was feasible.

Jack looked up from his desk. "Oh good heavens, Edward, go to Florence! Book yourself into a pensione somewhere central and plan to stay there the whole time — except maybe for the last couple of days. When you've seen all you can absorb of Firenze — not all there is, you understand, just all you can absorb — you might pack up and go to Urbino, just to see a few special things there. Round out your experience a bit."

Jack had made such trips himself while he was at university in Leeds during the twenties, had even made something of a miniature grand tour of Italy and Greece that in those days had cost next to nothing. He remembered walking in the streets of Paris and Florence and Rome, visiting the great museums and archeological sites without ever having to line up or struggle through crowds. There were no busloads of American tourists pouring into the Louvre to see the Mona Lisa — not that he faulted the Americans or for that matter the British who had begun to travel in Europe since the war, they were just as entitled as he was himself — but his early experiences were quite different from what Edward would encounter.

"What about Siena, and Pisa?"

"Don't try to do too much in one trip. There'll be lots of places to visit the next time you go — Siena and Pisa, certainly, Venice, Ravenna —"

Edward broke in. "I wish you were coming, Jack. I'd love to go on a holiday with you. You could be my guide. I feel so —"

"Absolutely not," Jack said. "Take a trip like this with some-one like me and you'd be listening to what I had to say all the time instead of using your own eyes. You don't want someone telling you how beautiful the frescos are, or that this or that building's actually a bastard piece of architecture you shouldn't like as much as you do."

"Well, I'll take your word for it."

"All you need is a pocket guide to get you around. Anyway, being by yourself and feeling lonely is a good thing — opens you up and makes you vulnerable. Gets you talking to people. I'll hear all about it when you get back."

It was a golden September afternoon when Edward got off the train in Florence. The pensione he'd booked through an agency in London was a short distance from the station, a small faded pink palazzo on the Lungarno Amerigo Vespucci, old and grace-ful and beautiful, like almost everything else in that city. As soon as he'd been shown to his room he'd flung open the tall double windows and filled his lungs with the exotic air of this wonder-ful city. The pensione overlooked the river on the front, but its inner side wrapped itself around a small courtyard where a foun-tain trickled gently into a shallow scalloped basin. He could see into the doorway of a room with a black and white tile floor that opened off the courtyard, evidently a kitchen. Just below his window a yellow dog lay dozing on the flagstones with half a dozen unconcerned mourning doves wobbling around him on their short legs, looking like so many wind-up toys.

Edward pulled himself away from the window, had a quick wash, and hurried down the worn marble staircase and into the street, setting out along the embankment toward the centre of the city. Everything he saw, every mellow, age-softened building, bridge, archway, and rooftop looked exquisite to his hungry eyes. The Ponte Vecchio spanned the river just ahead with all the odd little birdhouse shops clinging to its sides, the whole structure bathed in yellow afternoon light and flattened against a sky of the purest, deepest blue. He felt as though he might be making the whole scene up out of images from the paintings and photographs he'd looked at so avidly back in London. He came around a curve in the road and suddenly the Duomo leaped to fill the sky above the city, a cathedral big enough when it was built, so he'd read, to house all the citizens of Florence at one time. He gazed at Brunelleschi's glorious melon-shaped dome with tears blurring his vision, so moved that he was suddenly short of breath, and he stood for a few moments leaning against the balustrade, wondering if his heart could bear the weight of so much beauty.

Edward began his tours with a Baedecker in his hand, but after the first day he put it in his pocket and let his feet take him where they would. That way he could come unprepared on a famous sculpture with its contours defined against the cerulean sky, or emerge from a network of narrow shadow-filled streets into some sunny little square with a bustling market underway, or step out into one of the great piazzas surrounding a magnificent cinquecento church. He spied San Miniato from across the river and made his way to it, led by his nose through twisting streets, across a bridge, up a steep stone stairway to arrive breathless on the heights of the Piazzale Michelangelo. He hardly slept that first week, spent entire days walking, going through museums and churches, carrying on until his legs gave out or he suddenly noticed he was starving. He would stop at a café or trattoria for a bite to eat and a few moments rest, then charge on again. He returned to the pensione each evening long after dark, crashed into bed, rose at first light to gulp down his caffe latte and rolls in the little breakfast room of the pensione, and was off to catch the glories of Florence touched by the first rays of sun.

Every morning as he set out Edward felt as though he were entering a dream. Florence would not settle down to being, as London was, simply a city where people lived and ate and slept and went about their business in the midst of a rich historical and artistic tapestry of monuments and buildings. When he walked those streets he felt as though he were sinking through palpable transparent layers of time, with his eyes on fire. Standing in front of one of the great paintings in a church or museum he was willy-nilly transported to its moment of creation, into the mind of its creator, stunned, not only by the marvel of the art but by the passionate faith that so clearly lay behind it. He had never imagined there could be religious convictions as compelling as those obviously held by these artists. He gazed at *The Annunciation* of Fra Angelico for an hour, went out into the piazza for coffee and a sandwich, came back and stood staring at it for another hour. He came away from the *Enthroned Madonna* of Cimabue in the Uffizi hypnotized, dazed. His mind seemed to be dissolving in this atmosphere of religious fervour and overwhelming beauty.

Edward had never been remotely concerned with religious beliefs or practices, but now, seeing these works of art, he began to feel that he had missed something essential to his existence. He'd assumed that what went on inside churches was as meaningless for everyone else as it had always been for him. The obligatory Sunday services during his years at that school in

Canada had been dreary events — a stream of extemporaneous prayer spouted by some visiting minister, unenthusiastic hymn-singing by the students accompanied by thin notes from an electric organ. Since he'd come back to England he hadn't so much as stepped inside a church.

As his holiday time waned, the feeling that he was drowning in religious emotion became almost obsessive. He began to sleep badly, woke in the mornings feeling as if he'd spent the night in a crowded room where hundreds of people were all talking at once. One morning he realized, as Jack Turner had predicted before he left, that he could absorb nothing more in Florence for the time being, and after ten days in the city he reluctantly packed his bag, and, following Jack's advice, caught a train to Urbino. At the top of Jack's list of the marvellous works he must see there was Piero della Francesca's *Madonna of Senigallia,* or as it was sometimes called, *The Madonna with Two Angels.* He got off the train in the late afternoon feeling tired and hot but determined not to waste a moment of his precious holiday. He found a room in a pensione not far from the railway station, left his bag, bought a bottle of mineral water at a nearby café-bar and drank it down, and immediately set out for the Ducal Palace.

In the immense high-ceilinged room to which he was directed a ray of late afternoon sun from a high window seemed almost to be pointing out the very painting he was seeking. He crossed the floor and took a stance facing the work, stood there slowly letting his eyes take it in. Central in the panel was the exquisite figure of the Virgin, dressed in a persimmon-coloured gown with a dark shawl or robe falling around her shoulders. A sheer little veil lay in tiny pleats across her forehead. Her features were lovely in an exotic, almost oriental way, her expression gentle and maternal. The babe she held sat erect in her arms with a hand raised in blessing, looking more like a little emper-

or than a nursling. In both faces there was a feeling of remoteness and otherworldliness, of mystery and spirituality. Edward let out an audible sigh. It was so excruciatingly beautiful. He had seen wonderful painting before, but this was perfection. The colours were so delicate, the composition so harmonious, the whole painting aglow with such a magical stillness that it came close to bringing tears to his eyes. It was ravishing.

At last he looked away from the two central figures. To the right of the mother and child stood an angel gowned in pale pink with his arms reverently folded across his breast, gazing at the holy pair; to the left the artist had painted bars of sunshine falling upon a wall that had the effect of backlighting the golden hair of a second angel, who was standing in a doorway, slightly to the rear of the group. This personage was arrayed in silver and gold, and his face was framed in the gleaming tendrils of his bright hair as though by a halo. There was the suggestion of a smile on his lips. His almond-shaped eyes were staring, not at the madonna and infant, but straight ahead, looking, Edward suddenly realized with a jolt, directly and intently at him. He was transfixed by that stare. He stood gaping, paralyzed.

Those eyes were seeing him as he had never been seen before. He felt utterly transparent, completely known. Nothing could be concealed from that piercing gaze. He understood in that instant, and with blinding certainty, that this being had been waiting for him to arrive at this very spot for the past five hundred years, that his entire life to that moment had been nothing but the circuitous path of a journey taken in obedience to his summons. Edward's legs felt weak, he started to tremble. He sank slowly to his knees, unaware of anything or anyone but that seraphic creature who continued to look directly into his eyes. In the next instant Edward heard him speak, in a voice as pure and liquid as a note struck from a golden bell, words addressed directly to him, and to him alone.

"It is here, Edward."

The angel appeared to have the attributes neither of one sex nor the other, but was rather a fusion of the two. Edward's sense of his other-worldliness was profound, inescapable. He was in the presence of Creation itself. As he knelt, ecstatic, he became conscious of a shadowy sense of remembering, as though some long-forgotten repository of love and innocence within him had just been reopened. At that point he must have lost consciousness. He was only vaguely aware of his surroundings when two uniformed guards helped him to his feet and escorted him to an anteroom. They sat him down on a bench and one of them brought a glass of water, which he drank slowly, dazed, hardly knowing where he was or what he was supposed to do next.

17

"But of course art is powerful," Jack said, when Edward told him about his extraordinary experience in Urbino. "Art exerts a tremendous influence on people's minds, on whole societies, and always has. Why else would tyrants be so afraid of it? Dictators know very well that truth and beauty go hand in hand, which isn't very convenient if you're trying to sell a people a pack of lies. The aesthetic is always sacrificed for the ideological the minute the smoke has cleared. I'm not at all surprised at what happened to you in Urbino. You have a marked susceptibility to art in the first place, and the circumstances simply magnified it."

"I think I must have gone a bit crazy, Jack," Edward said. "It seems ridiculous now, but I believed at the time that everything about that painting in Urbino was absolutely personal, as though it had been painted just for me."

"Certainly it was personal, dear boy, and in a way it *was* painted just for you. The apprehension of art is absolutely personal and subjective. I'm sure the late Dr. Freud — whose writings on the subject you should look into, by the way — would say that something in you, perhaps some need of yours, responded directly to the mind of the artist. When and why a work of art was originally created has nothing to do with its power. It has its own reality, its own being, independent of time or the society in which it was painted, or for that matter, even the audience for which it was intended. You grasped what was in the mind of Piero della Francesca across all those centuries, and you don't even have to be a believing Christian to feel its impact. The fact that you responded to it so strongly demonstrates something remarkable in you, too, as well as in the painting."

"Well, if I'm so damned remarkable, why don't I know what it meant?"

"Are you sure you don't know, my dear? Didn't your angel say 'this is where it is,' or something to that effect?"

"More or less."

"Again I refer to Freud. You created that hallucination yourself, just as you create the story and all the characters in your own dreams."

Edward laughed out loud at that idea. "I always think my dreams are stuff that's sifted in from somewhere else, maybe from people I don't even know, like getting onto crossed telephone lines. Anyway, if what you say is true and I made up what the angel said, or what I thought he said, then I ought to know what he meant. And I don't."

"Aye, there's the rub. The reason your dreams — or your angel — speak cryptically, or so I understand, is that you really don't want to know what was meant, it's some truth about yourself you're not ready for — or not just yet, anyway. Your mind or psyche or whatever you want to call it doesn't want to accept the real facts, but it's willing to have them hinted at. Think about what you heard. Where is 'here' with regard to that — let's call it aural — hallucination?"

"Well, certainly not in the Ducal Palace in Urbino. Not a physical place. In the painting. In art, I suppose."

"And what does 'it' refer to?"

"That's where I get stuck. 'It' could be anything. Religion. God. My soul. The most important thing in my life. I don't know."

"Wouldn't you say that your great talent is your aesthetic response, your apparently infallible eye for discerning what is beautiful and precious, not just in art but in other manmade things too? It's a gift few people possess, you know. I don't have it. The way I experience art is nothing like the way you do. My reaction comes from the years I've spent studying not just works of art, but art history and aesthetic theory, too. My appreciation comes from the education I've managed to scratch together, not directly from within me — not any longer, anyway."

"I suppose you're right. I don't think of it as something special because I didn't have to do anything to get it."

"And what do you want from that talent? What do you propose to do with it? How do you plan to incorporate your gift into your life? Couldn't 'it' actually mean the essence of you, the finest part of you? What would an angel be talking about, for goodness sakes, but the best that's in you, your virtue, as it were. The part of you that must be cherished and nurtured?"

"Well, I suppose that could be what he meant. Maybe."

"Just maybe? Have you never thought of undertaking a real study of art? Devoting a few years to it instead of merely dipping into it in your spare time? And I mean world art, not just Western painting and sculpture. There's all the art and architecture of Egypt, India, China, pre-Columbian art of the Americas, the African art that's been such an influence on Picasso. You've only just begun. Why not see if you can get yourself into a university, even as a part-time student, read some philosophy and history and comparative religion, find out what's behind it all, learn more about the societies that have produced great art. You're intelligent enough, and I believe your natural gift is something you'll always have. I've always regretted I didn't find some way to go on with my own education when I was your age. I can tell you, if I'd taken my degree I wouldn't be shuffling paintings around at Christopher's today."

"What would you be doing?"

"Teaching, certainly. Writing, perhaps. For me art is a passion, but with your God-given sensibility and sense of discrimination you could be another Berenson, an authority people would seek out. A prophet, if you like. I'm sure you're aware you haven't begun to plumb your own potential, intellectually or any other way. I think it would be a shame if you were to spend the rest of your life just bobbing along on the surface."

Edward sat looking at Jack for a few minutes, thinking about what he'd been saying. The thought of going off to university at this late stage had never occurred to him. The next day at work he told Jack he'd tried to imagine himself at some great seat of learning, the Sorbonne perhaps, attending small intense seminars followed by long evenings in cafés engaged in discussions with other students. Or poring over illuminated manuscripts under a shaft of amber light in some silent Tuscan monastery. The idea had rather appealed to him. Jack laughed at the images he drew, and they both knew neither scenario would be impossible. Edward had a facility with languages; learning them came easily to him.

"What if this facility of mine is just a knack," he said, "like the superficial talent my mother said she had in music — nimble fingers and a quick read."

"If that's the case you'll find out. But you'll never know what you're capable of if you don't explore it. You're into your middle twenties, aren't you? If you don't begin to do it soon you never will."

He understood what Jack was getting at. Yes, his talent, his "eye," if you wanted to call it that, was a God-given sixth sense for which he was grateful, and now that he was aware of it he couldn't imagine being without it. For some time, though, he'd been thinking that what he really wanted to do was become an independent art dealer, and at the same time build an art collection of his own, one that might eventually even be notable. That was his goal. He believed he could do well as a dealer, and apart from that he wanted to be self-sufficient, at no one's beck and call. He couldn't quite see himself writing papers, worrying about exams, having to pursue studies that might not really interest him just to satisfy some professor's requirements or a university curriculum.

"I'll think more about what you've been saying, Jack," he said, "and I'm grateful for your advice, believe me. I know you want what's best for me."

18

After Edward had unpacked a few things he walked across the room and stood looking down through the window watching Paulo on the terrazzo, admiring his neat movements as he cleared tables and reset them, coming and going with trays of food. After a few minutes he went downstairs and set out for a drive around the back roads, through countryside blooming and burgeoning in the incomparable spring weather. After driving more or less aimlessly for an hour he parked the car at a particularly beautiful viewpoint on the brow of a hill, where a stand of mimosa was sending billows of pollen into the air like puffs of yellow smoke. On a distant steep hill, beyond a sea of tall grass strewn with pink and yellow wildflowers, he could see the tiny figure of a shepherd driving his flock slowly down into the valley, the animals pouring like cream over the undulating green terrain, a picture from a child's storybook. He yawned, leaned back into the corner of the seat, and stretched out his legs. The food and wine and the excitement of the afternoon had made him drowsy, and he must have drifted off, because when he opened his eyes again the shadows were getting long. He was dry-mouthed and his muscles felt cramped. He climbed out of the car and stretched, dusted yellow pollen off the windshield before he turned the car around and drove back to the trattoria. He showered, changed his clothes, and settled down with a book he had difficulty keeping his mind on, while he listened for the cessation of the sound of voices and the tinkling of cutlery and dishes below that would indicate it was time for him to go downstairs.

The tables on the terrazzo had all been cleared and the chairs propped against them for the night. Edward walked through the empty dining room toward voices he could hear coming from the direction of the kitchen. He stopped in the open doorway to take in the tableau spread before him — Paulo, his mother and father, a stout man dressed in chef's white, a similarly clad youth who was no doubt his assistant, and a young girl Edward hadn't seen before, all of them sitting around a long wooden table that occupied the centre of the kitchen. To the left, sinks and draining boards reflected the lights under long open shelves stacked with dishes. The back wall of the kitchen was dominated by a great black range under a steel hood, and in front of it an iron rack was hung with clusters of shining steel and copper pots and pans. A vast double-doored refrigerator occupied part of the wall to the right. The air was fragrant with aromas of cooking.

The table itself was a picture of *abbondanza* — cold meats on a platter, another of grilled vegetables, a bowl of green salad, what looked like a *fritto misto* of shrimp and calamari, bottles of wine and mineral water, golden loaves of bread on a board. A steaming pan of creamy *lasagne al forno* was giving off a heavenly aroma. Cutlery and white napkins gleamed at each place, wooden pepper mills punctuated the arrangement. The whole scene looked so happy and glowing with good spirits that Edward could hardly bear to look at it.

Something inside him burst open, something he'd been careful to avoid noticing, like a possibly cancerous swelling he'd hoped would go away if he ignored it. A terrible, agonized yearning rose up in him, suffusing him with stark awareness of his emptiness, of his undeniable, unbearable, overwhelming *need*. It had always been there, a cyst filled with the corrosive acids of abandonment, loneliness, lies. Sheer *want* burned in the pit of his stomach, in his bowels, flamed up into his chest, sucked the breath out of his lungs.

Before him was a scene of that basic human activity that confers a kind of holy grace on human lives — people who love one another sitting around a bountiful table, sharing good food and enjoying each other's company. Edward felt at that moment as though the grey forlorn fabric of his entire life, even those parts of it that he had considered the happier ones, was being held up and flapped in his face like a tattered banner. See, Edward, sad creature that you are, look at your trivial business successes, your feeble sexual affairs, your lukewarm friendships, your wretched little ambitions. Oh, and those all-important collections, don't forget them — the pocket knives and fountain pens, the sticks of furniture, the bits of crockery, the dabs of paint on canvas. Stack them up against real happiness. Look at these people. Evening after evening they sit around this table, laughing and talking, and there in their midst is this beautiful man, smiling, telling some story. He speaks, gestures with his hands, all faces turn toward him in admiration —

Bitterness filled Edward's mouth. He saw Rak's gloomy dinner table at Riverview, the shallow bowls of murky brown soup afloat with islands of cooling grease, grey nameless meat, large boiled potatoes draped in pale congealing gravy, colourless cabbage cooked to disintegration, doughy saccharine-sweet puddings, all of it poisonously sauced with Rak's steely gaze. Those gross crystal chandeliers suspended from the ceiling had been hooded in some curious way so they cast their blanching light only on the long mahogany table itself, leaving the rest of the room in deep shadow. The whiteness of her cap and apron revealed the presence of the maid who stood against the wall beside the kitchen door, waiting for a peremptory wordless signal from her master's bony hand. His mother silently stuffing herself to bursting, his own fair head bent over his unappetizing meal ...

Paulo's father looked up, noticed their guest standing in the doorway, half rose with difficulty, as though his joints caused him pain, and waved him with an outstretched arm to a place at the table.

"Do come and sit down," he said in Italian. "Edward, is it? I'm Herbert Jones. You've already met my wife, Chiara. That young lady is her niece, Elena, who's assisting us this year. This is our wonderful chef, Primo, and that tall string bean is his assistant, Luigi. My son, Paulo, tells me you and he have already become friends, so you're very welcome here. Sit down, sit down. You must be starved."

Edward did his best to conceal what he'd just been feeling, tried to smile affably and look relaxed. None of them seemed to notice his pallor or his trembling hands as he took his place and shook out his napkin. He supposed he was an oddity to them anyway, a foreigner. They took up the conversation where it had left off, the chatter so swift and boisterous and coming from so many directions at once that his knowledge of Italian was barely up to it. Primo seemed to be something of a raconteur, and now and then a wave of laughter following some story of his would roll around the table and peter out before he could catch the punchline. There was a tale about hunting for truffles in Piemonte with a dog that sniffed out, and enthusiastically dug up, something that wasn't a truffle. Edward never did find out what the thing was because the word was unknown to him, but he laughed along with the rest of them, not wanting to be the dimwit who didn't get the joke.

The little female cousin kept glancing sideways at Paulo with flirtatious eyes. Didn't she know, he wondered? Herbert Jones recounted some of his wartime experiences, how as an officer in the British Army he'd participated in the Allied drive up through Sicily after the retreating Hun, as he called the Germans. "I was camped for two weeks in this area," he said. "Fell in love with the country, even with all the shelling and bombing that was going on. The bloodshed was appalling. We had to stop to bury our dead, and some of the enemy, too. Awful, all of it. What human beings can do to each other. A dreadful time." He shook his head as though to rid it of those memories.

"But you came back."

"When the war ended I went back to teaching school in England. I kept thinking about Sicily, though. I ran into some health problems after a while, a weak chest as it was called. Probably from living in that perishing cold school."

"I know about those English schools from personal experience," Edward said.

"Ah. Then I needn't describe them. Anyway, I had a few bouts of pneumonia that laid me low, and the doctors told me I'd better take a few weeks off and go somewhere warm and dry. I went them one better. I'd never married, my parents were gone, I had no ties, nothing to keep me in England. I resigned from the school, put together my savings and came back and bought this house. I wasn't a restaurateur at that stage. Didn't know a thing about food. My plan was to run the place as a pensione. I looked around for someone to cook and serve the breakfasts, and guess who came and applied for the job? The most beautiful girl in the village!"

She was still beautiful. Her neck and arms were firm and round, her face unlined. When she leaned over to serve the lasagne the v-neck of her white blouse offered a glimpse of lovely bosom. A strong woman, Edward thought, nothing like his own poor mother. Chiara would have had Harvey Rak cringing in a corner, if he was any judge of character.

"I thought I'd better marry him," she said. "He needed looking after. The poor man didn't know how to boil water." She'd been watching her husband with tender eyes while he was speaking, and Edward more than once caught her gazing at her son with something approaching adoration. Her life obviously revolved around these two men.

She turned to him. "Well now, Signore Eduardo, are you going to make a famous artist of our Paulo?"

"I think he's going to do that by himself, Signora Chiara. All I need to do is show his work and advertise it a little. The paintings will speak for themselves."

"I wouldn't want him to be *too* famous. He might forget all about his home and family."

"Mamma," Paulo said, "that would never happen, and you know it. What's that English saying about home, Papa? Home is —"

"— where the heart is."

Edward felt a chill pass through him. All afternoon he'd been weaving a rich fantasy involving Paulo and himself. He would become the most important person in Paulo's life. They would be lovers, passionate, devoted, inseparable. Yes, he would make a famous artist of Paulo. They would come back to visit Paulo's parents, of course. Sicily was a wonderful place for a holiday. Paulo's real life, though, would be with Edward. His mother would accept her son's decision, would rely on Edward to take good care of him. Their mutual love for him would make a strong bond between the two of them.

He must have been insane. In a couple of days he'd be leaving and Paulo would still be here in the midst of his adoring family and he would be just as much alone as ever, only from now on he'd be miserable with longing for Paulo. For a moment he almost wished they'd never met.

"I think you're in a daze there, Edward," Herbert said, proffering a bottle. "Won't you have a little Marsala with your *dolce?*"

He felt a flutter of alarm, as though the man might have been reading his thoughts. When dinner was over he began to pick up plates and carry them to the sink, but the women and young Luigi wouldn't allow it. "Might as well leave them to it," Paulo said. "Come on, I'll show you my studio."

They set out along a narrow path behind the house. The night was warm, and Paulo began unbuttoning his shirt as they walked under the trees, peeled it off and carried it in his hand. Edward could make out a low stucco building gleaming palely against a row of cypresses looming up into the starry sky. "The studio used to be a little barn for cattle or goats," he said. "This was a real farm in the old days." He preceded Edward through the door to turn on lights. "I cleaned it up and had that skylight cut into the roof, put in plumbing and electricity, a new wooden floor — that was about it."

Edward stood and looked around the large open room. There were canvases everywhere, hung on the white walls or leaning against them, some evidently completed, others barely underway. A big wooden easel stood beside the ubiquitous painter's table covered with jars and cans and brushes, tubes of paint, a jumble of equipment in which only the artist himself could possibly have discerned some order. A short iron staircase led up to a loft under the slanted roof that appeared to be Paulo's sleeping quarters.

Edward breathed in the odours of linseed oil and paint and turpentine, smells which, to an artist *manqué* such as himself, were so sensuous as to be almost aphrodisiacal. "I arrange these things," he said, pointing to a still life set-up on a smaller table, "and then worry the life out of them, paint them this way and that way and the other way until I've exhausted all the possibilities. Even Mamma asks me why I don't get some new bowls and jugs and start on another batch."

Edward laughed. "I think your obsession, or whatever it is, is marvellous. What do you tell your mother when she says that?"

"I tell her it's like Primo making little variations on the same dish. It isn't a question of getting it right, it's more trying to find out just how much can be done using the same ingredients in different proportions."

Edward laughed. "What a wonderful analogy."

He was acutely aware of the nearness of Paulo's strong young body, the movement of muscles in his naked arms and torso, the springy mat of red-gold hair on his broad chest, the scent of wine on his breath when he was close. He was follow-

ing a pace or two behind as they looked at the paintings, surreptitiously raising the intensity of his yearning by leaning close
to inhale the lemony fragrance of some soap or lotion emanat-
ing from Paulo's hair or skin. He wanted so fiercely to take him
in his arms that he had difficulty keeping his attention focused
on the work. If Paulo had taken a backward step and their bodies had collided he would have exploded with desire.

When their circuit of the studio was finished Paulo turned
to face Edward. He laid a light hand on his upper arm. "Shall I
take you back to your room in the house? Or would you like to
stay here with me?"

"I would like to stay here with you," he said quietly, putting
both hands on Paulo's warm bare shoulders. Paulo was a few
inches shorter than Edward, and when he bent toward him
Paulo lifted his chin to receive his light kiss. Edward began to
draw away then, but Paulo grasped his head in both hands and
pressed his mouth to Edward's so forcefully that someone's
tooth, his own or Paulo's, bit into his lower lip, and he tasted
blood. Paulo slid one arm down Edward's back and drew his
lower body against his own.

"*Andiamo a letto, Eduardo.*"

Upstairs Paulo swept back the bedcovers and switched off
the light, leaving the loft bathed in pale starry illumination from
the skylight above their heads. He was brusque, muscular,
demanding, a robust partner who seemed to take it as his right
to be in command, moving Edward's body this way and that
with his strong arms, finding ways of pleasing himself and pro-
viding pleasure for his partner without the slightest inhibition or
restraint. After their first strenuous coming together they lay
back on the pillows, breathing heavily, wet with perspiration,
their arms still wrapped around one another. They were the true
gemelli, Edward thought, they were two unnaturally separated
halves that shared a single soul, reunited at last.

The spring night was too short. They made love, slept, made love again. As dawn bleached out the window above their heads they began to talk. Edward told Paulo about his long-ago epiphanous experience at the Ducal Palace in Urbino, the strange way in which that angelic being of Piero's that Paulo so much resembled seemed to have spoken to him.

"I still don't know what it's supposed to have meant," he said. "A friend tried to explain it away in psychological terms. He said it wasn't any kind of miraculous happening, just something I'd manufactured in my own subconscious, a sort of cryptic message to myself about something I really couldn't comprehend all at once and had to learn in this peculiar way."

"What was he, some kind of atheist? Why did you listen to him?"

"Are you a believer, Paulo? Do you believe in the Catholic Church, the whole thing?"

Paulo had propped himself up on an elbow and was looking down at him. There was enough light for Edward to see that amused expression he'd noticed the afternoon before, as though he'd surprised Paulo with his stupidity.

"I don't believe in the Church," he said, "I believe in God. The Church is just men, like you and me." He laughed. "And believe me, a lot of them *are* just like you and me."

"So you don't think what we've just been doing is jeopardizing your immortal soul?"

"I can't imagine God caring about such small details, can you? I think he has more important things to worry about."

"I've never thought much about God at all, or what He worries about. Or for that matter whether I really believe God even exists. I seem to get along pretty well without Him."

"That's like saying you're not sure if you believe in air, but it doesn't mean you can get along without it."

"Well, I wish I had your faith. It must be very comforting."

"I can't imagine what it would be like to live without it. It must be awful. Anyway, I don't just believe, I *know*. I'm not sure how it all goes together, but my painting has a lot to do with my soul."

"How can that be? What's the connection?"

"My talent's a gift from God. I never think it's me that paints so well, or my eyes that see everything so clearly, or my hand that's so clever with the brush. It's God working inside me."

Edward found it almost embarrassing to hear a grown man talk this way.

"I envy you," he said. "That same friend told me my particular talent was my ability to see and appreciate beauty, but that's nothing like being able to create it, the way you can. I can't see how my gift, if that's what it is, could be of much interest to God. I wish I had your belief that what we do matters to some being up there."

"Oh, I have a rational side, too. I'm sort of a split personality. My father likes everything to be reasonable and intellectual, you know? Mamma has her faith, everything's to do with the heart or the spirit or the soul. Papa made me read English writers and poets to balance what the priests put in my head at school. The stuff I had to memorize when I was a kid, you wouldn't believe it!"

"I never even met my father. I don't know what my mother believed in. She and I never went to church, anyway. Maybe my father was what they call 'Defender of the Faith' for a while, whatever that may mean. My mother told me she'd had an affair with the Prince of Wales, as he was then, and I was the result."

Paulo laughed. He probably thought it was mere fantasy. Maybe that's what it was.

"Mamma would have taught me a lot more than the catechism if she'd had her way and Papa hadn't kept checking up on things," Paulo said. "See this?" He dangled a little gold pendant shaped like a goat's horn suspended from a thin chain around his neck. "Mamma's made me wear one of these ever since my brother died. It's supposed to ward off the evil eye. There are words to go with it if I happen to run into the devil one day: *Crepa l'invidia e schiattono gli occhi.*"

"My God, what a curse! I hope you never have to use it. What if you got the wrong person and blew up his eyes by mistake?"

"There are things you do with your hands, too. *Mano cornu-ta.*" He folded his two middle fingers over his palm, leaving the index and little fingers up, like horns. "The other one is the *mano fica*, with the tip of your thumb between your fingers, to repre-sent the woman's parts. Even waving a clove of garlic under the devil's nose is supposed to scare him off."

"I wish I could have put my stepfather out of commission that easily. If anyone was a devil, he was."

"It must have been terrible, not having a real father," Paulo said, after thinking about it for a minute. He fell back onto the pillow, stared up at the skylight. "I suppose I take what I've always had for granted. Mamma's from a huge family — she's one of thirteen children. They're all very close. Oh, they have their little feuds and arguments, but they really love each other. Just let somebody give one of them trouble, and look out!"

"Do you ever feel lonely, Paulo? Ever feel the need for that one other person who'll make you a whole human being? The one you've been hoping to find all your life?"

Paulo thought for a moment. "I don't think so. I don't feel lonely that way. I suppose everybody wants a permanent partner sooner or later, but I don't think about it much now."

"I think there's been a star hanging in the Sicilian sky over this cowshed, guiding me toward you."

Paulo laughed. "That's blasphemous!"

"God won't care, you said so yourself. He's too busy with other things. Paulo, I think — no, that's not the right word — I *know*. I know I'm in love with you."

"Edward —"

"Don't say anything, not yet. I don't expect you to feel the way I do. It's too soon."

"All I was going to say is it's an awfully long way from here to Canada. It's not as though we could just jump in a car and see each other. We've just met, and now you're leaving —"

"I thought about that. Of course it's going to be difficult at first. I have a little plan though. I was working it out when you were asleep. I'm going to ask you if you'd consider coming to Canada in the fall. I'd give you a good reason to come — a solo show in my gallery. Say the word and I'll start things rolling, set a date for the show, get the invitations made, book your flight, everything."

"Edward —"

"— Think about it, that's all I ask. Write, or phone me after I get back to Toronto. Give yourself time. You have more than enough work for a show right here in this studio. I've seen it. You could ship all the canvases you want to exhibit and I'd look after the costs."

Paulo started to reply, but Edward pressed a fingertip to his lips. "Paulo, even if you decide you don't want to do this, if it all comes to nothing, even if I never see you again, I want you to know just being with you this little while will have been the happiest day and night of my life."

"Of course you must go to Toronto, carissimo!" Chiara said, as they sat over their coffee the next morning. "Your first exhibition, and you not there to see it? Besides, you can visit all my nieces and nephews, come back and tell me everything about them. Take photographs of everybody, too. Lots of them. They've got husbands and wives I've never seen, new babies — you're to go, Paulo! That's definite!"

149

Paulo looked at Edward over his bowl of caffe latte and rolled his eyes in mock dismay. "What can I do? When she gets an idea into her head, there's no arguing with her."

"Chiara, why don't you go with him?" Herbert said. "It's time you saw something besides this little corner of the world. What could be better than to go to Canada and see all your relations when Paulo would be there to look after you."

"Why, that's a wonderful idea," Edward said, his heart sinking a little. It hadn't been part of his plan to have Paulo spending his time in Toronto attending to his mother.

"And leave you here by yourself? Certainly not. I'm quite content with this little corner of the world. No, Paulo's to go and be our eyes and ears and come back and tell us about it. Every single little detail."

"But why don't you all come?" Edward asked gallantly. "Surely you'd like to see your son's first one-man show, Herbert. Wouldn't that be even better?"

Paulo and his mother were silent. Herbert finally spoke.

"I'm afraid I wouldn't be able to make a trip like that, Edward. This arthritic condition of mine keeps me tied to home. I'm not too bad at the moment, but when it flares up I'm pretty helpless. It's a nuisance, makes an old man of me before my time. I'd like nothing better than to go if I could. I wish you'd indulge me and go anyway, Chiara."

"She won't, Papa," Paulo said. "We both know that. Never mind, I'll go and bring back all the news."

"It's settled then," Chiara said. "And Paulo, you're to take the day off, spend it with your friend. Show Eduardo our Sicily so he takes a good impression away with him. Everybody thinks this island's just good for producing criminals and murderers. Go and visit the potteries and see the steps at Caltagirone. Show him we can make beautiful things here, too."

The rest of that day was an idyll, a dream. Before they left Paulo packed a wicker hamper with a round loaf of bread, a wedge of gorgonzola, blood oranges, prosciutto and salami, spring onions, olives, a handful of freshly washed arugula wrapped in paper, and a couple of bottles of red wine. Edward watched as he assembled food and plates and glasses in the basket and covered it all with a white napkin.

"Like picnics?" Paulo asked.

"I love picnics," he said. And oh, how he loved this man, his deft hands, his quick neat movements, his face, his eyes, that hair —

They skipped the potteries. Instead, Edward drove while Paulo directed him this way and that through the countryside on narrow back roads until they turned into an overgrown track leading into a fragrant olive grove in heavy-scented bloom. "My uncle's place," Paulo explained. "We can spend the afternoon here with nobody to disturb us. There won't be a soul around this time of year." They left the car and walked through the trees carrying the hamper, emerging from the lacy canopy of blue-green leaves and yellow blossom onto a long stretch of open grassy hillside that commanded a view of miles of the country-side. A winding highway ran through it like a thread far below, the sea glimmered in the distance under a cloudless cerulean sky.

They sank down side by side in the tall soft grass. "My God, it's beautiful, Paulo," Edward said. "It's paradise."

"Isn't it? I've always loved this place. I used to help my uncle with the olive harvest every year when I was a kid."

"What a childhood you must have had."

"I don't think I ever had an unhappy day."

Edward turned and looked at him, thinking how he'd craved what this man had been able to take as a matter of course. Paulo must have sensed his feelings, because he raised his two hands and took Edward's head between them, drawing his face toward his own. His kisses of the night before had been fierce and demanding, but now his mouth pressed gently, first on Edward's forehead, then his lips, now his left cheek, then his right, kisses soft as butterflies. "There," he said, drawing back a little, smiling. "I've blessed you with the sign of the cross, whether you believe in God or not."

Can you die of happiness?

19

The household in Richmond underwent a sudden and drastic change one December day. Rak was at his works, storming around the assembly floor in a fit of temper, slapping the back of his right hand against the sheaf of papers he held in his left. Rak Piano was getting behind on orders just when the Japanese were beginning to invade the market with smaller, cheaper pianos, and if Rak couldn't supply the demand people would shop elsewhere. The postwar generation had no sense of patriotism. Japan, indeed! Wind-up toys, maybe — but pianos? Bunch of rubbish.

While he was still in mid-stride Rak stopped suddenly and stood staring, wide-eyed, unaware that he'd lost his grip on the papers that now fluttered down to the wooden floor like a flock of pigeons, to be joined seconds later by Rak himself. A stout secretary came hurrying from her desk with a tiny bottle of smelling salts that she kept in her purse. She waved the neck of the vial back and forth under his nostrils, but the sharp fumes failed to rouse him. He wouldn't wake up. An ambulance was called and he was whisked off to the hospital, where doctors diagnosed a cerebral accident, or in laymen's terms, a stroke.

There was enough of his brain still working that he could understand what was said to him, but he was unable either to move — excepting to twitch his face — or speak, other than to grunt. One grunt yes, two grunts no. Dolly and Edward were told he was unlikely to recover. In due time solicitors and accountants figured things out between them and explained the financial situation to his beloved wife and dear adopted son in the presence of the immobilized man in the bed. Since Rak had taken care that his stepson knew nothing about his business Edward had little to contribute at the gatherings that took place at the bedside. He sat well out of the range of Rak's unmoving gaze so he could hear what went on and take note of the old man's grunts and twitches without his being aware of Edward's irritating presence.

During the next few months the business was sold and the substantial proceeds were put into a trust supervised by the solicitors, from which a monthly sum was paid out for Rak's care and the upkeep of the household and the needs of Dolly and her son. As to what would happen if and when Rak should die, they were told that according to the terms of a will Rak had made at the time of his marriage, his wife would be his sole beneficiary should he predecease her, a then not unlikely possibility considering he was so many years her senior, and furthermore, as his legally adopted son, Edward would be his beneficiary should Dolly die before Rak did, unless of course he recovered and made a new will specifically cutting Edward out of any inheritance. All in all, things would be well for Edward and his mother as long as Rak failed to get better and had the good grace to die first.

The nurse, Miss Flagg, supervised Rak's transfer from the ambulance to his bedroom the day they brought him home from the hospital. She took a professional look at the stricken man and marched straight into Dolly's room. "I'm very sorry, Mrs. Rak," she said, "but I wasn't engaged to look after a helpless man in nappies, and I have no intention of even trying. You'll have to get male attendants around the clock, there's no other answer for it. I'll call the agency at once and have them send a male nurse straight over."

Edward had reason to think, from the whispers and slight skirmishes he'd heard in the night now and then, that Miss Flagg's seduction of Rak had been well underway before he was struck down. The enterprising nurse now abandoned her earlier objective while continuing her pursuit of the larger project by trying to snag the one most likely to wind up with the money. Edward was lying in bed reading when she came to his room one night, clad in a diaphanous pink gown with a lacy collar and satin ties at the neck.

"Uh, hello, Miss Flagg," Edward mumbled. "Can I — uh — do something for you?"

"I imagine you can, Edward," she said, smiling confidently and settling herself on the edge of his bed. "May I slip in there with you so we can find out?"

He shifted over to give her space, feeling less than comfortable about what he was certain was on her mind. "I must tell you, Miss Flagg," he said nervously, "if this is about what I think it is you've come to the wrong person. I'm not at all experienced with women."

"Why darling, of course you're not. How could you be, locked up all those years with a bunch of horrible boys? I just wondered if you wouldn't like to learn something about girls. What do you think? Shall we experiment a little together?"

"If you like, I guess, but ..."

"But nothing! What a jolly time we're going to have." She slipped into the bed, covered herself with the blankets and began kissing him quite sweetly on his ear and cheek and down the side of his neck, occasionally letting the tip of her tongue do the work. After a few minutes of this she laid her head against his chest. "Well, your heart's got a good steady beat," she said, "and quite rapid. That's a healthy sign." She then began to run her hands slowly over his body, exclaiming over the wonderful muscles in his arms and chest. And thighs. He lay quietly with his eyes closed, getting used to this new experience. Her gentle caresses were extremely stimulating.

"Oh my goodness," she cried a few minutes later, "what a big man you are after all."

For his part, he was surprised that one so old (she was thirty-five) was still so soft and round and completely unwrinkled. Her body amazed him — the soft, silk-haired petals enclosing that firm little boss to which her hand led his, an anatomical detail he hadn't even known existed but which she made him understand was of the utmost importance; the lushness of breasts and buttocks that gave way under light pressure of his fingers and then bounced cleverly back into their original melon shapes. He pushed the covers back and looked down at the hillock of her hip as she lay on her side teasing him with her hand. She really was quite beautiful.

Her visits became an almost nightly event excepting for those few days of the month of which he had also been almost entirely ignorant but which she now explained to him in detail. Miss Flagg showed him exactly what she wanted during their lovemaking and seemed eager for it, which was another revelation to him. He'd rather got the idea, from novels and other writings by men who obviously didn't know what they were talking about, that generally speaking women — other than those of the lowest class — only allowed such things to be done to them because they wanted babies.

As for himself, he'd taken it for granted, without thinking about it too seriously or putting the matter to any test, that he was probably homosexual — a fruit, a fairy, as he'd heard such men being called — even though he'd felt no particular desire for any man in recent years, or for that matter, any woman, either. The sexual side of his nature that might normally have sought a partner had been so badly wounded by Monsieur Olivier that it seemed to have gone completely into hiding. He now found himself enjoying this new experience with Miss Flagg, who loved to feign exhaustion when he would rear up over her yet once more in the small hours of the morning. "Oh no!" she'd murmur, laughing at his zeal. "*When* am I going to get some *rest!*"

It was almost two years before a second stroke finished off what was left of Harvey Rak. Dolly expressed no emotion whatever when Edward told her that her husband was dead, neither distress nor relief. "Oh. Really? Well, I suppose things will be different now. Will we be able to go on living here, darling? Oh, what am I talking about? Why on earth would we want to? We can all go and live in London now, so you can be closer to your work. You know, Edward, I've always wanted to go back up to Amersham where I was born — just to look around, of course. I couldn't live at the hotel again now that Father's gone. Silly me, I couldn't live in a hotel at all, with only one good foot and needing my insulin shots and the rest of me not working properly. No, I'll still need my dear Miss Flagg." She smiled up at the nurse, reached out and squeezed her hand.

"I've always fancied it up Regent's Park way," Miss Flagg said. "Do you remember my telling you that, Edward, that time we were talking about which parts of London we'd like best to live in?"

"Regent's Park would be lovely, wouldn't it," Mummie said. "You could push me 'round the zoo in the afternoons. Would you like to live up there, darling?"

Edward was silent. He had some serious thinking to do. Much as he loved his mother, she was going to need nursing care for years, for the rest of her life, in fact, and some temporary arrangement wasn't going to be good enough. As his responsibilities at Christopher's grew he might not always be nearby when she needed him. There was already talk of his being sent around to smaller English towns and possibly even up to Scotland to seek out consignments of paintings and antique furniture. He didn't care for Miss Flagg's attitude, either, intimating that she considered herself a permanent feature in their lives. In *his* life. What did she mean "where *we'd* like to live"?

"We don't have to decide anything right now, do we Mother? Meanwhile, why don't we go up to Amersham for a visit? We could have lunch at the old inn. How would that be? There's no reason we couldn't go this very weekend if you feel up to it."

"Oh, Edward!" Dolly said, excited. "Could we really? Oh thank you, darling. I can't think of anything I'd love to do so much."

It made him feel sad to hear her, so small a thing, something Rak might easily have done to please her. "I'm eager to see Amersham too," he said, "after you've told me so much about it, and your life there when you were growing up."

The following Saturday Edward and Miss Flagg tucked Dolly up in a lap robe in the back seat of Rak's venerable Bentley, put pillows under her feet and stowed the wheelchair in the boot. Edward caught sight of his mother's face in the rear-view mirror as they rolled into Amersham, saw the tears on her cheeks and the bright sad look in her eyes. He parked the car near the old grey stone church on the high street where she said she'd been confirmed and taken her first communion; she shed more tears in the churchyard when they wheeled her through the bumpy grass and over some flat stones to see the place where first her mother and then her father had been buried. She pointed to a grave marked with the name of her old music teacher.

"Poor Miss Smythe," she said, "and poor Daddy. They both hoped to make a concert pianist of me. She was the one who encouraged him to send me up to London to study, you know, and then I went to the bad and never practised, just went to parties all the time. It was such a gay time in London during the twenties, and I was so young and silly."

"Do you think you could have been a concert pianist, Mother?" Edward asked.

"Oh, my darling, not in a million years. I had a great facility for sight reading, and very nimble fingers. I could play anything they put before me, quick as a wink, but it never got any better no matter how many times I played it. My teacher kept telling me to *think* about the music, to try to *feel* it, but even I realized I had no real musicianship. No art." She twisted around in her chair and reached for his hand. "Put me here, too, when the time comes, Edward. I'll feel at home here."

"Don't be ridiculous, Mother," he said. "You're still a young woman. You mustn't even think about such things."

Miss Flagg piped up with further encouragement. "I'm not worrying about where they'll bury me, my dear, of that I can assure you!"

Edward would have had to agree that there was a lot of life left in Miss Flagg.

His mother smiled her resigned smile. "Ah well, we'll see," she said. "We'll see."

The village of Amersham, set amid green rolling hills, looked the very image of rural English tranquility. Brick and stucco houses with sloping mossy tiled roofs tilted this way and that along the high street, with sagging shutters and crooked doorways, not a true right angle to be seen anywhere. There was a tea room, a greengrocer's, a butcher's; Miss Nettle's Yarns had a notice in the window advertising lessons in knitting and modern embroidery every Wednesday. There was a shop specializing in ladies' dresses, suits, coats, and accessories. A shoe store. A chemist. A poster at the newsagent's announced the annual exhibition of the watercolour society in the church hall, admission free.

They had lunch in the old half-timbered inn that Edward's grandfather had once managed, and where his mother had lived as a girl. She was overcome with happiness and nostalgia at seeing it again. "Oh, Edward! Miss Flagg! Look!" she cried, as they wheeled her into the dining room. "They've hardly changed it a bit!" She ordered her favourite dish, steamed steak and kidney pie in suet pastry, and a rich trifle for dessert, but for once she just toyed with her food.

"You can't imagine how I love this place, Edward," she said, reaching across the table to take his hand. "I'm so grateful to you for bringing me here, darling. I asked and asked Harvey to bring me for a little visit, but he never would, not even for Daddy's funeral. I don't know why."

"I have a surprise for you, Mother," Edward said. Prior to their trip that day he'd made enquiries and found that there was a highly recommended nursing home in Amersham, in a converted manor house at the edge of town. What's more, a pleasant ground-floor suite that overlooked the gardens would be available any day now, he'd been told, as its present occupant wasn't expected to last the month. After lunch, while Miss Flagg took Dolly off to the ladies' room, he telephoned the home to say they were on their way.

"Edward, it's beautiful," Dolly said in a quiet voice, after they'd toured the home and grounds. "It must be very expensive, though, and I don't want to be selfish. I know Harvey didn't leave us *that* much money —"

"He left lots of money, plenty for you to live here, if you like it," Edward said. "More than enough. I want you to be happy. Besides, you know, I have my own life to lead now; it's time I had a place of my own. I'm not a boy anymore."

Miss Flagg smiled and touched his arm. "He certainly isn't just a boy, Mrs. Rak, and he and I — that is, he has to make plans for the future, doesn't he?"

"It's going to be hard for me having you away up here in Amersham," Edward said, "but it'll be worth it, knowing you're comfortable and happy."

His mother started to sniffle a bit. "I do love it here, Edward, I can hardly believe it after all these years. I never did get used to living down there south of London, everything seemed upside down. And of course you need — it hasn't been easy for you — such a good son —"

Edward leaned down and hugged her. "Not another word. What do you think of this woman, Miss Flagg, she always cries when she's happy. When we come back to move you in, Mummie, we'll open charge accounts for you in the shops. The matron here says you've only to telephone and they'll bring you dresses and all sorts of things to look at and try on. They do it for all the residents."

"Lucky you, Mrs. Rak," said Miss Flagg in her merriest voice, taking a clean handkerchief out of her purse and handing it to Dolly. "What wouldn't I give to be in a beautiful place like this and never have to worry about anything again."

If Edward wondered a little at Miss Flagg's enthusiasm for his mother's move to Amersham, which she must have realized was going to make her own job redundant, he was soon set straight. Miss Flagg had expectations. A few days later he handed her an envelope containing a glowing reference and a cheque he'd had the solicitors make out for a generous bonus.

"What's this supposed to be, may I ask?" she said, turning the cheque over in her hand.

"It's for you, Miss Flagg. A parting bonus. Now that we're selling the house and my mother's going up to Amersham, we won't be requiring your services anymore."

She wheeled on him. "What? What are you saying? Do you imagine you can just dismiss me as though I were no more than a servant? You and I have an *arrangement*. You have an obligation to me. And *this*," she said, holding the cheque at arm's length as though it were giving off a bad smell, "*this* is an insult!"

"What obligation? What are you talking about?"

"You led me on! I've been your wife in all but name for nearly two years! That amounts to a commitment as far as I'm concerned. I could take you to court for breach of promise!"

"It never crossed my mind to marry you, Miss Flagg," Edward said, as calmly as he could. "I never thought of it and I never promised it. I wasn't the one who started the 'arrangement,' as you call it, either. It was you who came to my room that first night, remember?"

Her face took on such a look of rage he thought she might start clawing at his eyes with her pink-polished fingernails. "Did you imagine I would have wasted my time with a — with a — little greenhorn schoolboy? A half-baked, wet-behind-the-ears, fuzzy-faced — did you really think I found you *attractive?* If you're not going to marry me you owe me a thousand times more than this — this — insulting pittance!"

He was suddenly angry. "You can tear that cheque up if you like, Miss Flagg, but I won't be giving you another." He cast about for a suitable retaliation to her wretched tirade. "How could you imagine I would marry someone as old as you are?"

"You're a horrible man, do you know that? You let me waste my time on you, when I could have — could have — been making *other* friends!"

When he was helping his mother get settled up in Amersham, he told her about the scene with Miss Flagg.

"She expected me to marry her. I don't know how she ever got such an idea."

"We women have to try to get ahead any way we can, I guess, Edward. I used to think Miss Flagg was just waiting for me to die so she could marry Harvey. She was good for you, anyway."

"What do you mean?"

"Well, you will be getting married some day, I hope, and a man ought to have a little experience with — certain things — shouldn't he?"

"You mean you knew …?"

"Edward, I'm not deaf, dear. You were right in the next room." She smiled. "I was glad of it, to tell you the truth. All that time you spent cooped up in a boys' school — some of them come away from those places quite — well — odd, or so I've heard."

"You make it sound as if I was using Miss Flagg, instead of the other way around."

"What a harsh word, Edward, 'using.' What does it mean, anyway? Was the Prince using me when he invited me to his yacht? Was I using Harvey when I consented to marry him? I suppose we could say yes both times, but we could just as well turn it the other way around. I'd rather say we all try to get things going the way we want them to, give some and take some and hope it's going to work out. Of course," she said a little ruefully, "I'd be the first to say there's lots of times it doesn't."

His mother's outlook disturbed him. It seemed so cynical. Surely, he thought, there must be such a thing as love, real love, without ulterior motives. Surely one could express and be the object of physical passion that was without taint of exploitation. So far in his life he hadn't met it, but for some reason he believed it not only possible but a certainty that one day he would.

At his mother's insistence and the approval of his stepfather's executors, Edward was put in charge of overseeing the family finances. Their capital consisted of the house, which was to be sold, what was realized from the sale of the piano business — a substantial amount, as it turned out — and an annuity Rak had set up for his wife. The solicitors helped him make careful investments, the income from which would not only pay for his mother's care and any special nursing she might need during her lifetime but also provide him with a monthly supplement to his none too princely salary at Christopher's. When his mother died, the entire estate would be his to do with as he chose.

20

After a buyer for the house in Richmond had been found and Edward had settled his mother in the nursing home, he took a lease on a bright second-floor flat in a converted mansion off the Fulham Road. For the first time in his life he was free to come and go and live just as he wanted to. At his mother's insistence he had received an advance from the estate to get himself set up on his own and furnish and decorate his new flat. During those final two years at Riverview Edward had moved Rak's dreadful lumpen Victorian furniture out of his own bedroom and installed some handsome pieces he'd bought for himself, but there was no getting around the fact that it had still been Rak's house, and he could never get over the feeling that his belongings were uncomfortable and ill at ease there. Now he could give them the setting they deserved.

He had the walls of his new sitting room painted a warm white as a foil for his treasured collection of art. So far he had a Roualt colour lithograph, *Le Jongleur*, that he'd fallen in love with when it arrived in the auction rooms, not one of the artist's rarer prints but a beautiful one, full of pathos in spite of its glowing stained-glass colours. He owned a delicately tinted gouache of a standing nude by Pierre Bonnard, from his wartime years in the south of France. Bonnard was an old man by that time, but his vision had still been as fresh and direct as it was in his youth, and the lines and colours were lovely. On a trip to Paris Edward had bought a small Matisse drawing from a group of sketches the artist had left for the nuns at St. Paul de Vence to sell when he'd finished their chapel, a few of which had somehow ended up in a small left bank gallery. It was one of these, a brief sketch of a mother and child, that now hung on the wall behind Edward's Regency commode. One Christmas Jack had given him an illustrated book on the artists of the Vienna Secession, and as soon as he saw those reproductions he knew he'd have to have a Schiele or a Klimt painting one day, but until he could afford that he settled for an exquisitely provocative Klimt ink drawing of two entwined female nudes on a bed, and a little Schiele pencil sketch, probably a self-portrait, a disgruntled-looking male figure wearing only a singlet and his socks. He managed to snap up a small Odilon Redon oil of a bouquet of anaemones that the important buyers had somehow overlooked when it came up at Christopher's, a painting that was his most treasured work of art until he bought a painting by Giorgio Morandi.

He had first seen a Morandi still life in an exhibition at the Tate, a study rendered in the muted grays and blue-whites and buff tones the artist invariably used, a little canvas that was more disturbing to him than even that first Turner had been. The Turner had flung its message in his eyes, while the Morandi whispered something inscrutable about the secret life of *things*, about the metaphysical significance lying hidden in such common objects as those tremulously delineated bottles and jars and odd little boxes. Why that painting should carry such an emotional charge Edward had no idea, but it raised the hair on the back of his neck every time he saw it. He couldn't have put into words exactly how it made him feel, even after he'd gone back to see it again and again. After his fourth or fifth visit to the Tate he began to wonder if those common still-life objects were secondary to Morandi's purpose, if they were arbitrary, mere vehicles, and that the significance actually lay in the physical object that was the painting itself.

Whatever it was, when he saw a small Morandi oil offered in a catalogue from one of Christopher's competitors Edward knew he must have it. He sat poring over the reproduction in the catalogue like a hungry man gazing through the window of a restaurant, practically scrabbling at it with his fingers, wishing he could pluck it off the page. It was almost identical to the one in the Tate

— the same muted hues, and virtually that same collection of objects. Jack Turner insisted on coming to that sale with him in case he lost all sense of discretion in the bidding, but Edward knew that whatever the cost he would have the painting, even if it meant making a premature withdrawal from the estate. He placed it in the centre of a wall, where now, on a quiet evening, or sometimes on a Sunday morning, he would sit and gaze at it, stare and stare, until his mind slipped out of gear and flowed weightlessly into another dimension, where nothing existed but art itself.

In the main room in his new flat, which served as both sitting and dining room, he placed his cushioned George II settee in such a way that he could sit directly facing the Morandi. On either side of the two tall front windows were matching French Bergère chairs from the late eighteenth century, with a few green plants and a low table between them. On the floor he had laid a Persian carpet in hues of dull rose and blue, worn in places but of exceptionally fine quality. For what he designated the dining area he had acquired a Regency oval table and four chairs in good original condition, and a pretty commode for his china — all bought on slow nights at Christopher's top-end auctions — as well as a dozen classic Georgian forks and rat-tail spoons from the same period, and an almost complete service of early Spode dinnerware in a pretty apple green and white pattern with delicate borders of gold.

One winter night a relatively low bid got him a lovely little double-door display cabinet for his collection of crystal scent bottles, which now included, apart from the bottles he'd collected when he was young, three particularly fine ruby glass vials with silver caps, and several Baccarat and Lalique miniatures. He could never look at those tiny bottles without feeling a rush of love for his mother. Sometimes he would even take that one special bottle out of the cabinet and hold it to his cheek — although the perfume had long since evaporated and even the ghost of its scent had vanished — just as he had held it close for comfort on those lonely nights at his first boarding school. It had never lost its power to move him.

He bought a small flat glass-topped display table that was actually meant for showing off military medals, or so he learned, a simple piece of no exceptional value or virtue in itself, but perfect for displaying his collection of fountain pens, which had expanded far beyond the few early Watermans bought during his school days in Toronto. He was constantly adding to this collection, which now included, among others, four gorgeous Watermans with ornate eighteen-karat gold barrels and caps; two pre-1914 Montblancs, one with gold and silver filigree over a dull black ground, and one in ebonized pearl with silver mountings; a lapis Parker duofold; and a fearfully expensive 1910 Waterman Snake Pen. Just for the fun of it he bought two slender gold Victorian dipping pens he'd come across in a little shop behind Covent Garden, and a gold-lidded cut crystal inkwell to go with them.

In the centre of that display case he set the open plush-lined box holding the pen and pencil set his mother had given him just before Rak shipped him off to that hellish school in Canada, a matched Waterman set in a deep marbled red, with gold bandings around the top and bottom and a gold pocket clip on each. The box was red, too, stamped around the edges with gold to make it look like Florentine leather. Inside, the honey-coloured plush lining was now a bit worn and soiled, but the loops of black elastic to hold the pen and pencil in place were intact. It was the only thing in his display cabinet he never touched. The memories that writing set aroused still brought on a flurry of palpitations of his heart.

As for the rest of those pens, he would sometimes stand for half an hour with his elbows propped on the glass top of the case, gazing at his collection like a sultan looking over his harem before deciding which one he would favour and carry in his inside breast pocket for the next few days. Even after he'd pretty well made up his mind, he'd open the case and pick up each pen in turn, hold it in his hand for a few moments, feeling its weight and shape in his palm, sensing a subtle warmth that he often noticed when he did this, which he half believed might be an emotional legacy passed along from a previous owner who had treasured it as much as he did — or, if it were one of his more elaborately decorated pens, from the fingers of the craftsman who had worked the precious metals when he was making it.

He'd paid more than he'd intended to for a fine library bookcase with the original handblown glass in its doors, but his growing collection of books on art, many of which were first editions with beautiful bindings and colour plates, deserved it. He'd really only just begun to furnish his bedroom and was making do at the moment with a simple bedstead, which he covered with a piece of tapestry he'd picked up in France, but when he woke up in that bed in the morning he could look across the room at two elegant Georgian pieces, an armoire and a bowfront dresser, that gave him pleasure the minute he opened his eyes. His theory of collecting was simple: he acquired what he found beautiful, whatever the period or style, in the belief that his personal taste would be the catalyst that pulled it all together and give the whole ensemble its character and grace. As far as he could tell, it worked.

He often walked around his rooms for the sheer pleasure of it, deciding that everything was just about perfect — and then he'd notice a need for the one thing more that would give it all a better balance — a touch of colour in the form of a cushion or two, or a dark accent of some kind, something a bit exotic in ebony, or a small sculpture in bronze with a blackish patina — and he'd be off on the prowl again. The flat was already becoming more than a little crowded. The way things were going he'd soon need more space. His next flat would have to have at least two full reception rooms and a small den or library, because he knew exactly what sort of desk he wanted and he was already on the lookout for it at the sales.

Edward had been at Christopher's for more than eight years when he moved into that apartment. He was nearly twenty-seven, a fit five foot eleven, a little over eleven stone, with a slender but broad-shouldered physique — rather better built than many of those royal kin of his, if such they were. His hair had kept its blond colour when he emerged from adolescence, and he had the clear light complexion and blue eyes that went with it. Straight nose, firm jaw. Women turned and looked — and so did men.

One particular April day stood out in his mind. He had walked home through a still sunny late afternoon when every garden and park in London was misty with new green buds and pale blossoms, carrying a package containing a new white shirt he'd bought that morning on Jermyn Street. When he got home he washed and changed, slipped his arms into the new shirt and buttoned it over the fine blond hair that now lightly covered his upper chest. He stood in front of the looking glass trying to decide whether he would cut a better figure wearing a Windsor-knotted tie (named for that fashion plate his putative Papa!) or present himself as a slightly raffish chap with his shirt open at the neck. Leave it open but tuck in a foulard? He decided on the last. If he could never actually be one of those privileged, long-legged, crisp-haired young men he saw strolling about London with their tightly furled umbrellas and their air of bemused bore-dom, just away for drinks at the Ivy or tea at Buckingham Palace — or so he imagined — he could at least look like one of them.

He poured himself a glass of very pale dry sherry from the decanter on the commode. When he'd finished it he would go down and have his dinner in a pleasant little restaurant in the Fulham Road, smoked salmon and thin buttered brown bread, perhaps, or grilled sardines, and then rare beef and roast potatoes.

The owner greeted him by name when he arrived those evenings, and he often exchanged nods with one or two of the other regulars. With his glass in his hand he walked slowly around his home, looking at his pictures, noticing how a beam of late afternoon sunlight set the Persian carpet aglow and picked out the fine grain in the mellow wood of the tabletop. He became aware of an unaccustomed emotion washing over him, slowly, lightly, a gentle warm wave. It took him a moment to understand that what he was feeling was a sense of well-being, of lightheartedness, satisfaction, something very close to joy.

His mother was well looked after, he liked everything about his work, and the flat was just about perfect. It came to him that he was happier, right then, at that very moment, than he'd been since the day twenty years earlier when Harvey Rak had come sidling up to his mother in the piano department of Eaton's College Street store in Toronto. When he thought about those times Edward could scarcely recognize that child as himself. That boy seemed not to be Edward at all, just someone he used to know, a person he could barely even remember. Oddly, though, it was the beautiful, slender, fair-haired lady of his earliest memories that he carried permanently in his heart and in his mind's eye when he thought or uttered the word "mother." It was that woman he visualized when he held that little scent bottle in his hand, she whom he saw, just as she'd been when he was a boy of six. The faded sick woman he visited on weekends through that spring and summer at the nursing home in Amersham was someone else altogether.

171

21

Edward spent the occasional evening with someone he saw nearly every day at work, young Juliette, the secretary-receptionist who catered to the supreme beings in the office upstairs, she who had escorted him to the door of the holy-of-holies the day he was upgraded to his position as Jack's assistant. His becoming better acquainted with her had been less coincidental than it appeared, because, she confessed over their first little meal together, she had often stood watching from across the street before she went in to work so she could catch him at the employees' entrance and walk up the stairs at his side. On their evenings together they invariably ate an early dinner at a Lyons (her choice) right after work — Juliette tucking into egg and chips or beans on toast as though it were royal fare — and afterward caught a movie in Leicester Square.

"Your turn to pick the film, Juliette," Edward would say, as they looked around the semicircle of cinema marquees glowing in the darkening blue-green of a warm London evening.

"Oh no, you choose, Edward. You always know the best ones."

Juliette and Edward exchanged a friendly kiss before separating after the show to catch transport in opposite directions — he to his flat off the Fulham Road, she to her parents' home in the northern reaches of Barnet — but apart from that there was no intimacy between them, nor did Edward feel like pursuing the relationship further, which surprised him, considering how much he'd enjoyed the steamy affair he'd had with Miss Flagg, and Juliette's obvious interest in him. From little hints she gave it was clear she would be more than willing to go with him to his flat some evening.

Edward's own sexual nature was still a puzzle to him, and he was reluctant to put it to the test with Juliette, who might be hurt if he took her to his flat and didn't feel like making love to her, or what might possibly be worse, if they did become lovers and she took it as the beginning of a serious commitment. The blowup with Miss Flagg had left him unnerved, and much as he liked Juliette he was wary of being with her in other than public places. Still, though, he liked her and enjoyed being with her. One evening as they were parting company he mentioned on the spur of the moment that he was taking the train up to Amersham to see his mother the following Sunday, and wondered if Juliette would care to come along. They could have tea at the nursing home with his mother, he said, and have a meal afterward at the historic coaching inn his grandfather had once managed. Juliette accepted with enthusiasm.

Dolly seemed unusually chirpy and well that day. It was an early October afternoon of heavenly sunshine and warm breezes, and the staff had brought most of the patients outdoors to enjoy the treat of the unusually dry and summery weather. Edward and Juliette had tea with Dolly on the flagged terrace, the sun flashing pleasantly off the china and silver. Afterward they all strolled through the emerald lawns among drifts of fallen yellow birch leaves, Edward pushing his mother's wheelchair along the paths, Juliette walking along beside "your mum," holding her hand, the two of them talking and laughing as though they were old friends. Dolly squeezed her son's hand as he bent to kiss her goodbye.

"Your young friend is sweet, darling. I love her. I think she's just the right type for you, too."

That was the last time Edward saw his mother alive. Two days later the director of the nursing home called early in the morning to say that Dolly had died quietly during the night, undoubtedly from a heart attack. She'd been having spells of angina recently, although she hadn't been one to complain and she'd forbidden them to mention it to her son. Mrs. Cooper had been one of their favourite patients, and they were all very sad to see her go.

His mother's death was a turning point in his life, Edward reflected, but he felt peculiarly distanced from the hard knowledge that he would never see her again. There seemed to be a gap between what was going on and what he ought to be feeling. He remained dry-eyed all through the service in the church and the prayers at the graveside, and even when Dolly's coffin was being lowered into the ground the poignant sound of the handful of earth he sprinkled down on it, rattling and rolling over the varnished wooden lid, failed really to move him. Later in the afternoon he sat and watched while two men in rubber wellies and green coveralls filled in the space around and above the coffin and tamped down the soil, feeling somehow that these activities and ceremonies over Dolly's body were redundant, that he had actually lost his mother a very long time ago.

He went to the nursing home to settle up his mother's accounts and look through her belongings. He gave the clothes in her chest of drawers and closet a cursory glance, ran his fingers over the silver-backed toilet set laid out on her dressing table, heavily ornate stuff, a gift from Rak in the early days of their marriage. A vial of Houbigant Quelques Fleurs among her little array of cosmetics caught his eye, and he picked the bottle up, took out the stopper, and held it to his nostrils. Only then did tears come. He sat down on the side of Dolly's now freshly made and empty bed, holding the perfume bottle in one hand and the stopper in the other, and wept.

After a while he pressed the stopper firmly into the neck of the vial and slipped it into his raincoat pocket, took out a handkerchief and wiped his eyes, blew his nose, stood up and left the room, shutting the door quietly behind him. In the office he asked the director of the home if she would be kind enough to have someone bundle up his mother's clothes and arrange for them to go to charity. And oh yes, his knew his mother would be pleased if she would accept Dolly's silver-backed toilet set as a token to remember her by.

He'd had Dolly buried where she'd wanted to be, next to the graves of her own mother and father, even though doing so went against his own feelings. His own very existence had been reason enough for his grandfather to cut off his one child and condemn her to a life of uncertainty and grief, and his only grandson along with her. Before he left for London the next morning Edward went back and sat for a while on a bench near the mound of newly turned earth that covered Dolly's grave, and when finally he got up to leave he lingered for a moment longer, looking down on his grandfather's tombstone. He thought seriously about spitting on it, but there were other people around.

22

"No movement appears overnight like a mushroom, without antecedents," Jack said. "You can always trace roots that have been running along underground, attaching the new to the old, so the sprout that appears today is still taking nourishment from the parent plant, even as it rises from the earth — to drag the metaphor to its ultimate fatuity — no matter how much appearances would indicate otherwise."

"Oh, I believe you," Edward said. "Do you want to know how stupid I actually am? I never realized until long after you'd launched me on this artistic education what the Renaissance was a rebirth *of*. I thought the word just meant — oh, I don't know — a sort of spontaneous upsurging of interest in scientific measurement and naturalism."

"And what disabused you of that idea?"

"Well, what else? Going back to take another look at the Elgin Marbles at the British Museum. I stood there staring at that section of the frieze from the Parthenon, thinking how realistic and natural the figures were compared to those rigid figures on the portal at Chartres, and then I remembered the smiling angel at Reims that was done only one hundred years after Chartres, and how much more lifelike it was, more like the Greek figures. I literally said out loud, 'Oh for Christ's sake! Of course!'"

"Rebirth of the principles of classical Greece. The humanism behind Hellenic art. Man the measure of all things."

"Why didn't you ever tell me that, all the time I was plodding through the Middle Ages looking at gargoyles and barrel vaults and those hell-and-damnation tympani. I felt like a prize ass, discovering what everyone else in the world already knew."

"It never occurred to me that you wouldn't have known. Anyway, I'm glad I didn't. Look at the pleasure you got out of your 'eureka' moment. Darling boy, pull the blanket up over us, will you. It's getting chilly in here."

He did what Jack asked, and leaned over and kissed his cheek.

"That's because you were so steamed up a few minutes ago. You certainly were a bear for it this morning."

"Ah, Edward." Jack put his arms around Edward and pulled him close. "What a treasure you are."

"I love you, Jack," Edward said. "I don't know what I'd do without you. You're the best friend I ever had. It may seem like a funny thing to say, but I sometimes wish you were —"

"What?"

"My father."

"Oh my God! Don't say that. This is already a criminal relationship. Don't go adding incest to it!"

"Okay, I won't say it, but I do." He put his feet over the side of the bed and shoved them into a pair of slippers — Jack's, as it happened — and pulled on his bathrobe. "I'll make us breakfast. Want an egg? Stay right where you are, I'll put it all on a tray and bring it back to bed. Tea or coffee?"

Jack's flat in Putney consisted of four pleasant high-ceilinged rooms in a block of nineteenth-century flats whose great asset was the unimpeded view of the Thames from every window. It was summer, and warm moist air smelling faintly of mud and fish billowed in through the open window. The tide was running in, and patches of yellow light glancing off the water dappled the ceiling of the room. Jack loved his view of the river, loved this part of London where he'd made his home for so many years. When he needed fresh air or felt like taking a bit of exercise on a warm evening, he could cross the bridge and walk along to Putney Heath, have a pint outdoors at the Green Man while the sun was setting. The high street provided everything he needed in the way of groceries and other oddments, and the underground station was practically at his door. Now that Edward had moved to his flat just off the Fulham Road he was only minutes away by bus or tube.

Jack seemed to have become Edward's guide and mentor in more than matters pertaining to art without quite knowing how it came about. He found himself assuming the double role of lover and teacher while constantly worrying that the advice he gave might not be appropriate. If it hadn't been for his stepfather's hostility, Edward would have had no need to turn to Jack, but perhaps it was just as well that he did. From Edward's description of the man, Jack gathered that Mr. Rak thought it just the thing to dress from head to toe in green checks and speak the language of Shakespeare with whining vowels and hiccuping glottal stops. Until Jack had become his friend there hadn't been anyone to show Edward how to dress, or to correct his speech when he came out with some slovenly pronunciation. The young man was afraid that a few unfortunate Rakisms might have rubbed off on him and he wouldn't recognize them when they appeared. Jack obliged, picking him up on the odd word when they were together — including his North American tendency to change internal *T*s to *D*s. Budder.

One day, laughing, but obviously quite serious, Edward told Jack he thought he'd like to improve and polish himself to the point where he'd be somewhere between one of Gallsworthy's impeccably mannered Forsyte men and Virginia Woolf's stolid husband Leonard — elegant, fastidious, literate, a connoisseur of fine things even if he was not an artist himself. He imagined vaguely that he might become *eminence grise*, a patron giving support and encouragement to some talented person, as Leonard had with Virginia. At the moment, all his convictions and ideas — other than those pertaining to works of art and the finer things that came into the auction rooms — were unstable, subject to change with the next book he read, and yet even that was pointless because he had no way of judging the validity of any particular author's opinion. So he turned to Jack for guidance, and to Jack the fragments of Edward's unfocused self came swarming like iron filings to a magnet, attempting fuzzily to duplicate what Jack feared was his own far from perfect shape. It all made Jack uneasy.

It was a responsibility that seemed to have arrived on his doorstep full blown, and one that Jack found more than just a little daunting. Edward idealized him and expected more of him than he should have. Jack was flattered, there was no denying that, and although he wouldn't have admitted to fatherly feelings toward Edward while their relationship was at least for the time being a carnal one, a certain element of fatherliness was present in all their exchanges but the physical ones. At Edward's insistence Jack came along when he was getting measured for a suit; he taught him a little about food, often prepared a meal for the two of them in his flat, Edward poking his nose over Jack's shoulder to ask what this or that condiment was, or the name of some herb. Before he met Jack, Edward had neither seen nor tasted garlic, a substance which he had thought was merely a catchword for everything Rak had disliked about foreigners — French, Italian, Spanish, Greek — they were all one to Mr. Rak, it seemed, people he lumped all together as members of an inferior species he referred to as "garlic eaters."

The meals Jack prepared and the way he talked about them whetted Edward's desire to travel. "What did you say this was called?" he asked, as they sat down at Jack's table one evening. "It smells heavenly. Everything you cook is delicious. But what's this grey stuff?"

"The dish is called ratatouille. Quintessentially Mediterranean. The poisonous brown material you're poking so suspiciously with your fork is aubergine. The green is courgette. Onions, tomatoes, herbs, garlic, olive oil. Like it?" He broke off a piece of crusty baguette and handed it to Edward.

Edward ate a few forkfuls. "It's wonderful. Native to where, did you say?"

"Oh, you'll find this dish or something very like it in the south of France, Italy, Spain, Greece, wherever these vegetables grow. Before the war I used to spend part of my holidays in a little place in Provence, at Cap Negre. My God, the food! Smell it cooking all afternoon and if you hung around you'd practically faint before it was time for dinner. Soupe de poisson, grilled fish, sauté escalopes de veau in white wine, little potatoes tossed in olive oil and herbs. Those tiny French green beans. Local wines, soft-ripened cheeses that melt in your mouth." He paused, remembering. "I sometimes wonder how Madame and Victor made it through the war." He broke into his own reverie. "Anyway, Edward, it's more than the food, it's the whole thing — the sun, the air, the way everything smells — all of it."

Edward had a quality Jack could only think of as a natural gentlemanliness or refinement, he supposed one might call it, in his manners and gestures, and the way he moved and carried himself. He continually reminded Jack of someone whose features he knew well. The actor Leslie Howard? No, but someone like that, someone quintessentially English. It had never occurred to Jack during Edward's first two years in the art rooms that his new assistant had homosexual leanings, in fact he suspected he was having a little fling with young Juliette from across the hall. One evening, though, shortly after Edward moved into his new flat, Jack had invited Edward to a Mahler concert at the Festival Hall by way of a little celebration of his new independence. They'd been sitting side by side through most of the first half of the performance, shoulders touching now and then while they listened to that heavily romantic music, when suddenly Jack was startled to feel Edward's hand gently cover his own where it rested on his thigh. Jack turned and looked at him with amazement. A minute later the lights came up and Edward quickly took his hand away. It was still a time when any public expression of affection between men was unthinkable.

They stayed in their seats during the interval.

"You too, Edward?" Jack said quietly. "I never guessed."

"I didn't know about you, either, if you ... but I thought ... I had to find out."

"Have you had ... men friends before?"

" Some. At school."

"Happy experiences?"

"No, they weren't. To tell you the truth most of the time I don't even know what I'm feeling, or what I want ..."

The two of them went to a pub in Covent Garden after the concert and talked, and that night Edward went home with Jack to his apartment in Putney. Little by little, as his visits became regular occurrences, Edward began to tell Jack about his early life and the years at school in Toronto. He seemed to recall every detail with photographic clarity. Jack sat evening after evening, hearing how Edward had been shuffled back and forth from one continent to the other, of his feeling of abandonment and loneliness and exile. He seemed to have been waiting for someone to tell it all to, and if it was helpful to him, Jack was more than willing to listen. Edward managed to inject a little humour into his story from time to time in his descriptions of Riverview and its owner, but it was clear that his life had been full of unhappiness and betrayals — his mother the worst betrayer of all, as far as Jack could see, although Edward never once indicated that he laid any blame at her door, in fact it was clear that he felt an existential guilt for having been the cause of her grief in the first place.

Edward had had a so much wider an experience of the world than had Jack himself at that age that in some ways Edward's boyhood and youth sounded almost exotic to him. His own young days in Walsall had been so ordinary and regular, so absolutely without variety or unusual incident — his pink-faced bespectacled mother watching for him through the lace curtains in the front room when he came home from school on dark winter afternoons; his father coming through the door on the dot of a quarter past six after his day in the office at the steel mill, hallooing wife and son from the front hall while he hung up his coat and folded his umbrella; the completely predictable weekly rotation of dishes his mother cooked for their tea — all the memories so bland and undifferentiated, with so little incident to mark off each of the years that if asked he would probably have said he could hardly remember his childhood at all. It wasn't until he entered university that he began to recognize himself as an individual, separate from his parents and from that house with its neat little fenced front yard, the kitchen windows that were always steamed up in winter, the kettle on the hob that was hardly ever allowed to get cold. He couldn't decide, while he was listening to Edward, whether his own childhood had been mind-numbingly dull or absolutely perfect.

Jack was disturbed by the thought that his young protegé might go right through his life without discovering the breadth of his own abilities. Edward's instinctive response to art was exceptional, a gift much deeper and more rare than his own, strong enough to remain uncorrupted by study and analysis, he felt sure. Less gifted art lovers, people like himself, tended to look for facts to bolster the weak appreciation they already had, while those with a powerful and direct affinity with works of art probably found delving into academic studies a drab and tedious exercise. Even so, he would have felt remiss if he hadn't suggested that Edward give the idea some consideration.

As it turned out he needn't have worried. When the Christopher brothers offered Edward a post as art director in their new auction rooms in Toronto, Edward talked it over at length with Jack, and they both agreed that if he were to realize his long-term goal of becoming an independent art dealer it would be a good move. If he stayed where he was, it was unlikely he would move up in the ranks at Christopher's until Jack himself retired, which was still a long way off, and in any case it would be very much a continuation of his life as it was now. As for attempting to open his own business, there were already many long-established galleries and dealers in London with whom he would be in direct competition. His financial resources were far from meagre, but there would undoubtedly be many lean years before he could work up enough of a clientele to actually make a decent living in the business. He had toyed with the idea of locating himself in one of the smaller cities outside London — Bath, perhaps, or somewhere on the south coast — but no matter where he went in England he would still be a nobody with little formal education, no social standing, and entirely without family or any other kind of connection that might give him a starting boost.

The Christopher brothers had taken note of the fact that Edward had attended one of the better boarding schools in Toronto during the war. "Kept up with old schoolmates in Toronto, have you?" John Christopher asked. "Some useful contacts there for you still?"

"Oh, I should think so, Mr. Christopher."

"Like to go back for a while then? Renew old friendships?"

"Yes, I like the thought of a change."

" Any problems with leaving England? Family and so forth? Moving expenses would be paid, of course."

"No, I have no family here now, but I'm wondering about my pictures. I have a small collection I'd want to leave behind until I get settled, and some furniture. Perhaps I could have my things crated and stored here for the time being?"

"Of course, dear boy, of course. Nothing easier. We'll ship your belongings over whenever you ask."

It was late on a summer afternoon when Edward checked into the Park Plaza Hotel in Toronto. After the porter had deposited his bags in his room and handed him the key, he took the elevator to the top-floor lounge, ordered a drink at the bar, and wandered out onto the terrace with his gin and tonic in his hand. He leaned on the wide stone balustrade, gazing down at the city where he had spent so many of his younger years. Among the narrow Victorian houses and the stone and brick buildings of the university there were green spaces, parks and playing fields, and stands of trees. He could see the verdigris roofs of the Legislature in Queen's Park. Lake Ontario glittered beyond the downtown core, a patch of luminous turquoise streaked with aquamarine, dotted with the white sails of small pleasure craft on that beautiful afternoon.

The city seemed pleasantly unhurried. Peaceful. The air was fresh, the sun shone in a cloudless sky. A manageable place, Edward thought, one he could work his way into and make his mark on, a city he could handle. He would throw himself into the operation of Christopher's, get to know people, make a name for himself under the company's aegis, and choose his time for going out on his own as an independent dealer. Five years sounded about right. What would have been difficult if not impossible in London looked as if it might well be feasible in a city the size of Toronto, and if it weren't, well, he wouldn't have burned any bridges behind him.

His view over the railing on that rooftop terrace was southward. If he walked around the end of the terrace and faced northward, he would be able to catch a glimpse through the trees of the clock tower of that school where he had passed five years of his life without retaining from them one tolerably happy memory or the name of a single friend. Many of his schoolmates would no doubt now be well on their way to the positions of power the headmaster had predicted for them, rosy-cheeked financiers, pinstriped lawyers, surgeons with long pale fingers, directors of companies stepping smartly into the shoes of daddies gone golfing in Bermuda. There might even be educators among those bullying seniors who had once made his life hell, responsible now for enlightening the minds of other people's children. Perhaps they and their ilk would one day be his clients, and their patronage would be the source of the fine and beautiful things he hoped one day to own.

23

Edward flew home from Italy a changed man. Falling in love had turned him inside out like a sock, changed his empty hunger to an overwhelming need to give and provide. He felt an urgent sense of mission to take charge of Paulo's career and guide him to his rightful place in the world of art, and he knew he could do it. He had the resources and the contacts. As a way to endure the gulf of empty space that was yawning wider and wider between them during his flight back to Toronto, he began jotting down plans for Paulo's exhibition. He would set the date for early in October, when the weather would still be mild, a gala champagne affair, probably on a Friday evening. There would be beautiful invitations with full-colour reproductions, good-sized ads well ahead of time in the newspapers and arts magazines. Perhaps he'd have posters printed to put up in restaurants and public places the way they did it in Paris, something a bit different for staid Toronto. A small photograph of the artist on the poster would stir interest — how could anyone not want to meet such a beautiful and interesting-looking man? He mustn't forget to contact the Italian consulate and the Cultural Institute and invite them to send representatives. Pull out all the stops.

Paulo's shipment of twenty-eight canvases arrived in June. Paulo himself would come just before the show and stay for a month so he could see all those relatives — not long enough to suit Edward, but it was a start. He looked on Paulo's coming to Toronto and this first exhibition of his work as a beginning, not only for Paulo as an artist, but as a personal renaissance for himself. He went about his work in a state of youthful lightheartedness — at least that's what he took it to be, he couldn't be quite sure since he hadn't been remotely lighthearted during his own youth — feeling something of what he supposed the parent of a gifted child must feel.

Paulo's success would be his success, Paulo's happiness his own. Everything was for Paulo.

A new maturity seemed to be settling comfortably around Edward's shoulders, too. To his own surprise he was finally being released from the weight of the grudges and hatreds he'd been carrying around since his childhood, throwing them off like a burden he'd decided not to carry anymore and wondering why he'd bothered lugging those grievances on his back in the first place. Harvey Rak dwindled in Edward's recollection until he was now little more than a poor withered ghost, a shade for whom Edward could even feel something close to pity. What his stepfather had hoped for when he scooped Dolly up out of the piano department at Eaton's and what he ended up with a few years later were two very different things. If he'd chosen to, Rak could have shut the door on Edward when he came back from Canada at the age of eighteen, told him to go away and live somewhere else. He could have argued with justification that his obligations to his now-adult stepson had been met. He could have relieved himself of the burden of an invalid wife, too, by simply consigning Dolly to a nursing home, but he had done neither. In fact, all things considered, he'd behaved rather decently. It was a strange experience, feeling sympathy for Harvey Rak, even a certain — Lord, could it be? — gratitude toward the man. With his plans dropping into place one after the other, Edward hardly recognized himself in this open-hearted fellow who hummed along to popular tunes on the radio in the morning and even executed the occasional dance step while he was waiting for his coffee to filter.

He was standing behind a barrier in Pearson airport, locked into a crowd that appeared to be composed entirely of fat men six and a half feet tall, when he caught sight of Paulo through a chink between the shoulders of two beefy bozos in baseball jackets. He at once became aware of a feeling that was familiar, but somehow out of context, and it took him a moment to recognize it for what it was. What he felt, as he watched Paulo come through those doors into the arrivals area, was exactly what he invariably felt when a wonderful new work of art he'd purchased through an international dealer or from an auction was at last delivered to his door. Whenever he uncrated one of those paintings — like that fourth Morandi he'd acquired recently — and lifted the work from its excelsior and wrappings, he would experience a feeling of triumph. Once again he had thrown out his net and drawn it in filled with the living essence of a great artist. Morandi had stretched this canvas with his own hands, his fingers had held the brushes that applied the paint, had added this dark touch here, smudged that line there. It seemed to Edward that a part of the artist's creative soul had been delivered into his hands, and the knowledge brought such a surge of elation to his heart, such a feeling of empowerment, that it left him breathless. He had become addicted to that sensation of omnipotence, and like any addiction it was only ever temporarily satisfied. This time, with Paulo, there was no dichotomy, this time he would possess not just the essence of the artist, but the whole man. Both art and artist would be under his roof, both would be his.

He tried to catch Paulo's attention by waving his arms in the air as he pushed forward to claim him from the crowd that surged toward the barrier. Paulo was wearing a white turtle-necked sweater under a black leather jacket, looking even more heart-breakingly handsome than Edward had remembered him. When a girl standing nearby said loudly to her friend, "Look at the hunk in the white sweater!" Edward wanted to tell her, "Hands off, he's mine!" What the turbaned limo driver thought when he glimpsed their more-than-affectionate embraces in his rear-view mirror on the way home, Edward had no idea, and didn't care. The man should have had his eyes on the road anyway.

"The pictures arrive all right? How do you like them?" Paulo asked when they finally released one another.

"They're wonderful. Absolutely wonderful. By the way, I love the male nudes, they're stunning, but I'm not sure we can show them just yet. This city isn't quite ready for that. It's a pretty square sort of town."

"Really? That's kind of crazy, isn't it? They're not *doing* anything. Are female nudes banned, too? I've never heard of such a thing."

"For some reason female figures are perfectly acceptable, but males are not. It is crazy. I think it's that *men* don't like depictions of frontal male nudity. Don't ask me why."

"Maybe we ought to show them and shake the place up a bit."

"I know, I know, we probably should. Look, here we are. This is it, driver, stop right here. Paulo, I know what you're saying, but we just can't do it, not if we want this show to go well."

He could tell that what he'd said displeased Paulo, as he'd known it would, which was why he wanted to get that discussion over with right away. Those male nudes would not only be unlikely to sell in Toronto, they could be just enough to spark a flurry of unpleasant notoriety and turn people off the rest of the exhibition. He couldn't chance risking the success of the whole show just to make a point. Another time perhaps, when Paulo was better established. Was he being too timid? Paulo probably thought so, but this part of the business was his responsibility. He wanted to sell the work, not turn it into some kind of polemic.

Once inside, Edward turned on all the lights in the gallery and watched while Paulo walked slowly through the two large rooms, stepping back now and then to scan a whole wall full of pictures.

"I always wonder if there's going to be enough connection between what I did last year and what I'm doing now. But I think it all works pretty well together," he said finally, turning to Edward. "Don't you?"

"Paulo," he said, "I think it's wonderful. I've never had an exhibition I was so proud of. But then I've never been in love with the artist before. Do you think that could have something to do with how I feel about it?"

"Do you expect me to believe that? I'll bet you fall in love with every new artist you take on. Like me falling in love with the guys I get to pose for me. When I'm finished with them as models I feel as though I've used them up. Don't care if I ever see them again. Wait and see."

Edward didn't want to think about Paulo and his models, or what they did in that studio when the sessions of drawing and painting were over. He wanted him so much himself at that moment he felt sick. "I could never have too much of you, Paulo. Or even enough. And if I had been making a habit of falling in love with every new artist — which I haven't — I never would again."

He waited for a reassuring response, but instead Paulo slung an amiable arm around his shoulders. "You look so serious when you talk about love, Edward, like you were going to cry. It's supposed to make you happy, you know?"

He supposed he did look serious. The way a person raised in poverty will look serious when the talk turns to money.

"Let's go upstairs, Paulo," he said. "I feel as though I've been waiting forever."

The gallery was packed on the evening of the opening. Edward's loyal regulars did him proud, came in throngs, strolled around looking at the pictures, quaffed up the champagne, introduced themselves to the artist — and bought nearly half the show before the evening was over. A rave review in the *Globe and Mail* the following day described Paulo as an artist of dazzling virtuosity. Of the thirty canvases in the show only twelve remained unsold by the end of the first ten days. During the first week Edward showed the two male nudes to a client he thought might be interested and sold those too, and then quietly bought all twelve of the remaining paintings himself, one by one, adding another red sticker or two each day. As far as he was concerned it was an investment in their future, his and Paulo's, and a testimony to his faith in his protegé. Incidentally, of course, he wanted this first show to be a complete sellout. The bills of sale he wrote up for his own acquisitions turned out to be an unnecessary subterfuge. Paulo didn't seem to have the slightest interest in who his patrons were.

"Does it make you feel as though you've lost all your children?" Edward asked. "I don't know how I'd feel if I'd painted those pictures and had to watch them all walk out the door."

Paulo seemed amused at the idea. "It doesn't bother me a bit. I'm glad for your sake it's gone well. Glad for both of us. I'll be happy to have the money, too. But it doesn't bother me to be clearing out my studio. I'll feel like starting something entirely new when I get home."

Edward couldn't bear to think about his going home. "This is a great accomplishment, Paulo. With your first show a sellout like this you're well on the way to real recognition. Fame, if you like."

"Really? I never think about being famous. I just want to keep on painting. If my work sells well enough that I can live off it, that's all I care about."

How do you persuade a man that unequivocal acceptance by public and critics is something to be savoured and enjoyed? Edward had positively to push him into sitting down with an interviewer from one of the leading arts magazines.

"Why don't you just go and talk to her, Edward? I don't know what she wants."

"Well she doesn't want *me,* that's certain. The personality of the artist is as interesting to these people as the art is. It's too bad, but that's the way it is. Do come now, Paulo, she's waiting for you."

He watched and listened from a little distance as Paulo adroitly fielded the woman's questions. Was he married? No, still single. Haven't met the right girl yet? He laughed. Something like that. How did he like Toronto? Beautiful. Wonderful city. What's it like being a painter in Sicily? Do the mafia control the art world, too? Oh, I may be paying them something indirectly every time I buy a tube of paint, but I never think about those people if I can help it. They're a curse. Do you think you'll go on living in Sicily after this great success you've just had? Of course. Why wouldn't I?

On Sunday morning Edward sat at breakfast with Paulo, watching as he drank his coffee and turned the pages of the newspaper, loving him so much, wondering how long it would have to be before they could get their lives sorted out and Paulo would be sitting across from him at breakfast every morning.

Paulo set his cup down suddenly. "I forgot to tell you. I was talking to Giancarlo and Rosa. They want us to come for *pranzo* today — that okay with you?"

"Of course, whatever you like. We have an invitation to a cocktail party later on that I accepted for both of us too, without consulting you, I'm afraid. Think we can cram both of them in? "

"Don't worry. *Pranzo's* at noon — it'll be a big, hot meal, if I know Rosa. What do you do at a cocktail party anyway? When Italians get together we *eat*."

"According to T.S. Eliot you wander to and fro talking of Michelangelo."

"That sounds like something I can handle."

"There'll be fifty or sixty people standing around drinking dry martinis and talking at the tops of their voices. If it's so noisy you can't hear the person next to you it means the party's a success. As for food, you'll probably get little hot sausages wrapped in pastry and stuck on a toothpick."

Paulo laughed. "It sounds awful. Why would anybody give a party like that? Or go to one?"

"Well, dearest, you go to make social contacts, do business while you're pretending not to, show off your clothes, be seen. I don't know that anyone really enjoys cocktail parties, but everybody goes to them."

Paulo looked at him with his head cocked sideways as though wondering if he were joking.

"Is that why we're going? To be seen? Do business? These people aren't your friends?"

"Does that seem a bit like prostituting ourselves? I suppose in a way it is. They're customers rather than real friends. If I give them a little of myself and a little of you, they'll keep coming to the gallery and bring other people like themselves who'll buy our pictures. If I snub them they won't. Unfortunately it's what you have to do to get along in this business."

Paulo frowned, digesting what was obviously an unpalatable idea. "When does it start?"

"We're invited for six. Our hostess bought two of your paintings at the opening, so I could hardly refuse. They'll be lionizing you, so watch out. There's nothing these women like so much as a handsome artist to get their teeth into. Anyway, I'm looking forward to the *pranzo*. How are you related to Giancarlo and Rosa?"

"She's one of Mamma's half-million cousins. Gian's in the construction business. They have five or six kids. Mamma wants a full report on everything — and this is only the first bunch, by the way. There'll be lots more before I leave. We'll both be fat as pigs before this month is over."

"What will all these cousins think about — us?"

"Us? They won't think anything. You're my friend. I don't lie to people, but I don't tell them more than I have to. Why get them upset? They'll be happy to see me and whoever I bring along. Don't worry."

Rosa and Giancarlo lived in the northern part the city in a bleak pancake-flat subdivision that had been christened Forest Park by someone with a sense of irony. Edward had never explored the residential developments that sprawled around the periphery of Toronto, and this one was completely terra incognita. They found themselves cruising slowly around endlessly curving streets of virtually identical houses, bungalows, or split levels with wide picture windows, each front lawn with its thumb-sized sugar-maple sapling stuck squarely in the middle of it. Edward was peering at the street names and house numbers when all at once Paulo shouted, "That must be it!" pointing to a house had been made to look a little different from its neighbours by the addition of an ornamental iron railing around the front stoop and a grape arbour built across the area meant to be a carport. A blue pickup truck with lettering on the cab door stood in the driveway.

Edward had already imagined this family gathering — a substantial Rosa and her burly husband and a half-dozen dark-eyed kids with whom they'd spend the afternoon stuffing themselves on pasta and veal and passing a jug of homemade wine. He loved Italy, but its customs and cuisine transplanted poorly, and since he'd been in Toronto he'd found something almost sad in the efforts people made to reproduce them in Canada's less than hospitable climate. Without the golden light and the cobalt sky, the smells and the sounds, the crumbling paving stones and time-worn walls, even the dust in the hot dry air, the food never seemed more than the sum of its ingredients.

They were met at the door with cries of joy and moist kisses by Rosa and her husband, both looking much as Edward had imagined them. After an excited five-minute pileup at the front door they were led straight through the main-floor rooms, past an unused tract-house kitchen and down the stairs to a big tile-floored room that was kitchen and sitting room and dining room all rolled into one. From a stereo in the corner a tenor was belting out "Nessun Dorma" at a decibel guaranteed to keep everyone on the whole block awake. Edward glanced around: a big gas range at one end of the room was jumping with steaming pots, and a long table with a dozen chairs around it took up most of the centre. Everywhere you looked there were children, enough to populate a nursery school. One small girl who was crawling on the floor immediately scrambled over to Edward and pulled herself up to a standing position by clutching fistfuls of his trouser leg, which immobilized him until a slightly older child came and pried the baby loose.

Paulo melted into this heaving mass as though he were sliding into a warm bath. Within moments of their arrival he was sitting in a chair holding a child on each knee while Cousin Rosa stood behind him alternately squeezing his shoulders with both plump hands and compulsively stroking his curly hair. He looked as though he were thoroughly enjoying the massage. Giancarlo doggedly spoke English over Edward's protests that he could handle Italian, while Rosa, who spoke little English, switched at every third word from standard Italian to a Sicilian dialect Edward had trouble following. The kids shouted to the adults and each other in all three languages, their English quite unaccented; the oldest boy kept himself busy correcting his father's pronunciation.

"*Il professore*," Giancarlo said, nodding toward his son with admiration.

They were served great bowls of penne arrabiata followed by mounded platefuls of roast pork with potatoes and rapini. A dish of apple compote came next, and one of those yeasty high-and-dry Italian cakes. Paulo had one child or another climbing on him throughout the entire meal, ending up with the infant, to whom he fed his dessert. What with the quantities of food he was obliged to put away and the heat and din under that low ceiling, Edward thought the top of his head might come off before the meal was over, but Paulo came away from that house luminous with happiness, looking the way Edward had expected he might after the wonderful success of his exhibition. During the drive home Edward glanced over at Paulo's flushed and glowing face from time to time, his heart filled with love, and his mind with misgivings. He felt as though his very survival depended on finding a way to have Paulo always at his side, become his partner for life. How was he ever going to make this man his own?

Things were so much simpler between heterosexual couples. They married, took vows, pledged fidelity, lived together under one roof, became a social unit. Edward wanted Paulo to be married to him in just that way. If he'd been a woman it would have been the most natural thing in the world for him to leave his parents, to move in and join his life to Edward's. He wondered if such an idea had even crossed Paulo's mind during the months since they'd met, while he'd been thinking of almost nothing else. He was running out of time. Before he knew it he'd be fifty, his teeth and hair would be falling out, and Paulo would still be a young man. It didn't seem fair.

They went home for a minor re-outfitting before going on to the cocktail party. Paulo had taken off his jacket before everybody sat down to lunch, so the pasta sauce and apple compote flung on him by the children had landed only on his shirt, which he changed, but the one tie he'd brought was a write-off, which Edward thought was just as well. It was a wide affair woven in bold stripes of metallic silver and green, and Edward could now replace it with one of his own without seeming critical of Paulo's taste. He looked at Paulo approvingly when they were ready to go. His suit was of the unrelieved dull black cloth that was appropriate for Sicilian weddings and funerals, Edward supposed, and in combination with a starched white shirt and Edward's expensive silk tie it gave him something of the air of a twenties New York mobster. The paradox of the angelic face atop that vaguely sinister getup conveyed just the sort of piquantly dangerous look that would appeal to Edward's Rosedale matron and her friends.

Their hostess's house was large, furnished and decorated in the fashion of the fifties — wall-to-wall broadloom overlaid with Oriental carpets, panelling and woodwork painted foam green, heavy gold damask draperies and pelmets at the windows. There was a conservatory full of palms and ferns, a bay-windowed music room containing a gleaming grand, a couple of music stands, and a cello case set in a casual arrangement that suggested *soirees musicales*. Sets of beautifully bound classics filled the shelves of the library. There were paintings, of course, several from Edward's gallery, including the two recently acquired from Paulo's exhibition that were now hung in places of honour, one facing the door at the end of the marble-floored entrance hall, the other in the dining room over a candle-lit sideboard.

Edward lifted dry martinis for himself and Paulo from a tray carried by a passing waiter. Maids in black and white uniforms were slipping through the crowd with platters of hors d'oeuvres — iced prawns, caviar on toast rounds, mille feuille pastries layered with fois gras. Not a sausage to be seen. He was still stuffed from the *pranzo*, but the freshness of ice-cold gin went down nicely. Their hostess came rushing forward to kiss him and take Paulo into custody, grasping his arm with both manicured hands and leading him off into the crowd. During the next hour or so Edward only occasionally caught sight of his bright head and black shoulders

197

through chinks in the wall of bodies. When the time came to leave Edward had to go searching for him, discovered him in the conservatory tête-a-tête with a slender young man who had unnaturally yellow hair and gold rings in his ears, a faun-like youth whom Paulo introduced as a dancer with the National Ballet. Jealously rose in Edward's throat like hot bile, but he managed a smile. "I think we should be leaving now, Paulo," he said, sounding prissy and overbearingly possessive in spite of himself.

"Where's Kingston?" Paulo asked as they were driving home.

"Oh, two or three hours' drive east along the lake. Why do you ask?"

"That fellow I was just talking to? Raffy? He offered to drive me there next weekend. Rosa's sister Maria lives in Kingston. I promised Mamma I'd see her if it wasn't too far away. Raffy said his brother lives just outside Kingston and we could stay over with him if we want to."

"Paulo, I'll take you to Kingston —"

"You've been doing enough, Edward, you haven't stopped since I got here. You'll be getting sick of having me on your hands all the time."

He felt as though he'd been stabbed. Curses on bloody little Raffy. He knew very well what he had in mind, staying over at his brother's house. Maybe it was in Paulo's mind, too, and if he made a fuss he risked antagonizing him. "I could never get sick of you, Paulo," he said, when he'd regained enough control of himself to speak, "but of course, go with Raffy. I'll catch up on my paperwork while you're gone."

After Paulo had dropped off to sleep that night Edward lay awake with his mind roiling. Something had to be done, but what? There was no way he could persuade Raffy to withdraw his invitation. The only solution would be to bring this Maria and her husband to Toronto so Paulo wouldn't have a reason for going to Kingston. He could throw a party next weekend, that was it. A surprise. Paulo couldn't find fault with that. He'd call Cousin Rosa first thing in the morning and get them in on it, gather up all the clan, book one of those Italian reception halls on College street, lay on a banquet.

A couple of days later he told Paulo what Rosa and he had cooked up.

"They're all coming! Even the Kingston contingent. Your cousin Rosa says Maria and her husband will stay with her. I think we'll be about thirty all told. We've got the hall booked for a sit-down dinner and Rosa's ordering the meal — everything's all set. She's a great organizer, that Rosa."

"Edward, you're doing too much. You make me embarrassed."

"Paulo dearest, I love doing things for you."

"I'll have to get hold of Raffy and tell him I won't be going."

"Why don't you invite him to the party?" Edward suggested, feeling magnanimous.

"Maybe. I'll think about it. Probably not. Everybody'll be speaking Italian."

"I'm going to take you touring for a few days before you leave," Edward said. "Where would you rather go — up north to stay in some rustic lodge, or take a drive around Lake Ontario? If we did the lake trip we could make a stop at Niagara Falls and drive across upper New York State. Lovely countryside. And if we come back home along the north side of the lake we could pass right through Kingston and stop off for a visit with your cousin Maria too, if you like."

24

Before Paulo arrived Edward had come up with the idea of making his largely unused third floor into a studio space where Paulo could do a little painting if he felt like it, while he himself was busy in the gallery. The studio would be quite private — Paulo could use the back door and go up the old servants' staircase at the rear of the house without having to go through the gallery at all. He cleared out the space and had the walls painted white, put up lights, found a work table and an easel and some shelving, even bought an array of the kind of paints Paulo used, a roll of canvas and various sizes of stretchers, and gesso and brushes. As an afterthought he added a few dozen sheets of good rag paper for drawing. After the first flurry of activity surrounding the show was over Edward led him up the back stairs and showed him the little studio. "All yours, Paulo, any time you want to spend a few hours painting or drawing."

"You're so generous, Edward," Paulo said, looking pleased. He stepped back and looked at Edward, frowning slightly, as though he were checking out his features for the first time. "Do you know what I'm going to do first? Paint your portrait. I'll stretch a canvas this afternoon, and you can come up and sit for a few drawings tomorrow."

The portrait turned out to be a small head and shoulders in strong colours, laid on in thick impasto with a palette knife — actually a butter spreader borrowed from Edward's kitchen — a wonderfully lively little painting and an excellent likeness, one in which Edward could see a strong resemblance to the man he had by now come to believe was his father. He loved the portrait, and loved Paulo for painting it. Unfortunately, or so he thought at the time, as soon as Paulo let them know the studio existed his relatives began flocking up there, groups of youngsters and their parents who seemed to be coming and going on those back stairs whenever Paulo was in the place. Edward was jealous of Paulo's time, which Paulo patently was not, and it upset him to see his protegé sidelining his precious talent for these people. Then he began to notice that from the rapid pencil sketches Paulo made while his cousins were chatting over cups of coffee or sucking on cans of Coke, Paulo was painting a series of brilliant, quickly executed little portrait studies, all in the same limited palette of intense hues that he'd used in his own. He saw that there was a relationship developing between the canvases — no pun intended — that gave them great authority as a group, a little series that would make a wonderful small exhibition on its own between Paulo's larger shows.

One morning toward the end of Paulo's visit Edward helped him put the portraits up on the walls of the studio, and they walked up and down looking at them, Paulo pointing out who was whose sister or nephew, remarking on the resemblance to Mamma in the features of this or that cousin. "That's Gus, he's studying law, he's the smart one in the family. Carmela there is getting married next summer, her mother just about gave up hope, she's thirty. Look at 'Tonio's boy, little Joey. 'Tonio sure doesn't need to worry if Joey's really his own kid."

"I love these portraits, Paulo, they're absolutely alive, every one of them."

"I've had a good time doing them," Paulo said casually, almost dismissing them. He seemed to be looking on them as little more than snapshots and painting them had been merely a pastime. It was while they were looking at those paintings that Edward told Paulo about his own aunt and cousins.

"You know," he said idly, "I actually have some relatives in Toronto myself."

"You have? Here? I thought your mother was English."

"She was, but her aunt lived here, and the aunt had three sons. They were all older than I — they'd be in their mid-fifties by now, I imagine. My mother and I stayed with them for a few weeks when I was a baby. I remember going around to say goodbye to Aunty Kay before we left for England. I was very young at the time."

"Do they still live here? Were they here for the opening of my show? I don't remember meeting them."

"No, they weren't. To tell you the truth I've never even bothered looking them up. I remember they lived in a little house near High Park and my uncle drove a streetcar for a living. My great-uncle, of course. Anyway, that's all I knew about them. When I came back to live in Toronto I suppose I just couldn't see the point of stirring up the mud."

"Stirring up the mud! They're your cousins!"

"Once removed. Not precisely first cousins."

Paulo turned and looked at him, stared so long Edward could see the shape of his own head in Paulo's eyes silhouetted against the light from the window behind him. Finally he looked away. "What a strange man you are, Edward. Practically neighbours with the only relatives you have in the world, and you don't even let them know you're alive. What does that mean, anyway, once removed? In my family a cousin is a cousin. Blood is blood."

"I'm not really sure of how Aunty Kay felt about my mother and me. Maybe we were both a disgrace to the family. She did take us in for a while, but then maybe she didn't feel she had a choice. Anyway, I have no idea where they are after all this time. All I remember is that their name and the name of the street they lived on was the same. Garden."

"It wouldn't be hard to find them, would it? Is your great-aunt still alive?"

"I don't even know that. She was older than my mother, of course. I suppose she might be in her eighties."

Paulo looked hard at him again, frowning, shaking his head in amazement. Most of the people in his village in Sicily were related to him, and from what he said they were continually involved in one another's lives. "I can't imagine not wanting to know your family."

As the time when Paulo would be leaving for Sicily came closer, Edward's feeling of desperation grew. The thought of being separated from him again for months and months seemed just about intolerable. Paulo was always affectionate and their lovemaking was never less than passionate, but he had never given any indication that to him their relationship was anything more than a friendly affair mixed in with the business of showing and selling his work — never intimated that he thought Edward might become a permanent fixture in his life or that he ever planned or even wanted to leave Sicily. Was it possible, though, that Paulo was unsure of how Edward felt? As the younger person, could he be waiting for Edward to declare himself? He took heart from the thought. For their last evening together Edward booked a quiet corner table at a French restaurant for their farewell dinner.

Paulo scanned the elaborate menu. "Madonna mia! You could eat for a week in Sicily for the price of dinner here."

"Paulo," Edward said, "I could enjoy a plate of sawdust as long as I was sharing it with you, but this is a special occasion and it calls for a special dinner. Let's just enjoy it."

When they'd finished their meal and the waiter had brought them espresso and snifters of cognac, he decided the moment had come to speak. "I love you, Paulo," he said quietly, leaning across the table. "I can't find the words to tell you how deeply I mean that. I don't know whether you've been unsure of my feelings, or if maybe you've been waiting for me to say it first. I want you to come and live with me and be my partner. I want to dedicate my life to you."

Paulo's eyes widened over the rim of his brandy glass. Had it never occurred to him that this was where it had all been leading? Edward wondered. Paulo coughed, put his glass down, and cleared his throat a couple of times, while Edward watched with anxious eyes. Paulo looked embarrassed, as if Edward's declaration had been the last thing in the world he'd expected to hear and he didn't know how to deal with it. He began to shake his head slowly back and forth.

"Edward, I'm really touched, believe me, but for one thing, I couldn't possibly leave my family. I'm sure you can understand that. You've been wonderful to me, right from the start, when you first came to the trattoria — showing my work and now giving me this exhibition, taking me everywhere. It isn't that I don't like it here, either, because I do. It certainly seems to be a good place to sell my paintings — look what's happened, every piece gone, more work than I've sold before in my whole life. But —"

Edward tried to hide the tremor in his voice. "Perhaps it was too much to hope for, Paulo, too soon ..."

"— in any case I wouldn't leave home for any length of time as long as my father is living, Edward. You've met him, you've seen how frail he is. And it's more than the arthritis, you know, he has a bad heart too. Mamma keeps telling me I should get away more and see the world, but I couldn't leave her with Papa to look after and the restaurant, too. I might spend more time away from home some day, but ..."

Edward's heart sank. It was Paulo's youth speaking, of course. Life looks endless when you're in your twenties. He didn't feel the pressure of time as Edward did, and besides, he probably shared his mother's belief that what would come would come, everything was either God's will or the work of the devil, you didn't really have to make plans for yourself because one or the other of those two entities would decide everything for you.

He didn't know just what he'd expected — maybe that Paulo would say he'd need time to think, that he'd have to stay with his family for another year or two. Edward could have readily accepted that if there'd been any hint of a commitment, the suggestion of a promise, at least something more positive than what he was hearing right now.

Then he tried to imagine what must be going through Paulo's mind and cursed himself for his own impatience. He'd been in too much of a hurry, he should have known better. He ought to have waited until the next time they were together before coming out with all this. Besides, what had Paulo seen here that would have made him want to come and live with Edward? The place he was calling home at the moment was utterly inadequate for two people; his living quarters were barely big enough for one, with his antiques and collections occupying every foot of floor space and wall space and every other kind of space. There was hardly room for the pots and pans in the kitchen. Four crowded rooms above an art gallery, already full to overflowing, a makeshift studio on the third floor thrown together at the last minute, hardly room to swing a cat in it. As they drove past it one day Edward had pointed out the big house that he was in the process of buying, but they hadn't been able to go inside so Paulo could see the place. They hadn't even walked around to look at the garden and the solarium at the back. He'd been stupid, altogether too precipitous. Paulo obviously needed more time, it was his first visit. In a year or two perhaps, now that the seed had been planted —

"We'll still see each other," Paulo was saying. "There'll be another show, won't there? I'll be coming over again."

"Of course there'll be another show, Paulo," Edward said, pulling himself together. "Nothing has to be decided now. We'll have lots of time to work things out. I'm going to be pretty busy myself in a few months after I get possession of the new house.

The whole place needs doing up. But — in the meantime — do you think we might take a little trip together if I came over next year? Late next summer perhaps? Would you take a couple of weeks off so we could go somewhere together?"

"That's a wonderful idea," Paulo said, sounding pleased to find a way through the impasse, if that's what it was. "I could meet you in Rome and we could drive down the coast to Brindisi and take the ferry to Corfu, if you like. I've never been there. Or maybe you'd rather go to Venice, or Ravenna. Would you like that?"

"Of course I would, Paulo. God, though, I hate to see you go — even more, now that we've had this time together —"

Paulo leaned across the table and touched Edward's hand. "Edward, I'll be ready for another show before long. You've made me such a rich man I won't need to work in the restaurant except when there's some kind of emergency. I'd probably have enough new work in — what — eighteen months? How many pictures would you need — would fifteen or so be enough?"

"Even twelve would be enough. I'd like to keep you in the public eye for the next few years, and it certainly could be with smaller shows. We don't want to flood the market. Make them wait. It's good business."

"So we'll plan another show, and you'll come to Italy for a visit in between. How's that?"

"All right, Paulo, that's what we'll do. It'll have to be enough for now, until we can work out something better."

25

Soon after Paulo left to go back to Italy, Edward happened by odd coincidence to glance at the deaths column in the morning paper — by no means a regular habit — and his eye was caught by an obituary for a woman who could have been none other than his mother's Aunty Kay. Katherine Garden, née Cooper, in her eighty-fifth year, dearly loved by sons Melvin, Webster, and George, sadly missed by seven grandchildren with names all ending in "y" like Disney's dwarfs. Services to be held two days hence in the chapel of a west-end funeral parlour. Remembering Paulo's shock at his indifference toward these relatives, he thought he might attend the funeral, slip in unnoticed and hang about at the back, get a look at these cousins once removed. His curiosity was aroused, and besides, he'd be able to tell Paulo he wasn't as stonily indifferent to his kin as he'd seemed to be, although he still couldn't imagine having anything in common with that severe-looking great-aunt he barely remembered, and even less with her large uncouth sons. Of their motorman father he had no recollection whatsoever. Possibly he was out driving his streetcar the day he and his mother and Rak had visited to make their farewells.

Before the service got underway he joined a slow-moving line of mourners shuffling their way up the side aisle to gaze on Aunty Kay's stilled features. When he reached the open coffin he stood for a few moments, trying to equate what he was looking at with what he remembered. It wasn't so much that this woman looked old, because to him she'd looked old when he was five, but the mild and pleasant expression and the lines of good humour on her face even in death — which he decided were too much impressed into her features to have been contrived by the mortician — weren't at all in keeping with his memory of knitted brows and pinched mouth and glower of disapproval. It occurred to him that she might have made an accurate assessment of Rak that day they came to say goodbye, and that it wasn't Edward and his mother of whom she'd been so disapproving but his mother's choice of husband. Maybe she'd had some inkling of how badly things were going to turn out for them. He looked down at her subtly rouged and powdered face, beginning to wish that he'd tried to get in touch with his Great-Aunt Kay while she was still alive. As he turned to walk down the aisle and find a seat his glance swept over the somberly clad individuals occupying the first two pews: three grey-haired women in black hats and coats interspersed with three large men displaying varying degrees of baldness, all of them much mottled about the face and looking uncomfortable in their starched collars. Melvin, Webster, and George, without a doubt, and their wives. Those kids he'd last glimpsed playing with a dog at the end of the hall looked ready for the old-folks home themselves. And could that tired-looking group of whey-faced adults in the second row be the seven dwarfs? He'd expected tots.

He felt like Rip Van Winkle, getting up from a nap to find the world grown old. If the lives of his cousins had flashed past while he blinked, was his own rushing away on the same high-speed track? A moment of panic overtook him, a slight shortness of breath. He proceeded down the aisle and found a seat, running his fingers nervously through his own still quite luxuriant hair that was barely beginning to turn grey, unconsciously plucking at the flap of slack skin that had begun to manifest itself under his chin during the past year or so. The place suddenly seemed too hot, and the heavy smell of the bouquets of roses and lilies heaped around the bier was suffocating.

He abruptly changed his mind about staying for the ceremony and making himself known to these people. What did these sad grey strangers have to do with him? What interest could he possibly have in their dreary lives, or for that matter, they in his? He stood up and stepped crabwise out of the pew, making it into the anteroom just as canned organ music began revving up on the loudspeakers. He passed a picture of the Queen on the way out, a reproduction of that glamorous Annigoni portrait she sat for when she was still young and beautiful, her regal expression outshining the trappings of her office. *There* was his cousin, if a cousin he needed. A proper first cousin at that, no once removed about it. The mud could remain undisturbed. If Paulo ever asked, he'd tell him they'd all moved away and couldn't be found.

26

When Edward and Paulo met again in Rome the following September, a few breathlessly happy moments in the midst of a milling crowd in the arrivals level of the airport turned out to be just about the best part of the whole trip. After that everything went off the rails. Instead of having booked them into a hotel as Edward had expected, Paulo announced that they'd been invited to stay in the apartment of a friend for a couple of nights before they headed north to Ravenna. The friend turned out to be a handsome actor in his thirties introduced by Paulo simply as Lupo. Wolf indeed. Lupo was welcoming and amiable towards Edward and disconcertingly affectionate with Paulo.

"Paulo darling," Lupo said, showing them to the room they were to share, "I forgot to put fresh towels out for you and Edward, but you know where to find them." So Paulo'd been here before, often, perhaps, Edward thought, tasting bitter jealousy. This Lupo could see Paulo as often as he wanted.

A drama festival was underway in Rome that week, and there was a party in progress the entire two days and nights they were in Lupo's flat. People came and went, drinks were poured, pot was smoked, food brought in and passed around. Edward got the impression that many of Lupo's guests stayed up all night — when he and Paulo emerged from their bedroom in the morning the same party they'd left the night before still seemed to be going strong. Their host appeared to be almost tireless; he hardly slept as far as Edward could see, just disappeared into a bedroom for an hour or two now and then or took a nap on the sofa. The guests were mostly men, although there were a few young women among them, all of them theatre people and dancers. In the evening everyone swarmed out to a local restaurant and commandeered tables to be assembled so they could sit together, and the dinner conversation was mostly theatre gossip, from which Edward was necessarily excluded. He would have been ready to leave after the first night, but Paulo seemed in no hurry to go, in fact Edward got the disturbing impression that he was — what? — intimating subtly that he wouldn't be offended if Edward happened to be interested in one of the other men — which of course he was not.

"Giorgio thinks you're wonderful," he said, when they finally got to bed the second night.

"Georgio? The one with the beard?"

Paulo laughed. "No. That's Dom. He's straight. Giorgio's the big guy without much hair. He looks like a wrestler but he's actually a set designer. He said he was having trouble keeping his hands off you."

"Well, I'm sure he's a very nice person," Edward said, aware of how horribly prim he was sounding, "but you can tell him I'm not interested in anyone but you." In fact he was more than a little shocked and very glad they were to be on their way to Ravenna in the morning.

They never got to Ravenna. Paulo had been calling home frequently to check on his father, who had been having one of his arthritic flare-ups, and the morning they were to start on their trip he came away from the phone frowning. His Papa's condition was worse, he said, and his mother had sounded frantic because two of the kitchen staff were off with the flu. "They need me," he said, and that was that. They took a taxi back to the airport and caught a flight to Catania.

At the trattoria Paulo immediately set himself to caring for his father, helping him from his bed to a chair every so often, massaging his arms and legs, lifting him in and out of the baths that soothed his painful joints, and as soon as the old man was comfortable and resting he'd put on an apron or a white jacket and start in to work in the restaurant. Chiara was as busy as he was. They were hospitable enough, but after a few days Edward felt he was in the way, just an added burden. He made some phone calls, changed his bookings, and flew to London. He would call every day, he told Paulo, and if his father improved in the next few days and the restaurant staff came back to work, he would return to Italy. As he boarded the plane for the short trip to London, a feeling of despair began to settle over him. If Paulo's family were going to need him at home for years to come, then he himself would have to find a way of being closer to Paulo. But how?

Edward and Jack sat facing one another across a lunch table at Sheekey's, in Leicester Square.

"You know, Edward," Jack said, looking at his friend's lean and somewhat drawn face, "I never really believed your mother's account of who your father was supposed to have been, but seeing you now I think she was telling the truth. You're the Duke himself of thirty years ago."

Edward laughed. "Do I really look that jaded and world-weary? As for you, there's a bit more grey in your hair but otherwise you're the same old Jack, haven't changed a bit."

"Oh come now. I'm what's called 'well preserved' — in other words just short of mummified. But enough of that, let's talk about this dilemma between you and your young Italian friend, Edward. There has to be a solution, you know."

"That's what I keep telling myself, but I can't think what it is."

"Have you considered reversing the procedure? If your young man can't leave Italy and you're both so desperate to be together, what about selling everything up and moving to Italy yourself? Maybe you could find a little villa somewhere and just live on the income from what you have."

"And call the place *I Tatti*? I suppose I might have just barely enough to live off for the rest of my life if I sold everything I own — but I wouldn't be living the way I want to, and I could hardly bear to think of selling my beautiful furniture and paintings, all the things I've spent so many years collecting. Can you see me living in some little sun-baked hillside town making do with a deal table and a few bits of local pottery? But even if I were willing to do that, I have Paulo's career as a painter to think of. I truly believe he's going to be among the great artists of our time, and I've made it my project to see that he arrives where he belongs in the world of art. It's more than a project, it's a responsibility I've dedicated myself to, and it's tremendously important to me. I couldn't do much for him eking out a hand-to-mouth existence in Italy."

Jack sighed. "I remember when I felt that kind of responsibility for you, Edward. It's not easy, taking on the future success of someone you love. I don't envy you."

"I don't have any choice, Jack. I can't imagine my life now without him. It's as simple as that."

"Have you thought about moving back to London, then? Selling your business and starting a gallery here? You'd be able to spend more time with Paulo if you did that, wouldn't you? You thought about having a gallery here at one time, maybe you could do it now. The art markets are pretty heated up in England these days, and on the continent, too. Have you been watching the sales? There don't seem to be any upper limits. I think you might do very well."

"I've tossed around the idea of doing something like that, Jack, only the gallery in Toronto is doing such a land-office business I'd be insane to walk away from it or sell it. This year I've had to increase my staff to three full-timers, not counting myself. The boom in business generally has trickled down into the art market with a vengeance. Big corporations are scrambling for major pieces of Canadian art for their boardrooms and offices, and the various government departments and agencies are all buying. The independent consultants are having a heyday, and so am I."

"Then how about keeping what you have and starting up a second business over here? A sort of auxiliary to your home base."

"I thought about that, too, but it would really squeeze me. I'm buying a rather expensive house and doing it up, and that's put a big dent in my finances. Oh Lord, just listen to me. You're coming up with all these helpful ideas and all I do is say 'Yes but, yes but.' I'm a hopeless case, Jack, it's my problem, and I'm sorry to be troubling you with it."

Jack laughed. "Oh, I don't see you as hopeless, Edward. Not at all. Here's another idea. How about going into partnership with an existing gallery here in London, or making some kind of exchange arrangement with one of them. Show one another's artists and split the commissions. At least it would bring you over to this side of the Atlantic fairly frequently, and you could get to Italy to see Paulo when you came, or he could come here. It'd be a foot in the door, more time together until the two of you get your lives straightened out. Maybe you'll both wind up in London eventually, who knows?"

Edward put down his knife and fork and gazed across at Jack, turning his friend's newest suggestion over in his mind. "That's something I hadn't thought of, Jack, a partnership of some kind —"

"It might be the way to go for the time being, until you see how things work out."

"I like it, Jack, I like this idea." Edward played with the stem of his wine glass, ruminating. He could take a little flat here, why not, a quiet place where he and Paulo could meet, be together on their own ...

"I can think of a couple of dealers who might be interested in what you have to offer. Can you stay on a few more days while I see what I can come up with?"

"Of course I can. You're wonderful, Jack. You always were."

Two days later Jack called Edward at his hotel. "Could you put together enough of Paulo's work for an exhibition, Edward? I dropped in on an old friend yesterday, a man named Christian Gauthier who has a gallery in Cork Street, well established, very high standards. Shows what I'd call classic modern work. I took along several of the catalogues you've sent me over the years and he was particularly interested in the one from Paulo's show, dead keen in fact. He has a slot early in the new year — February, I think he said — where one of his artists has backed out and let him down. I think he'd put Paulo's work in there if it were available. Christian's getting along in years, he must be my age at least. We got to talking about you a bit and he said he might even be interested in taking on a partner eventually. Do you want to meet him? Have a look at his gallery?"

"Absolutely!"

"This afternoon, then, right after lunch."

27

The arrangements for Edward's fiftieth birthday luncheon were all in place. The caterers would be delivering their equipment later that afternoon, the chef and his assistants would arrive to prepare the food first thing in the morning. He had chosen the flowers, great fat pale roses the florist was going to bring and arrange in Edward's own vases. A white marquee was at that very moment being put up in the garden; a string quartet had been laid on to play through the warm afternoon. Everything in the house was perfect, right down to the plants he'd begun cultivating in the solarium a year ago that were now rewarding his care with bloom and exuberant foliage. His many friends were invited, and his clients; several of the consultants he dealt with regularly; the curators of the major museums in the city; all the people he'd worked with at Christopher's Toronto branch before he went out on his own. His gallery staff would be coming, and of course all the artists he represented, the foundation of the business. There would be close to two hundred guests in all. It felt like something of an apotheosis, this party, more than a milestone in his life, something like a vindication of the years he had devoted to building his business and acquiring the beautiful things with which he'd filled his home, the furniture and objets d'art and paintings that gave him so much pleasure and which he would now share with his friends. It would be a housewarming as much as a birthday party. He put his hand into his pocket to touch the talisman that he slipped in there every morning when he got dressed — the tiny silver penknife that represented the beginning of it all, which was now on a ring along with all the tiny brass keys to the cabinets and breakfronts and commodes behind whose glazed doors his precious collections were displayed.

He walked slowly through the main-floor rooms, giving each of his works of art a few minutes of his attention: the dazzling Klimt oil sketch of beautiful Adele Bloch-Bauer; his two glorious Bonnard landscapes from the artist's early days at Le Cannet; a small subdued brownish canvas by Bonnard's friend Vuillard — one of those interiors of his mother's stuffily draperied-and-wallpapered parlour. In this version the old lady sat with two other black-clad matrons drinking coffee from the shiny black-and-white service that turned up frequently in Vuillard's claustrophobic interiors. There was the small Picasso oil, classic rose period, the head of a young girl, and near it a large ink drawing from a later period of Picasso's oeuvre — a dark window, a lamp, and the skull of a bull. Edward stood for long moments staring at an attenuated monochrome figure painting by Giacometti which affected him now, as it never failed to do, with a prickly feeling of alarm — a sensation that he had decided some time ago was what he might feel if he were suddenly to come face to face with himself on the street. The slight shudder the work evoked was interesting, and not at all unpleasant.

Edward moved on to the unwholesome little Balthus figure, a painting of a spooky-innocent young girl holding a doll, a work which carried, for reasons he had never quite figured out, a slight overtone of obscenity. He gazed in turn at each of the five small Morandi still lifes, assemblages of pots and bottles, bowls and kettles and cooking implements, painted in those ubiquitous Morandi muted blues and buffs, works that came second in his affections only to Paulo's. Paulo's paintings were not on display in these rooms; they were hung in his private sitting room upstairs, the only art in that room, unless you counted a seventeenth-century Faenza pitcher that sat on the Sheraton half-round table between the windows. He never took guests up there.

He moved out of the drawing room and stood for long moments gazing at the works of art in the hall — the two

Matisse figure drawings, a group of five Roualt lithographs of kings and clowns. He took another long concentrated look at his first important acquisition, the tiny Odilon Redon oil of anemones in a bowl. In the dining room he paused before two sunless Cape Cod scenes by Edward Hopper hung next to one another; a Milton Avery of two reclining figures on what might have been a beach; a wonderful erotic Diebenkorn drawing of a partially nude woman, her head turned to one side as she lounged in a deck-chair with open legs, casually displaying her crotch. The banality of the subject of a Burchfield painting — a wooden-fenced back yard in upper New York State — was transformed by a billowy radiant spring sky hanging above it that invested the whole scene with magic. He devoted a few minutes to his four Milne watercolours; a few more to a small oil by Glackens of a young girl standing in a doorway. Of the three Fairfield Porters, two were the artist's typical raw New England landscapes that made one shiver with chill in spite of strong shadows and hard blue skies, and the third a sunny interior with a young girl, undoubtedly one of the artist's daughters, lying on the floor reading in the company of a calico cat.

Each painting or print was an example of the particular artist's finest work, always from the best period, and if some were small, none was second-rate. They had been chosen entirely without program or thought of putting together a national or geographic sampling. One evening a dinner guest had stood looking squarely at the Havana street scene by J.W. Morrice hanging over the regency serving table — Morrice being, in Edward's opinion, the best artist Canada ever produced — and asked why it was Edward didn't have any Canadian art in his collection. No rocks, no snow, no pine trees, how could it be Canadian? Did Van Gogh stop being Dutch when he went to Provence? The idea that a work of art could have a nationality was fatuous anyway.

As for his furniture, almost entirely English and French from the seventeenth and eighteenth centuries, any single piece could stand alone as a work of art in itself. Not one item had ever been restored or repaired or subjected to the ministrations of some so-called refinisher. If the thing had been changed in any way since the day it was made, if the drawer pulls weren't the original ones, for instance, he wouldn't have bought it. His eye never let him down. He could spot anything spurious — a bit of replaced inlay in the marquetry, a remade drawer, the insertion of a tiny lozenge of modern glass in the door of a cabinet — as instantly as if it had been marked with red paint.

Recently he'd had photographs taken of each piece of furniture and work of art, and of his rare fountain pens, the scent bottles, and the snuff boxes he'd begun collecting during the past year — several French boxes in gold, silver ones of English make, and most precious of all, a Meissen miniature from the eighteenth century that was less than two inches long and had a delicious little Watteau-like painting on the underside of the lid. The sets of Meissen and Sevres and Spode dinnerware had been photographed, the silver and crystal, the fine antique oriental carpets on the floor of every room, and then all reprinted in colour to make up the pages of a catalogue with dates of acquisition, provenance, country of origin, and a biographical note on each artist or maker. In future years, when he added new items, he would have supplements to the catalogue printed.

This was not just idle collecting. These treasures were going to have a future. He had decided during recent months that he would bequeath his house and its contents to the city, or possibly to the university, as a permanent museum bearing his name, a bequest more modest than the Frick in New York or London's Wallace Collection, to be sure, he wasn't out to compete with those, but Toronto wasn't New York or London, and collections like his were few and far between in this vast young country.

It had taken Edward a long time to bring what had happened into perspective. More than a year had passed since that time in London, and only in the past few months had he been able to think about it rationally and with some degree of objectivity. It had been like trying to recall the details of period when he'd been seriously ill, delirious even, in the grip of a prolonged fever. He realized now, intellectually at least, if not fully with his heart, that between those two points in space and time — his first meeting with Paulo in the trattoria in Sicily, and the final one at the exhibition on Cork Street — he had completely relinquished his will, as one is often obliged to do when one is ill. He saw that he had given over the safekeeping of his life, his heart, and his mind into other hands. He still flinched at the memory of the exquisite vulnerability that condition had brought him to, and the anguish it had cost him. He had stood too close to the edge, he had nearly lost his life — or what counted as his life. One can be dead without the soul actually having left the body; one can die of emptiness, of inanition, and still go on breathing.

Paulo had known the name of the hotel. He knew where the gallery was. He could have phoned and left a message in either place, got in touch somehow. After days had gone by and Edward hadn't heard a word from him, he telephoned the trattoria in Sicily. A woman whose voice he didn't recognize told him rather brusquely that as far as she knew Paulo had gone to Rome and wouldn't be back for some time. *La signora e il signore* were in Catania today, they wouldn't be back until the evening, and no, Paulo was not with them, of that she was certain.

Something must have happened, Paulo had fallen ill or there'd been an accident. Maybe he'd been hit by a car or mugged.

Rome could be a dangerous place if you weren't careful, there were parts of the city a person ought to stay away from at night. Paulo was so trusting, too much so, naïve, even. His openness was part of his charm but it could have gotten him into trouble. Edward worried and stewed while he managed somehow to fill the days. He dropped in at Cork Street frequently, mainly to see if Paulo had telephoned there, but preparations for the exhibition were all under control, and Christian Gauthier was beginning to give him funny looks when he asked yet one more time if Paulo had called. He went down to Putney to have dinner with Jack, who had been expecting to meet Paulo. Edward found himself making up a story to account for Paulo's non-appearance, spinning a yarn about his having been held up at home on family matters. It made him feel ashamed to have to lie, and he had the feeling Jack had seen through him, although he didn't say anything, of course. Jack was tact itself.

He wandered the streets of the west end, drifted in and out of the shops thinking vaguely about finding a gift for Paulo, a watch maybe, something special to mark the occasion of his protegé's first London exhibition, but worry spoiled the impulse and nothing he saw seemed just right. He spent half a day touring the Wallace Collection, mostly because it was so close his hotel. He'd been absolutely dazzled by the place during his early years at Christopher's, when he'd gone there again and again, sometimes just to stand in front of a particular painting for half an hour and let it saturate his eyes, but that day there had been too much going on in his mind for his eyes to be properly receptive, and when he'd finished his rather desultory tour he felt a little as though he'd dined on an entire meal of rich desserts. The ornate artifacts in that collection seemed cloying now, suited to the taste of the late Victorians, he supposed, but no longer to his. All that elaborately decorated furniture and those precious and extravagant objets d'art lacked the classical restraint that marked everything he himself invariably chose. When he left the building his mood was even darker than it had been when he went in. He'd planned to stop in for dinner at a nearby Greek restaurant that had been going strong since his early days at Christopher's, but when he was halfway there he slowed his pace. He wasn't up to mezethes and fat roast lamb and bouzouki music tonight. In the past few days his appetite had waned to such a degree that he'd just about given up eating proper meals and instead had been picking up snacks and sandwiches in pubs, eating them in a hurry, washing them down with a glass of wine or a whiskey or two. He turned around now and made his way back to his hotel. He would get himself a sandwich and a drink in the dark little bar at Durrant's and call it a day. He'd enquired for messages so often that now when he entered the lobby the solemn-faced porter in his green-striped waistcoat automatically said, "No messages, Mr. Cooper," as he handed Edward the key to his room.

Paulo still hadn't been in touch on the morning of the vernissage. Edward had fallen into bed exhausted with worry the night before only to find himself wide awake at three in the morning, feeling as though he were suffocating. He opened the window wide and sat for an hour with his elbows on the sill, staring down into the dark empty street. He went back to bed and finally dozed off as dawn was beginning to lighten the sky, waking with a start some time later to the sound of crates of bottles being slammed down on the pavement in front of the hotel. The background blare of street noises told him the workday was well underway. He dragged himself to the bathroom and had just stepped into the shower when the phone rang in the bedroom. Dear God let it be Paulo. He grabbed up a towel and hurried to answer it, leaving a trail of wet footprints on the flowered carpet.

"*Buongiorno Eduardo. Sono io, Paulo.*"

"Paulo! Thank God, I was so worried I was ready to start calling the hospitals. What happened? Where on earth have you been?"

"Sorry, I should have called from Rome, but I got tied up. I kept thinking I'd be getting away in another day, and then something else would come up. Never mind, *tutto va bene*, I'm in London now."

Edward collapsed on the side of the bed, sagging with relief. "I'll forgive you anything, I'm so glad to hear from you. Are you still at the airport? Get a cab, Paulo, and come to the hotel, Durrant's, on George Street. I'll be downstairs waiting. I'll get them to hold us a table for breakfast."

"I'm not actually at the airport, Edward. The thing is, Lupo's with me, or I'm with Lupo, I'm not sure which. Lupo takes over when you travel with him. Our flight was delayed taking off from Rome and it was pretty late when we finally got here, after midnight I guess. We didn't want to disturb you so we came to this little bed and breakfast where Lupo always stays when he's in London. I think it's near the theatres in the west end, I never know where I am in this city. But sure, let's have breakfast. Your hotel can't be too far from here. I'll be there in a few minutes."

Lupo. While he'd been awake stumbling around in this stuffy room worried sick and gasping for air, Paulo and Lupo had been together. In bed.

"What the English call breakfast always amazes me," Paulo said, wading into a plate of poached eggs and back bacon and grilled tomatoes. Edward's breakfast was in front of him too, but he had yet to pick up his knife and fork. The look of those yellow egg yolks next to the watery red tomato made him feel queasy. Paulo's insouciant attitude, the implication that everything was perfectly normal, was incomprehensible to him. Was it possible he didn't even know how his late arrival and this Lupo thing was knocking him sideways — or didn't he care? Day after day without so much as a phone call, turning up at the last minute with

Lupo in tow? Edward picked up his glass and swallowed water with difficulty.

"I'm sorry, Paulo," he said, "but I can't seem to concentrate on the strangeness of the English breakfast right now. I don't think you realize how worried I've been, I've been just about out of my mind, and now you tell me — I mean, I gather you and — *Lupo* —" He could hardly bring himself to pronounce the name.

"Oh, me and Lupo. That's nothing new. We're off and on all the time, we have been for years." Paulo took a thin square of crustless toast from the little silver rack that sat between them on the table and began examining it carefully on both sides as though he wasn't quite sure what it was. He apparently satisfied himself that it was edible and bit off half of it. He raised his eyes to Edward's, chewing his toast. "I'm sorry you were upset. But you know, Edward, you didn't give me an awful lot of warning about this exhibition. I did tell you on the phone I had appointments to see some people in Rome."

"Have you been angry then? Was that it? You didn't like the show being a surprise? Has this been a sort of punishment?"

"No, of course not, it wasn't intentional, but I did have business to attend to. And now that you mention it, I am a bit of a big boy for surprises, Edward. I would have liked being consulted about this show before you set it up. I would have done things differently if I'd know about it, put in some of my new work, for one thing. I wish you'd told me about buying those pictures from my show, too." Paulo was smiling, but there was an edge in his voice. "It *is* my work, and it *is* my show, after all. You could have told me the truth back in Toronto, you know. I'm not ten years old. I could have taken it."

It was dreadful listening to Paulo talk like this, when all he'd ever wanted was to please him. He could hear the tremor in his own voice when he spoke. "I'm sorry, Paulo," he said. "I won't ever do anything like this again, I promise you. I couldn't be sorrier. It was stupid of me."

Paulo had been twisting in his chair while Edward was speaking, glancing around the dining room. Now he raised his hand to catch the waiter's attention and pointed to his empty cup, smiled as the man approached with the coffee pot. Had he even been listening?

"Do you think we might put it behind us now, Paulo, and have a fresh start? The pictures look wonderful, I know you'll be happy with the way Gauthier's hung them." It suddenly struck him that Paulo had arrived at the hotel empty-handed. "Paulo, where are your bags?"

"I left them at that B and B. I might as well just stay where I am. It isn't far from here; it only took me ten minutes in the taxi."

"Stay where you — Paulo — aren't we going to be together? I thought —" Edward leaned across the table. "I don't understand what's happening."

"Nothing's happening, Edward. Well, that's not quite true. My big news is I've signed an exclusive agreement with a dealer in Rome — exclusive after this show in London, of course — one of the big ones, Galleria Primavera. They have a second location in Milano, they move their artists' work back and forth. That's what's been holding me up, meeting with the director and their business people, talking about dates and whatnot. You know what Romans are like, everything's done over a three-hour lunch or a four-hour dinner. Everybody wanted to look at my slides —"

"But Paulo, what about us? For God's sake, let Lupo look after himself and come and stay with me here. We have to sort all this out. What has Lupo got to do with you and me anyway? You and I belong together, we're the *gemelli* —"

Paulo broke in. "Edward, listen," he said, leaning across the table, "I'm sorry. Somewhere along the way you got it wrong.

225

Think about it. You came to Sicily and took an interest in my work, and that was great. You sold some of my pictures. You gave me that show in Toronto. We had some good times together, great times, and I'll never forget any of it. But I never told you I was going to spend my life with you. I never even thought that for a minute." Paulo rubbed his hand across his eyes. "How can I make you see this? We've been fine together, just fine, but you've never been the only guy in my life. Don't you remember what it was like to be young, Edward? All these months, did you really think you were *il solo?* I never promised to be faithful to you, I never said I was going come and live with you, any of it. I have half a dozen close friends. Lovers, if you want to call them that. If you'd asked me I'd have told you."

Edward tried to lift his coffee cup, but his hand shook so badly he had to give up on it. He was in shock, sat there stunned, watching Paulo's lips move. His mind seemed to be floating away, he was starting to feel strangely detached, as though he were drugged or half anaesthetized. Paulo pushed a piece of toast around in the egg yolk on his plate, then popped the morsel into his mouth, chewed it up and swallowed it, put down his fork.

"Listen, Edward," he said, looking intently into Edward's eyes, "this isn't the end of the world. I'm sorry, it just never was the kind of relationship you thought it was, but it isn't just you, you know. I don't want to be tied down, I don't want to belong to anyone. Maybe I never will. But you and I will always be friends, really good friends, you know that."

He shouldn't have chosen this side of the table, facing the window. Paulo's figure was silhouetted against the dappled brightness of the day, and the contrast made it difficult for Edward to see his features — just the kind of arrangement of light and dark that often brought one of these damned headaches on. As he stared, half of Paulo's face began to melt and disappear into the white fog that was gradually obliterating the left side of everything in front of his eyes. A running arc of multicoloured lights started streaming from the centre of the fog toward the outer corner of his left eye and back down along the bottom of his vision, like the running coloured lights on a movie marquee. Did they still have those lights on theatres, he wondered? He hadn't bothered to notice. In the old days Leicester Square used to be completely lit up with them.

Now the nausea welled up. In a few minutes he would lose what little he'd eaten of his breakfast. "You'll have to excuse me, Paulo," he said, getting up out of his chair. His napkin slipped from his knees as he rose, and his jacket cuff caught the handle of a table knife and sent it clattering to the floor. He didn't appear to notice. "I've got a migraine coming on. I'll have to go up and get my pills and lie down for a few hours."

Paulo was on his feet. "Let me get the pills, Edward, you're white as a sheet —"

"No no, don't get up. Finish your breakfast." Edward signalled the waiter to bring the bill, scrawled his signature on it when it came, holding his left hand over the blind eye. "I'll be better by this evening. Don't be late getting to the gallery. That interviewer from the BBC's coming at six. I'll see you there."

It was mid-afternoon when he woke up. He lay quietly for some time with his eyes closed, letting his mind roam over the events of the morning and of the past week. After a while he raised himself very slowly on one elbow and carefully shifted his pillows against the headboard, inched himself up in the bed so he could lean back propped in a half-sitting position. He had drawn the heavy flowered curtains across the windows before he went to bed, and the room was in dim partial light. His head felt as it always did after those attacks, thick and unresonating, as though it were stuffed full of some dense material, like asbestos or kapok. Somehow he would have to find the energy and the will to get through the rest of this day and the evening that lay ahead, put one foot in front of the other for the next few hours. Tomorrow he could go home. He looked at the luminous dial of his watch. Half past three.

The pain had abated. He'd been lucky this time. The pills had kicked in right away and he'd slept soundly for several hours. His present feeling of sluggish inertia was not unfamiliar; he always felt passive and stupid after he'd taken those pills. There were four of them, an analgesic to block the pain, an anti-nausea pill of the kind they gave for sea-sickness, a tranquilizer to help him relax, and a tablet that delivered a strong jolt of caffeine which had the effect of clamping down the arteries and slowing the roar of blood behind his eyes. Migraine headaches were not caused by the constriction of the blood vessels in the meninges, as was generally thought; quite to the contrary, so Edward's doctor had told him, the pain arose from the sudden expansion of those blood vessels. The throbbing was due to their over-dilation when too much blood was allowed to flow through them too quickly. Blood was clearly something that had to be kept under firm control.

The thought crossed his mind that, drugs or no drugs, there was actually nothing for him to be anxious about anymore. After all these months of yearning and longing and desire and worry, he had nothing left to hope for. Perhaps despair ought to be welcomed for the comfort it offered. That wry thought almost made him smile. He picked up the phone and pressed the number for room service, asked them to send up a pot of coffee, a couple of sweet rolls of some kind, and a small cognac.

Edward waved aside the doorman's offer to whistle him up a cab and stepped out into the gathering dusk of the soft afternoon. He needed to walk. He paused on the front steps of the hotel, noticing that the pavement was wet from what must have been a recent shower, but the sky, or what he could see of it, had cleared now to a washed blue that glowed redly to the west, with wisps of gold cloud trailing through it. A Turner sky, possibly, if one could see more of it.

During the past ten days he'd traversed just about every possible route between his hotel and the Cork Street Gallery, and he hesitated for a minute on the curb, deciding which one to take now. He had plenty of time, all the time in the world when it came to that; no one really cared whether he turned up or not. But then, what else did he have to do? He crossed the street, heading south to Oxford Street and along to Davies, where he turned south again. His feet seemed to be picking the route on their own, because he shortly found himself, a little to his own surprise, in front of the pair of old buildings that had once housed Christopher's Auctioneers, long since vacated for more spacious premises. So this was where he'd been going. The old familiar brick wall beside the door was now adorned with a series of brass plates engraved with the names of accountants, a theatrical agency, the offices of something called The Holism Society. The top floor appeared to be devoted to a dance studio or rehearsal hall. He didn't really understand why he'd walked this way; he'd known that Christopher's wasn't here anymore, and even if it had still been here and the place still full of china and chairs and old paintings, what difference would it have made? There was nothing left here for him now, not at Christopher's, wherever it might be. Not in London. Not in England. Not in Sicily.

He walked on, thinking he might get a better look at the sky in the open space around Berkely Square, but by the time he got there and stood gazing upward it had all faded to a uniform translucence that was rapidly dimming to a milky grey.

On Cork Street he paused on the pavement for a moment, looking through the window into the brilliantly lit interior of the gallery. There seemed to be a good turnout, if that mattered, a large number of people were milling around. Paulo was there, standing apart from the rest of the party with a small group in the middle of the room. As Edward came through the door, Paulo caught his eye, raised a hand in greeting, and turned back to a tall woman in a red suit standing in front of him proffering a microphone. A black-haired man in a leather jacket stood to one side with a bulky camera on his shoulder; a skinny youth held aloft a pole bearing a spot that cast Paulo and the woman in a showerbath of white light. A waiter hovered on the fringes holding a tray of filled wine glasses in his two hands, absorbed with the spectacle.

"So, Paulo Jones," the woman was saying, "perhaps we could start by having you tell us how an Italian artist comes to have a good old Welsh name like Jones."

Paulo laughed. "My father's English. As a matter of fact the name causes me problems. Italians find Jones hard to pronounce. I get all sorts of thing, like *Ho-ness, Gio-ness*. The only J's in the Italian language are on foreign words, and people don't know what to do with them."

"I gather you've lived all your life in Italy, but you speak English like a native. That's your father's doing, too, I suppose."

"Yes, he started speaking English to me the day I was born, so I don't know whether it's my first language or my second. Mamma only speaks Italian. When I was a little kid I just began speaking two languages instead of one."

"I understand you've exhibited your work in Canada, and now you're having this show here in London, but never a solo show in Italy? Why is that?"

"Just the way things happened, I guess. That's going to change, though. From now on I'll be with a gallery in Rome. I won't have to leave home to show my work."

"No more exhibitions planned for Toronto or London then?"

"Not a far as I can see. Rome and Milan from now on. I'll just get on with my painting and leave everything else to my dealer."

"Then we'd better enjoy these wonderful paintings while we can. I'd say from what I see of your work with all this gorgeous colour and light that you draw heavily in your art from your surroundings in Sicily."

"I do. Everywhere else I go the light seems weak, everything looks sort of grey. The shadows aren't sharp. You can't do anything with shadows in the kind of light you have here."

"It sounds as if you were born in the right place for your work then."

"Oh, I was. I've never doubted that. Some artists have to go searching for their right place — like Gauguin going to Tahiti. I think Matisse went to Morocco for a while, didn't he? Van Gogh had to leave the north to find what he needed. I could never work anywhere but Sicily ..."

The interview was beginning to be tiresome. Edward had positioned himself at a little distance from the group, and now he let his eyes stray. Over Paulo's shoulder he could see half of one of the larger paintings, the one that had struck him so vividly that first day in the trattoria, the interior of the dining room and the scene through the window onto the terrazzo where he'd eaten his lunch, and the landscape beyond. He loved that painting; it was glorious. Next to it was one of the still lifes, the bowls and jugs, some fruit, the whole thing radiating heat and light and harmony. He could only see part of the next one, a glowing landscape, part of the vineyard and the hills beyond, seen from the terrace.

Someone moved just then and blocked the painting from his vision, and he brought his eyes back to Paulo. A gap had appeared in the cluster of people, leaving a clear view of Paulo's whole stocky, black-clad figure. The lights gleamed on that rather oily looking curly hair. He'd let it grow since Edward had seen him last and it was very long now, the curls not merely surrounding his head in a corona but lying on the collar of the ubiquitous black Sicilian suit. That hair colour was unusual for an Italian, of course, but quite commonplace here in England. Go to Ireland and half the population had coppery curls. He continued to stare while the interview droned on, now just a background noise to his thoughts and observations. He'd hadn't noticed before, for instance, that Paulo was quite so bandy-legged. It was a rather less than heroic-looking figure he cut standing there in that glaring white light. Edward saw with surprise that he was really quite an ordinary young fellow after all, one who looked very much like what he was: a waiter in a Sicilian restaurant. One of Rak's repellent words leapt to the front of Edward's mind before he could suppress it. *Wop.*

But he had produced such wonderful work, this ordinary little fellow, such priceless, miraculous work, utterly gorgeous paintings that Edward loved beyond reason. He readjusted his focus away from Paulo and back to the wall of paintings, when suddenly it struck him. *My God, the paintings! These were all his own paintings! And they were being sold!* He looked quickly around the room. Christ! Three were already marked with red stickers, no four! Five! Five out of the twelve, only seven left. He had to stop it all, withdraw them from the sale, get them back. No, that wouldn't do, he'd have to buy them back, tell Gauthier — he wheeled around and walked swiftly across the room to where

Christian Gauthier was leaning with ankles crossed and arms folded, his ample backside perched on the edge of his desk.

"Christian, I've made a terrible mistake, I'm buying back all the pictures that haven't been sold. I can't let them go." He looked around and counted again. "Five — six — seven. All seven of them. Don't ask me to explain, I absolutely must have them back. Of course I'll pay your proper share, and the costs and the return shipping and anything else you want to specify. The exhibition will be sold out, you'll get your commissions, Paulo will get what's due to him. Just treat me like an ordinary client, work it whatever way you like, but I absolutely must have these paintings back."

Gauthier stared. Judging from his round-eyed open-mouthed expression he thought Edward had gone barking mad. "All right, Edward," he said finally, after blinking and swallowing a couple of times. "If you're sure that's what you want, why not? I think you'd better calm down, though. You don't look well. You've gone very pale."

"I can write you a cheque right now —"

"Oh tut tut, my dear fellow. Tomorrow or the next day. Don't worry, I won't sell them to anyone else." He picked up a small brass box from his desk and began to circle the room, going from picture to picture, taking red discs from the box and sticking them onto the cards beside the paintings. "A sellout show," he said when he returned, setting the box back down on his desk with a satisfied little flourish. "That suits me fine."

Edward finished his tour of the rooms downstairs and began to make his way up the wide graceful staircase, enjoying the feel of the satiny cherrywood bannister under his hand, his eyes taking pleasure in the way the faded rose and blue tones of the Persian stair runner were set off against the gleaming white of the risers. At the landing the stairs met three wide casement windows and a cushioned window seat, and then another short flight led to the gallery-like upper hall. He walked across to the door of his sitting room, opened it, and went in.

A day seldom passed that he didn't come to this room to spend a little time in quiet meditation among Paulo's paintings. A feeling of calm descended on him here that confirmed his acceptance — even his satisfaction— at the way things had turned out. There was a profound sense of relief in letting go, giving way, abandoning the struggle, although what it was he had been struggling for — or against — through most of his life, he wasn't even quite certain anymore. Whatever it was, he would struggle no more. He was tired. His heart was tired of wanting this nebulous something that he couldn't name and might well not even exist. He'd trapped himself in a prison of his own making, and he'd had enough of it. As he eased himself down in the cushioned settee the fragment of a poem he'd had to memorize at school filtered up into his consciousness. *The heart must pause to breathe, and Love itself have rest ...*

What he'd come to realize, slowly, was that he already had everything he wanted from life, all the things that mattered, anyway. He'd been born with a talent, his God-given aesthetic sensibility, or whatever you wanted to call it, and he hadn't buried it, his Lord would have no cause for complaint, there would be no weeping and gnashing of teeth when the time for accounting came. He had put his abilities to good use. He'd brought many promising young artists along, and whenever he'd come across exceptional talent he'd put all his resources behind it. The work in this room attested to that. And he had collected beautiful things, rare things, paintings and fine objects that gave him immense pleasure now and would still be here after he was gone to give pleasure to others. He had only just begun to realize to what a degree these things completed him.

What had Paulo signified in his life, then? Where did he fit in? Edward had done a great deal of thinking about just that ever since the exhibition on Cork Street more than a year ago. He'd made those arrangements with Gauthier that night and had even managed to hold himself together long enough to embrace Paulo and congratulate him on the success of the show.

"I'll be getting along now, Paulo," he said, with his hand on the younger man's shoulder. "That migraine's still hanging around, I'm afraid."

"Okay, Edward. Have a good night. I'll call you in the morning. *Mille grazie per tutto.*"

Edward smiled and nodded. Next morning he checked out of Durrant's, went back to Cork Street to conclude his business with Gauthier, and then took a cab to a hotel at Heathrow and booked a room where he could rest for a few hours before his plane was due to take off for Toronto. Paulo had called a few times since he'd been back, but there was, after all, such a thing as self-respect. Edward kept the conversations short and casual, and after a while the calls ceased.

If an essence of the divine, or of genius, if some element of eternal spirit lived within great works of art — and this Edward emphatically believed was so — then such an essence was here, in these paintings. Paulo had been the medium through which Grace — there was no other word for it — had been transmitted. Grace was lodged in these paintings and would remain in them as long as they continued to exist, because truth and beauty were elements as indestructible as gold. It was possible that when these canvases finally crumbled into dust, the essence they had harboured would be released to move along and take form somewhere else. Who could tell about such things? For now, though, for his lifetime, they belonged to him. There had

been a time when he'd believed that Paulo *was* that eternal spirit, that genius, that Grace, but of course, he had been wrong.
Paulo had simply been the catalyst that acts upon the eternal
essence to give it concrete form — the means whereby Love is
transformed into art.